CHERRY BEACH

CHERRY BEACH

A NOVEL

DON GILLMOR

BIBLIOASIS
Windsor, Ontario

FIRST EDITION
10 9 8 7 6 5 4 3 2

Library and Archives Canada Cataloguing in Publication

Title: Cherry beach / Don Gillmor.
Names: Gillmor, Don, author
Identifiers: Canadiana (print) 20250304732 | Canadiana (ebook) 20250305720
ISBN 9781771966900 (softcover) | ISBN 9781771966917 (EPUB)
Subjects: LCGFT: Detective and mystery fiction. | LCGFT: Novels.
Classification: LCC PS8563.I59 C44 2026 | DDC C813/.54—dc23

Edited by Daniel Wells
Copyedited by Vanessa Stauffer
Cover and text designed by Kate Sinclair
Cover image: Mario Amé/pexels.com

Published with the generous assistance of the Canada Council for the Arts, which last year invested $153 million to bring the arts to Canadians throughout the country, and the financial support of the Government of Canada. Biblioasis also acknowledges the support of the Ontario Arts Council (OAC), an agency of the Government of Ontario, which last year funded 1,709 individual artists and 1,078 organizations in 204 communities across Ontario, for a total of $52.1 million, and the contribution of the Government of Ontario through the Ontario Book Publishing Tax Credit and Ontario Creates.

PRINTED AND BOUND IN CANADA

To abandon oneself to principles is really to die—
and to die for an impossible love which is the contrary of love.

—ALBERT CAMUS

ONE

WE WERE ON JARVIS, talking to a sex worker named Infinity who was saving up to have the operation done in Belgium.

"You could have it done here," I said. "It would be cheaper."

"I don't want a Canadian vagina."

"They're subsidized."

"They lack personality."

It was early June, the heat still sly, not yet unwanted. A half-dozen women lingered in their summer clothes: halter tops, heels, a festive boa. There had been a series of assaults against sex workers over the last two months. We talked to the girls, they were jittery, didn't know anything.

"Have a nice night and pay your taxes," I said.

Davis drove, eyes on the road, hands at ten and two, heading south. It was just after 7 p.m. The houses we passed were once the grand homes of the city's ruling Methodists, solid citizens who had created a city in their own image: righteous, prosperous, and dull. But cities have their own dark thoughts and the downtown spread out, prostitutes and thieves arrived at their doorsteps, and the Methodists moved north to Rosedale, putting a ravine between themselves and sin. And their abandoned mansions became rooming houses or were turned into separate flats. I'd been in some of them, squalid, dank, high ceilings with crown moulding. A stained mattress on the floor, someone crying.

Davis was telling me about something her daughter did in school, something uplifting, when the call came in. St. James Town, two bodies.

I took the call. "Less than a minute away. Anything else?"

"Two bodies sixth floor, crying, screaming."

"Crying screaming in progress?"

"No, discovered."

She gave us the address and unit number and I repeated it.

Davis had already made a U-turn. I was scanning the street. Whoever did it could be walking our way, a walk that had a studied nonchalance, the weapon in the trash, their adrenaline still swamping their system, breathing a little off, eyes too eager for contact, helpful in a non-helpful way, calling me *Officer* like Eddie Haskell.

St. James Town was a collection of high-rises that were built at the one moment in history when that seemed like a good idea. The towers were mostly filled with immigrants who were trying to grab on to something larger, and despite having the highest density in the country, it had a crime rate that was unremarkable. Until a year ago, when it started to become truly remarkable. An unexplained spike in assaults, car thefts, vandalism, and, most remarkably, a graffiti blitz that was staggering in scope and ambition. And now a double homicide.

We were the first to arrive but the sirens were close. Already a small crowd was outside, exchanging unreliable information. We moved in quickly, waited a full minute for the elevator with three women asking us different questions in unison. There was an old couch in the foyer, beige and brown colours, harsh lighting, the floor worn. The elevator lurched upward, the machinery whining.

The sixth floor had almost every door open, people huddled, some crying. We walked to unit 651, Davis with her hand on her holster. Inside were five people, all of them sobbing or wailing. On the floor, the bodies of two women, girls. A woman was draped over one of them, keening, a primal sound. It had to be the mother. It looked like both victims were teenagers. The blood spread for almost a metre. The wailing was piercing. I stared down. We had to clear the room for forensics. The mother wasn't going to budge, hanging on to the last of her daughter. Davis cleared the rest of the room, left the mother with her daughter for a few more minutes. The other girl was a few metres away, on her back. Maybe seventeen. The living room furniture was intact, no sign of a struggle. Uniforms arrived and secured the scene. I left Davis and went to find the security cameras.

It took ten minutes to find the super and get access to the footage. By then, forensics was all over the apartment and the bike cops were spread out on the streets. The camera outside the main entrance didn't work. The one in the building directly across did, though there wasn't a clean view. I took a quick look at the footage from 6 to 7 p.m., speeding through it, dozens of people, twenty different guys in hoodies, hands in pockets, heads down. Nothing that was immediately helpful. I went back upstairs.

Davis had taken the mother to another apartment and was interviewing her. Forensics was going through the scene. We had the victims' names: Angela Blair, aged sixteen, and Dashika Moore, seventeen.

I went across the hall to the neighbour in 652, identified myself as Detective Abel, flashed my badge. She was maybe fifty, shocked at the deaths, frightened of me, not sure she should tell me anything but afraid not to. She had grey hair, tired eyes. Her hands were folded in her lap, and she worked them when she talked.

"Did you hear anything?" I asked.

"No."

"No screams."

"No."

"Did either of them have a boyfriend that you knew of?"

"I don't know. I saw boys sometimes." She shrugged.

"Can you describe any of these boys?"

She stared at the coffee table. There were burns on the edges, like you used to see on pool tables.

"White?" I asked. "Black, brown, Asian."

"I saw white and Black."

"Age?"

"Maybe a bit older. I don't know. It's hard for me to tell these days."

I took her statement and took another statement from a man down the hall who said you could see this coming.

Dashika Moore's mother arrived, distraught, and screamed when she saw her daughter. Her world had been taken away. She had to be restrained, let forensics gather evidence. There was nothing to say other than the boilerplate: *I know this is difficult, but anything you can tell us may help us catch whoever did this*. Thelma Moore was close to fifty, short hair, a strong face. I led her to the apartment where Davis was interviewing Susan Blair, Angela's mother. The two women sobbed and embraced one another.

Davis and I were with the two mothers for an hour. Angela Blair was the younger one. She lived in the apartment with her mother. Susan Blair had short blonde hair, freckles across her nose. She was visiting a friend in the hospital, came home to find this. Dashika and Angela were on the same track team. Both straight-A students. Dashika was heading out of town in three days—an academic scholarship to Michigan State, had a job on campus. She had three athletic scholarships as well but decided to go the academic route. Dashika and Angela were going to go to a restaurant, have a nice farewell dinner.

We asked them about enemies, we asked about boyfriends. Thelma Moore told us that Dashika was sort of seeing a guy, but it was off and on, she thought maybe Dash had given him a pink slip. He wasn't the kind of guy who was heading to college. Delroy Staples was handsome, not tall, she thinks 5′8″ or so, slight build, pretty eyes, shaved head. Your first boyfriend, before you get smart. I left the room and called in an APB on Delroy Staples, then went back to the scene.

Belisle from forensics was crouched beside one of the girls. Her neck was lacerated. He looked up at me, anticipating my question.

"Fourteen stab wounds on the Black girl. Can't tell which came first yet. White one stabbed twice."

The killer was after the Black one; the other was collateral damage.

"Weapon?"

"Serrated blade, probably six–eight inches."

"Same weapon both girls?"

"Maybe."

Both girls were tall, slim, athletic. I nodded and left, went down to the car to wait for Davis. A handful of cops were talking to alleged witnesses, most of them witnessing each other, just wanting to be part of this.

Pierce and Toussaint walked over.

"Fucking barn dance," Pierce said, gesturing to the cars, EMS, fire, ambulance, news trucks.

I was looking over Pierce's shoulder. There was a guy at the back of the crowd. Something about him. Some perps hung around crime scenes.

"Good thing the black and white got here first," Pierce said. "Public relations coup."

The guy at the back of the crowd, maybe twenty, his face almost luminescent under the street light, like one of those fish that lives at the bottom of the ocean.

There was an elaborate mural on the wall of the building across from us, a scene that showed two women working in a field, a bit bigger than life-size. It was done as thick black outlines, no colour, stark geometric lines. The women were being overseen by a giant lamb wearing a straw hat, holding a whip. In what looked like biblical script were the words TO THE SLAUGHTER. It was evocative, had an odd power. I'd been through this way three nights ago and hadn't seen this. There were five others this size or larger on the southern buildings.

"You see this before?" I pointed to the mural.

Pierce glanced at it. "I don't know art but I know what I don't like."

"I think this is fresh."

"Fucking kids are on a tagging streak here," Toussaint said. He was heavy, bored. Pierce was wiry and mean. They looked like Lennie and George from *Of Mice and Men.*

"This guy is busy," I said.

"Crew most likely." Pierce said.

"What we have upstairs?" Toussaint said, checking his phone.

"Two dead girls."

"What's it look like?"

"Like a headline."

DAVIS FINISHED WITH the mothers and drove back to the station. Davis thinking about her own daughter, about those mothers.

"You think a jealous boyfriend maybe kills Dashika, and Angela is collateral," I said.

"Possible. No robbery. Both girls star students, no obvious sign of drugs, gangs, nothing that puts them into a risk category."

"Dashika's, what, five-nine? Strong. And her friend's there. She'd fight."

"Which maybe explains all the stab wounds."

"Or there is more than one killer."

"Mothers raise their kids to take on the world and everything is taken away. You don't get more devastated. I can't even imagine, and if I could, I wouldn't."

Everyone on that floor would carry this forever.

"Neighbour didn't hear any screams?" Davis asked.

"Yeah, no one heard anything."

"So either this is some kind of gang play where no one hears anything because they're scared, or there were no screams."

"You think two guys."

"You wonder how it could be one guy. He stabs one, the other is going to make some noise. They're standing in the living room, a few metres apart, maybe less. So why no screaming. The security cam?"

"There isn't a clean look at our door," I said. "We'll have to comb through it. There might be eighty people on it for our time slot. Wait for forensics for time of death."

"Or they knew the killer. Didn't expect it. That's why no reaction."

THE NEXT DAY, this was what we knew. We were looking for Delroy Staples, age twenty-one, left school at fifteen, no known address, surfaced in a city-sponsored work program for underprivileged kids, disappeared. And we knew this was a headline. Cities don't like senseless killing, they don't like beautiful promising girls taken away, leaving a psychopath with a knife. There were eighty murders in the city last year, spread over 630 square kilometres and seven million people. Of these, twenty-seven were gang related, the losses rippling through a few neighbourhoods, but from a broad civic perspective, essentially happening offstage. Another twenty-two were domestic, man kills his wife in a rage, family destroyed, street is shocked, it radiates a few blocks. There were a few random murders committed by angry motorists. All of these were page five in maybe two of the city's four papers. And then there were murders that caught some part of the civic subconscious, that tapped into collective fear and grief, and this was one of those situations. It would be front page, in the papers for weeks, then again when the trial started. The deaths of these two girls would ripple out from the city core and past its edges. At the same time, they would burrow into the city's psyche, change the way it saw itself. They would produce a handful of narratives, which would be in turn hopeful, hateful, contradictory, unreliable, and self-serving.

PRIORITY ONE, SUPERINTENDENT Harvey Mellon said. We were lead because Davis was young, female, and Black and the division already had optics issues; our lone female Muslim officer was suing both the force and the city, claiming systemic racism, sexual harassment, and Islamophobia. Davis had essentially replaced her, someone to point to when the word *diversity* came up, an effective ambassador to send to schools and speak to community groups, a face for recruitment posters. That she was extremely effective in this role was cause for both relief and worry in the division. Relief that she took some of the heat off the Boys' Club, and worry that she was dragging them into the future.

Mellon was mid-fifties, struggling with a complex neighbourhood, closing in on retirement. He had a sparse crew cut, a large gut, thin white arms, a face that was almost Irish cop, but there was something softer there, something unconvincing. His control of the station was tenuous and would have been non-existent if he hadn't been months from retirement. The hard nucleus of the station saw no point in steamrolling him and he had a dim awareness of this and it made him nervous and loud.

He was also putting Jimmy Lloyd and Mad Max Maxwell on the case. His reasoning was that Davis could gain access to the Black community, be the face of the investigation, while Lloyd and Max cracked heads, getting results the old way. At some point Lloyd would tell a reporter that this violence was imported from the islands, and he didn't *have a prejudiced bone in his body*, he's just *telling it like it is* and at what point did we all become *so afraid of The Truth.*

Mellon sat behind his desk and stared at his splayed hand, then looked up at us. The mayor was on the police chief, who was on him, he said. Whatever resources we needed.

"I understand there's a boyfriend," Mellon said.

"Yes, sir," Davis said. "We're looking at him."

"Seems pretty clear. We need to find this guy, get this thing done. City mourns alongside Mrs Moore, Mrs Blair, we bury the guy, justice is done. So, yesterday we need this."

The reason we needed it yesterday was that every day that the cruisers were stopping every Black kid with a shaved head and Jimmy and Max were working their magic, was a day that risked some fresh PR disaster.

Mellon took our intel, assembled the division, gave a speech about how this needed to be solved, how we were carrying the weight of the entire city on our shoulders. He was trying for something stirring.

WE DROVE EAST to Delroy's father's place, past a strip mall with discount electronics and shawarma and a cheque-cashing service.

Audley Staples lived in a tiny bungalow, one of those houses that had been spun out of the first suburb, the homes getting smaller as they radiated outward from that three-bedroom-two-cars-two-kids centre that was white as snow when it was built in 1952. He was sitting on a plastic chair on his small porch, reading what looked like a community newspaper, the kind that comes free to your door.

We parked and got out. Audley looked up at us. He was fifty or so, grey, thin with a paunch, wearing grey shorts and a wife beater that had Lebron's number written on it in what appeared to be felt pen.

"What are you going to do about the aliens?" he asked. His voice carried the islands in it.

"Illegal?"

"Illegal? Yes man they're illegal. They are taking slaves up in their spaceships." He held out the paper with one hand and slapped it with the other. "Right here." There was a fuzzy grey still from a 1950s alien movie: large head, big, dark eyes.

"That's our very next priority, Mr Staples," I said. "But right now we're looking for your son, Delroy."

"You find him, give him a licking."

"Did you give him a licking, Mr Staples."

"I haven't seen the boy in three years. What has he done?"

"We don't know if he's done anything. We just want to talk to him."

"I know how the police like to talk." He looked at Davis and said, "Where are you from, darlin'?"

"East York."

Audley chuckled. We stood on his lawn for another twenty minutes and found out that Delroy had come to Toronto from Jamaica when he was eleven, had lived with Audley, then with his grandmother. After that, who knew. He had his life, Audley had his. Delroy's mother had come up first, had a job to come to, was supposed to get settled, get a place, then Audley and Delroy would join her. Except when they arrived, she was gone, run off, Audley said, waving his hand.

"Let me tell you something," Audley said, his finger pointing at me. "In Jamaica, he was a beautiful boy. He went to church, he sang, he was an angel. Anything that he did, anything that he has become, that all comes from here." He gestured around himself with one stick-like arm, then pointed that finger at me again. "If the devil is in him now, this is all you people."

We drove north, the wide main streets devoid of people in the afternoon glare. We talked to the grandmother, Audley's mother, a diminutive woman who looked like she had just stepped out of the 1950s, wearing a print dress and a hat that you would wear to church. I asked her about church. She was Baptist, there was a church six blocks away. She was active, helped with their outreach program, she baked molasses cookies and helped new immigrants get acclimated. She offered us lemonade and those cookies. Her house was small, immaculate. Seven portraits of Jesus and a porcelain statue of our saviour on the cross, blood leaking from his bright blue eyes.

"There is so much suffering in the world," she said sweetly. She hadn't seen Delroy in several months. There was something inside of him that was good, she said, some place in his heart that would get him into heaven.

Davis and I drove back to the station.

"Hard to imagine her telling a lie," I said.

"I doubt either of them has seen Delroy for a while."

We watched the city slowly roll by, everyone looking at us, not looking at us. The east side went by, its monumental malls and empty spaces.

We had planned to talk to both mothers again. I had told Davis it might be better if she talked to them alone, that the presence of a woman, another mother, might feel more consoling than the both of us. But Davis said I had to come, had to carry the pain of these women.

We drove to Thelma Moore's house in East York, not far from the hospital. Susan Blair was going to be there. Davis had grown up around here in one of those bungalows. I thought she might say something about that as we drove, but she didn't. We'd been partners for eight months and in that first month we'd given each other thumbnail sketches of ourselves. She was thirty-six, had a master's in criminology, divorced, one kid. My previous partner, Travis Fell, had retired at fifty-one and moved to a small town an hour and a half away. I drove out to see him a month after he left, found him in the backyard of his house, tending to his garden and his alcoholism. You rely on your partner. You don't have to like each other, but you have to trust one another.

The street was mostly prim post-war bungalows that had been put up for returning Second World War veterans. There was a Toyota in the driveway, a crab apple tree in the front yard. The small lawn was mown. A garden up against the house had yellow flowers.

We rang the bell and Thelma Moore pushed aside the chintz curtain and took a look at us. She'd probably had reporters coming by, photographers. The papers had already run a story saying that Delroy was a person of interest, they'd been fed some details from someone inside. Moore looked at us for a moment, then opened the door.

Inside, Susan Blair was sitting on a floral-patterned couch. She was barefoot, wearing jeans, a polo shirt. Her face was a pale grey. There was a maple coffee table with two coffee cups on it, two chairs, a television in the corner, a dozen framed photographs of Dashika on the wall, a few school photos, one of her in her track clothes, outside, smiling.

Davis sat on the couch, I took one of the chairs.

"Can I get you coffee? Water?" Thelma asked.

We both shook our heads: *No, we're good.*

Thelma perched on a chair.

Davis gave her the preamble: *We're sorry to put you through this again at this incredibly difficult time, but anything that will help us catch your daughters' killer*...I let Davis do most of the talking. She asked Susan Blair about Angela—vibrant, full of life, a good student, dedicated athlete. She was crying, but kept talking through her tears.

"Did Angela have a boyfriend that you knew of?" Davis asked.

Blair shook her head. "No. No one serious. I don't think kids really date these days. Not like we used to anyway."

"She and Dashika were close."

Both Thelma and Susan nodded, tears smeared across their cheeks. "They ran track together," Thelma said. "They were a year apart, but it was kind of a big-sister thing. Neither of them had any brothers or sisters."

"Your husband..." I started, turning to Susan.

Blair waved the question away with one hand. "Gone for thirteen years," she said.

"Gone..."

"He's not dead. He left when Angela was four. I don't know where he's living. I doubt he's in the city."

"He wasn't part of Angela's life."

Blair shook her head. "No. He disappeared, moved to Thunder Bay with someone he met. We never heard from him."

"And he hasn't been in touch?"

Blair shook her head.

We stayed for forty minutes, collecting whatever we could. Their tears turned into sobs, and Thelma held her hands to her face, heaving. We waited for the sobs to subside. Davis asked a few more questions, then we left. We hardly spoke on the way back to the station.

I MADE A call to Delroy's last school, named for an explorer who everyone had forgotten. It had been six years since Delroy was there, but maybe someone remembered him. The principal said she did, had read the papers, had been thinking about Delroy, wondering if he could have done it.

I looked at the security cam footage once more, slowed it down. There were twenty hoodie guys caught on camera in the right time frame, all of them alone, three of them with sunglasses, all the faces obscured. The pavement was a pastiche of shadows, but another one briefly flashed, near the corner, something between an oval and a rectangle. A head. Another hoodie. Leaving at the same time as one of the others. So maybe two guys.

I drove out to the school. There were kids out on the field. The grass was dry and brown with large patches of dirt. There were only a few weeks left of school and those kids could feel it. They kicked soccer balls and pushed each other and stood around, trying to look cool.

The principal's name was Patricia Kozdaw: tall, weary, my age. She had looked up Delroy's file.

"He was a smart boy," she said, holding a paper, not really reading from it.

"But?"

"He got into a fight with another boy."

"There must be quite a few fights in the course of a school year."

"Too many. But Delroy came back the next day with a knife."

"He use it?"

"No. He threatened the other boy, though. I expelled him. It wasn't a happy decision, but I can't have weapons or even the threat of weapons in the school."

"Do you remember him having a girlfriend?"

"No, I wouldn't have any idea. I doubt any of the teachers would know something like that. But I remember Delroy. A beautiful young man."

Everyone remembered an angel.

TWO

I GREW UP IN the first suburb in the country, a planned community modelled loosely on Ebenezer Howard's Garden City idea that, surrounded by green space, we would return to Eden. The developers added the mid-century utopia of our own shopping centre. We had our own industry, and the people working in the Westinghouse factory on the edge of Don Mills spent their days making washing machines, then bought those washing machines from the store at the mall, and we were the poster children for progress, the middle class at its brief, glorious apex. There were three-bedroom split-level bungalows with car ports. The kids played ball hockey and worshipped the Maple Leafs. The dads all worked and most of the moms stayed home and followed a recipe on the back of a package of Shirriff instant potatoes and met for morning coffee and did exercises in front of the TV, and this veneer of Rockwellian order heralded a new civilization.

By the time I arrived there was boredom and drugs and mothers who drank in those arid afternoons and fathers who built basement lairs with wood panelling and wet bars to contain their rage.

My father went to work every day in the Westinghouse factory, where he was an assistant manager, and came home and lit a Du Maurier and watered the grass. When I was twelve he drove our Buick Skylark through the guard rail on the parkway and plunged into the ravine. A police car took my mother and me to the scene. It was daytime, traffic was light. The road was dry. The red and blue police lights were going and we stood by the broken guard rail and looked down at our car.

There was some life insurance, but it wasn't much. After three months we sold the house and moved into one of the high-rise apartments on the edge of the neighbourhood and my mother and I both started different lives. She had what was then called a nervous breakdown. None of her old friends came by. It was just the two of us in a seven-hundred-square-foot apartment on the tenth floor. I could see our old house from there, see our old life.

It was the end of birthdays. I didn't want to invite kids to the apartment and my mother didn't always remember anyway. A few weeks after my actual birthday she'd buy a cake that was on sale and I'd unwrap a sweater or a toy I'd outgrown with the TV on in the background.

She recovered enough to get a job, working as a waitress in a Greek restaurant in a strip mall. She had to take two buses to get there and when she got home after the dinner shift she was exhausted and sometimes fell asleep on the couch. On weekends we went to movies, taking a bus, then a subway, downtown, going to the early matinee and sometimes staying for six hours, watching three or four movies or parts of them. We always sat in the front row; she didn't want anyone between her and the screen, wanted to lose herself in it. She made popcorn at home to save money and brought it in a plastic bag in her purse and we shared the popcorn and stared up at all that glamour.

I went to the University of Wisconsin on a hockey scholarship and studied English literature and history. I felt guilty leaving my mother, but it was liberating to be in another country, to recreate myself. I came home for Christmas and summers and each time I came back I would find less of her. She took a bus to see a therapist, worked at the restaurant, watched television, no longer making the trek to the movie theatre. I went to law school at the University of Toronto and waited tables at night. Her cancer was diagnosed late. The oncologist said a matter of months, maybe a year. It turned out to be months. I quit law school in my third year and spent three months watching my mother slowly disappear. She had been thin and became almost transparent, a wisp. Her eyes were ringed red, blue veins bulging on her skeletal hands. In palliative she was on a morphine drip, semi-conscious, and I would sit beside her in the orange plastic chair in that dimmed light and hold her hand, trying to summon the life she might have had, a life framed by a central tragedy and then doled out in small punishments. Two days before she died, her eyes opened wide and she delivered a ten-minute stream-of-consciousness soliloquy—a jumbled conversation with my father from decades earlier, followed by a recitation, mostly the names of brands, like a preacher reciting books of the Bible: Deuteronomy, Leviticus, Numbers, Westinghouse, Du Maurier, Buick, Kraft. Forever and ever amen.

It took me two days to write her obituary; it was twenty pages long. There wasn't a service. Her ashes caught the west wind and scattered across Don Mills, landing softly on all that perfection.

A VISIT TO the track club that Angela and Dashika belonged to didn't yield much. The track club worked out at a high school in East York that had a nice track and a scoreboard that said HOME OF THE FIGHTING BADGERS. The coach and some of the kids remembered seeing Delroy occasionally hanging around. Seven of them didn't get a stalking vibe. Two thought he was a bit creepy. One said she knew the minute she laid eyes on him he was a killer, she could just tell. He was always alone, as far as anyone remembered. They were all devastated. And they were all scared. We said we were doing everything in our power and it was just a matter of time and they nodded and didn't look reassured.

The coach's name was Addison, Adidas sweatsuit, a loose walk.

"You saw Delroy up in the stands?"

"I saw him," Addison said. "There were others, boyfriends, girlfriends who came to watch practice. I finally had to ban them. Too much of a distraction."

"Delroy stopped coming?"

"He stopped sitting in the stands. He'd wait across the street. Sometimes in a car."

"You remember the car?"

"Old, someone's crappy first car."

"What can you tell us about the girls?"

"Dashika turned down three track scholarships, one of them to Florida State, full ride. Went with an academic scholarship. Angela worshipped Dash. Hung around her all the time."

"Would they come to you if they had a problem?" Davis asked.

"Boy problems? Probably not."

"Is there anyone they would go to?"

"You mean a teacher maybe?"

"Yeah, a teacher."

"You could talk to Alice...something, don't know her last name but Dash mentioned her a few times. Taught English, I think."

We thanked Addison. I went into the school to find Alice something. Davis left to go to Thelma Moore's. She had rounded up five friends of her daughter's, who would all be there. Davis would talk to them on her own.

I checked in with the principal's office, introduced myself, showed her my badge, asked if there was an Alice someone, taught English. There was a kid waiting in the office, not in trouble, waiting to do something, maybe for the principal after school. He looked at me.

"You're a policeman?" he asked.

"I am."

"Can I see your gun?"

"Can't take it out. If I do I'd have to write a whole report about why I took it out."

"How many people have you shot?"

The secretary said, "Mr Abel, Alice Fraine. She's in 211B. She's expecting you. Up the stairs, down the hall on your left."

I went to 211B. Alice Fraine was sitting behind her desk. She got up and shook hands and I sat down in one of the slightly undersized chairs. Alice sat down in her chair.

"You want to talk about Dashika," she said.

"What kind of student was she?"

"Top of the class. Worked hard. She had tremendous discipline. She approached school the way she approached track—train, get up early, beat the person beside you."

"Did you ever see Delroy Staples?"

"He waited for her sometimes. I'd see him out in the parking lot."

"Was he ever with someone?"

Alice thought for a minute. "He was usually alone. I think there was another boy with him sometimes."

"You remember this other boy? White, Black, Asian, older?"

"Wearing a hoodie. From this distance, hard to say. My guess would be Black."

"Did Dashika ever say anything to you about him?"

"She didn't say much. I had the sense that she was kind of ashamed of him. Maybe not ashamed, but you're dating someone and you don't introduce them to any of your friends. Like you're getting something from the relationship, but they don't fit into the rest of your life."

We talked for an hour. She was devastated by the deaths and started sobbing. I made soothing sounds and thanked her and left.

I WAS AT my desk when Jimmy Lloyd and Mad Max came in. Lloyd was mid-forties, 210, solid, son of a cop. Mad Max had a pocked face, a few years younger, few pounds heavier. There are essentially three kinds of cops. There is the guy who does everything by the book, who most of the station thinks is a useful idiot to send out to schools, do PR, ride-alongs with journalists. Then you have the Real Cops, who don't believe in rules, who do whatever needs to be done. In between these two poles is the Wise Officer, who understands the essential hypocrisy of the organization and finds some balance between the need for formal rules and the need to get things done. Lloyd and Max were in the second group.

"You anywhere on this?" Lloyd asked.

I shook my head.

"The heat coming down," Lloyd said. As a rule, Max didn't say much. When they talked to anyone, Max just stood there with that reptile sense of menace.

"*Where are you hiding, Delroy?*" Lloyd asked in a schoolboy voice. "*Come out come out wherever you are.*"

Lloyd took out a cigarette. He liked to wave an unlit cigarette, something between a prop and a threat. He'd sometimes light it inside a restaurant or bar and some guy would tell him *You can't smoke in here* and Lloyd would say he's the law and fuck that. "You still looking for the second gunman behind the grassy knoll?" he asked.

"Still looking."

"Once we find Delroy, there's a second guy, he's going to tell us."

"St. James Town," I said.

"Proud home to New Canadians."

"You answered some of those calls. Stolen cars, assault."

"I think the Tamils brought a war over with them. You'd think that's one of the things you leave behind when you come to the New World."

"Those murals there. Any leads on who's doing them?"

"We have a handle—Maestro."

"Like Banksy."

"Like who the fuck is Banksy."

"You see them anywhere other than St. James Town?"

"Hard to say. Apparently this guy is legend. Has imitators, so fuck knows. There's a tag on the bridge looks a bit like him. Maybe some of the splendid artwork along the retaining wall in the valley."

It wasn't clear if Mad Max had actually blinked yet. His eyes were dead.

"Nothing from any of your CIs," I asked.

Lloyd shook his head. "Guy has to be somewhere. And your current not-producing-any-results theory?"

"A girl," I said. "She's in love with Staples. He's lying low, watching the news, eating takeout that she is getting for him. She has a job, he's home all day with the TV. They feel like they're living in a movie. Bonnie and Clyde."

"Happy ending. Guy like that, he'll get itchy. He'll poke his head out." Lloyd held out the hand with the cigarette and pointed it at me and pressed the thumb trigger down and made a clicking sound.

DAVIS'S GROUP INTERVIEW gave us what we already knew: both girls beloved and talented, terrible waste. Everyone cried most of the time. There had been a vigil in St. James Town, a larger one planned for Queen's Park. There were flowers and messages and small gifts all laid in a shrine outside Dash's building. It dominated the news, tearful testimonies from classmates, some of them manufacturing some drama for the camera, maybe. The story was getting bigger. Davis did get one small piece of information; one of the girls said she'd seen Delroy with another kid, white, hair in cornrows, the kind of white kid who acts Black, moved his hands around like he was in a rap video.

DAY 4, MELLON calls a meeting, tells us he got a call from Miami police saying they had busted a young woman on a prostitution charge and had reason to believe that Delroy may have been working her. Fit the description, was from Toronto, just arrived, still had some of the island accent. The girl thought he may have been trying to get back to Jamaica, talked about it a lot. How it was paradise. Mellon said he was following up with Miami but not to take our eyes off the ball. Davis and I left.

"Credible?" I said to Davis.

"He gets to Miami, finds a girlfriend, turns her out, all in four days. Hard to see it. How does he get across the border?"

"Maybe some sleepy small-town crossing from Quebec into Vermont?"

"I don't think they do sleepy anymore."

"Takes a bus to New York or Buffalo?" I said. "Someone's car? It's a stretch. Kid is smart but he doesn't seem to have any kind of network. He'd need help."

"He's beautiful, vulnerable-looking. Gets some woman to help him out."

"What kind of paper would he have?"

"He'd have a passport."

"What time is our thing with the mayor?" I asked.

"Two tickets to the shitshow, 1:30."

OUR MAYOR, BOBBY DALE, was an alcoholic populist who used to sell hash in high school and who had the support of the suburbs and was an embarrassment and political *bete noir* to everyone south of Lawrence Avenue. He had a limited understanding of how to run a city but was a shrewd politician. He had sparse, dark hair cut short, a paunch, small eyes, a pug face, a graceless everyman who could connect to the anger that sat in every modern life. He was sprawled behind his desk, tie askew, one collar point turned up. The sweet rancid scent of alcohol leaked out of those suburban pores.

His assistant, who in her brief career had had to clean vomit from his suit and listen to jokes about pussy and find him pancakes and vodka at 2 a.m., was sitting in a corner with her phone in her lap.

"Detectives," he said. He didn't get up, motioned for us to sit. He smiled. "You know how I feel about cops."

He loved cops. He loved the cops who found him passed out in his SUV with an empty bottle of vodka on the floor and arranged for him to be driven home. He loved the idea of beefy old-school Irish cops twirling nightsticks, keeping the city in line, and he wanted desperately, almost evangelically, to return the city to the version he grew up in, a pale kingdom where it was safe for a suburban white kid to sell drugs in math class.

"This city..." He looked at Davis for the first time. "We're grateful for your work on this."

Neither Davis or I said anything. Keep this as short as possible.

His assistant held up her phone and snapped three quick photos of the three of us.

"This kid, the Jamaican you're looking for, we need this ASAP. I hear from friends on the force that we're close."

His *friends on the force* included Jimmy Lloyd. There were about ten cops he met with on occasion, most of them from the western suburbs or from central. I'd heard they met in a cop bar in the West End, a few drinks, a few sex workers who needed to cut a deal.

"We're close," I said. I felt it best to say something, wrap this up. "We're interviewing a suspect..." I looked at my phone. "They've got him in the box right now." I stood up.

Dale gave me a thumbs up. "Do what you need to. We need results. Got my blessing."

Walking out of city hall, Davis said, "What the hell was that?"

"I don't know."

"His 'friends on the force?'"

"Jimmy Lloyd is one of them. He's royalty—father, uncle both cops, the thin blue bloodline."

"So why do we get the uplifting pep talk?" Davis asked. "He barely stayed awake. We were in there for two minutes. He almost said I was a credit to my race."

"I think you're projecting."

"He's got Lloyd on it, he's got his own guy."

"Photo op maybe."

"Can you remind me again why we don't just bust his ass—driving under the influence, I'm guessing possession of an illegal substance, monumental stupidity, incipient racism..."

"We'd turn him into a martyr, a freedom fighter who is pushing back against the downtown elite, and his voice—the voice of the people—will not be silenced by the guerilla tactics of an overeducated Black revolutionary who wants to overthrow a democratically elected government."

"Jesus wept."

AT 7 P.M., driving home, I stopped in St. James Town and parked and got out. It was still hot. People walked to their buildings holding the same yellow bag from the No Frills down the street. The smell of cooking, spice in the air.

I looked at the mural with the women in the field. It was an impressive piece of work. You didn't have long with these things. You had to get it up in minutes. It taught the artist economy. How do you project misery and a hint of defiance in those faces with quick slashes of black lines? How do you get that lamb to convey menace? It did, though. Something about the eyes, the angle of the mouth. I walked farther along the sidewalk. There was another mural on one of the northern buildings. It was more elaborate. It was in a more protected spot and he would have had more time. It featured a bright red version of the letter C, more than two metres tall, a few red drops falling from the top. Below it, an elaborate figure that looked like an Egyptian hieroglyph, with the head of a malevolent fox. It was abstract and dramatic. Whoever Maestro was, he had talent.

"Money, phone, watch, motherfucker."

I turned around to a man, late twenties, my height, bad skin. He had a knife at his side, almost nonchalantly, an eight-inch blade. We were out of sight of most people passing by. Anyway, people walked with their heads up until they saw something that could be trouble, then their heads went down.

Adrenaline shot through me. He didn't look nervous, didn't look like he was using. Usually they're a bit jumpy. They talk fast, look around quickly, heartbeats racing, repeat what they just said louder. This guy was calm, another day at the factory.

"Hurry the fuck up," he said evenly. He maintained eye contact, didn't raise his voice.

"My wallet," I said, reaching into my jacket. I came out with the gun. It wasn't fast but he wasn't expecting it.

"Drop the knife," I said. "Lie down. You run I won't chase you, you understand."

He thought about it for five full seconds, then the knife hit the concrete with a scraping sound.

"Lie down, face first, put your hands behind your back." The adrenaline bouncing around.

He did it and I cuffed him and called it in. *Send a cruiser.*

"What's your name?" I asked. Silence.

I asked him a dozen questions, he didn't say a word. The cruiser arrived and took him in. I followed in my car, booked him on attempted robbery, assault with a weapon.

I went home and made a vodka martini. My condo was in a new building, a lot of glass. I could walk to artisanal muffins, fair trade coffee, artisanal bread, three tattoo parlours, artisanal sausages, and two dozen restaurants filled with exotic haircuts. Most of the force lived in the suburbs, away from what they had to deal with in the city core. I looked out the window. The sky was pink in the west. There were people heading down King Street, going for dinner, moving in small, animated groups.

I turned the oven to 400°F and took out broccolini, grape tomatoes, and a red onion, sliced the onion, cut the grape tomatoes in half, placed them in a bowl and drizzled olive oil and lemon, then added cumin and hot pepper flakes and tossed. I laid it all out on a cookie sheet, then added a slab of feta cheese on top. I mixed maple syrup and soy sauce and brushed it onto a fillet of salmon. I put the vegetables in the oven, then added the salmon on a separate sheet five minutes later. When everything was close to done, I turned the oven to broil and brushed the salmon again, and put it back, the salmon skin side up so it would get crispy and the fat would percolate down into the flesh. The skin was a stellar source of omega-3 fatty acids, which were good for something I couldn't recall. When it was done I took it all out, poured a large glass of a Cotes du Rhone that had been recommended in a newspaper column titled "French Overachievers Under $30," and sat down and watched the news.

THE NEXT DAY I came in at 10 a.m. and asked the desk cop to see the guy who'd tried to jack me. Ambrose Fortier was his name.

"We cut him loose."

"He threatens a cop with a knife and you cut him loose. You are aware that he was picked up fifty metres away from the biggest case in the city, which, by alarming coincidence, happens to be the stabbing of two girls by an unknown male." Though it was hard to believe that the killer would be that stupid.

"Didn't have a choice. Last night, guy comes in, $5,000 suit—not that I'd have a clue once you get above 299—but he's got bail."

"You have this guy's name."

The desk guy looked it up. "Here it is. Devin Nunes. Lawyer. Works with Delaney Hutch."

I nodded. A kid who is jacking people in broad daylight for pocket change and iPhones has a law firm that charges $900 an hour on retainer. And gets bail before the sun comes up. Nunes must have worked a deal with the Crown on bail terms, so no contested hearing was necessary. His case was called at 9 a.m., first on the list, and Fortier was on the street before I got in. Fortier had some kind of juice.

I looked up Fortier's record. He was twenty-nine. Six assault charges, did eight months for assault with a weapon. Was on a federal watch list for hate crimes. May have been involved in the defacing of a mosque in Scarborough. Was the singer in a white supremacist rock band called White Lives Madder.

I called Davis and told her the story.

"What the fuck," she said.

"Yeah. Something going on over there."

"You think there's a connection?"

"I do. But I don't have the slightest idea what it could be."

Most cities reach a certain size and they become a version of the Zapruder film, blurry and sick, combining tragedy and ten layers of conspiracy. A filament of money and drugs and politics and sex links a thousand people in a daisy chain of rumour and grift, the heart of every city. Whatever connected Fortier to that kind of money would be a glimpse into something.

IN FIVE DAYS, forty-one Black kids who more or less fit the description of Delroy Staples had been detained. There were twenty-two complaints about being unnecessarily stopped, searched, and manhandled. On Day 6, three things happened. One: Lloyd and Mad Max arrested a kid and broke his jaw. He was U of T, first-year medicine, following in the footsteps of his mother, Dr Susannah Paul, who hired high-profile counsel, and the three of them called a press conference and were suing the department and the city for a substantial but not unreasonable amount, which meant they were serious. This had the potential to haunt the news cycle for weeks.

Two: I couldn't sleep and got in my car and drove through St. James Town at 2 a.m. with my lights off. I backed into a parking spot, turned off the car, left the radio on very low and listened to a satellite show about Miles Davis. *Kind of Blue* was one of those college albums you'd hear everywhere, even Wisconsin. I listened to that mournful horn, slumped down in the seat.

I was almost asleep when a shape walked by, just off the sidewalk, dark hoodie, backpack. A kid, maybe 5′ 7″. He stopped, crouched down. He was looking toward Parliament Street. I started the car and stepped on the gas and he flushed like a rabbit in the lights, crashing out of the bushes, racing across Parliament. He tried to climb the fence into the cemetery. I jammed the car up on the sidewalk, got out and got an ankle. He kicked and I pulled him down hard onto the sidewalk. Kid looked maybe sixteen. Scared.

"I wasn't doing anything," he said.

"What's your name?"

"I don't...I don't have to tell you."

"You'd rather be arrested?"

"For *what*? I wasn't *doing* anything."

"What's in your backpack?"

"You need a search warrant." He was still scared. Someone had taught him this, someone who had a murky reading of the law.

"Get in the car." I pulled him into the front seat, locked the doors, did a fast U-turn, drove to a parked car on Parliament and pulled up within two inches of it so he couldn't open his door.

"What are you going to do?" Now he was wondering if I was really a cop or not. I wasn't in a cop car, didn't have a partner, hadn't shown him a badge.

"What's your first name?"

He hesitated. "William."

"Give me the pack, William, or I'm going to take it."

He took it off. "Here," he said. "It's not even mine."

"Of course it isn't."

I opened it up. There were four cans of spray paint. I looked at William. Difficult to believe he was Maestro.

"You know it's a crime."

"It's not a crime to have spray paint in a backpack." He was less scared now. And he was right.

"These colours match anything in St. James Town and that's enough." Probably not, and certainly not worth the paperwork.

"I'm an artist." William had short blond hair, maybe 125 pounds. "It's not a crime to be an artist."

"It's a crime to deface public or private property even if said defacing is believed by the artist-slash-perpetrator to be art. You do the piece with the sheep on the west side, William?"

"No. But if you're smart, you'll get a chisel and take it home. It's going to be worth a million dollars some day."

"The next Banksy."

"Banksy sold out, this is next level."

I hadn't heard Banksy had sold out. I was vaguely disappointed. "Maybe Banksy only pretended to sell out." I said, "Wouldn't that be in keeping with his persona?"

William looked out the window to the Subaru two inches away. "You'll never catch him, you know."

"I caught you."

William looked down.

"You want to tell me his name?"

"Banksy?"

"Maestro."

If William was surprised, he didn't show it.

"You work with him."

"He's a genius. People look at the *Mona Lisa* and see something different every time."

"I'm pretty sure that was a different guy." I put the car in drive and pulled away, heading south. "Where do you live, William?"

"I'm . . . it depends."

I guessed one parent or the other, and he was weighing which one would be less receptive to him being brought home by a cop at 2 a.m. "An international man of mystery."

I pulled onto Wellesley and stopped. I reached across William and opened his door. "Tell Maestro I think his work is derivative."

William grabbed his backpack and was out the door, racing into the darkness.

THE THIRD THING that happened was there was another murder.

THREE

THE CALL WENT OUT while I was at home asleep. In the morning, my cell rang. It was Davis. "There's another body in St. James Town."

"Victim?"

"It's Infinity. The Belgian vagina."

"Jesus. I'll be there in an hour."

Infinity's legal name was Audrey Meadows, a sunny name, a name from another era. Born Kevin Lundquist in Dryden, Ontario, a pulp and paper town, probably not a joyful place to grow up LGBTQ. She was twenty-nine years old and had been strangled with what may have been a necktie.

We went to Belisle in forensics. He was gaunt, humourless. Word was he never slept.

"Any thoughts?" I asked. "Angry customer?"

Belisle shrugged. He didn't like to speculate. He was, he regularly reminded us, pure science. "She was found in that field at the northern edge, near Bloor, by the historic house that has to be moved. She was face down. Strangulation. Maybe a tie. There are some fibres. We'll know soon."

"Something that was at hand."

Belisle shrugged.

"Infinity didn't usually work St. James Town," Davis said. "Any sign she was dumped there?"

"From the position of the body, she may have been dumped out of a car. It might have been moving, judging from the scrapes."

"She's in a car," I said. "Maybe some guy doesn't put it together who she is, gets a surprise when he puts his hand down there, loses it."

"He's wearing a tie..."

"Possibly," Belisle said.

"So white-collar guy, takes off the tie, strangles her..."

"You're acting in the moment, you take off your tie?" Davis said. "Doesn't really fit..."

"No, but if it's premeditated, he'd have a better plan for the body maybe. This guy drives a few blocks east, pulls into first open space he sees, keeps moving, reaches across, opens the door, pushes Infinity out. She's what..."

"One-forty," Davis said, "Give or take."

"So not an easy thing to get her out of a car while driving."

"A big guy?"

"Or two guys. Any bruises, contusions?" I asked Belisle.

"Some bruising."

"From being dumped or being beaten?"

"Too early to judge."

"But one is probably post-mortem," Davis said. "One is pre-, so..."

Belisle looked at us, his Nosferatu stare. "I'll have a portrait for you tomorrow, fibres, scrapes, time of death." He went back to his work and we left him.

"Portrait," Davis said.

"Belisle honestly believes he's an artist," I said.

"Maybe he is."

MELLON DIDN'T WANT any connection between the Blair and Moore murders and Infinity made solely on the basis of geography.

"This stays on page five," he said. "We already have the advocates on us, feeding the papers. *Need to protect the lives of sex workers*, et cetera. Priority one for you two remains Moore and Blair. Eyes on the prize."

Mellon told me I was heading to Kingston, Jamaica, said Miami had liaised with the Kingston cops, that Delroy Staples was headed there. Kingston police heard murmurs from their people, he might be on the island. It sounded thin and Mellon wasn't convincing.

"How solid is this intel."

"Solid enough we have to follow up."

In the five seconds of silence that followed, Mellon's face looked a bit blank, as if he were trying to remember something he'd memorized imperfectly. "Be a public presence," he said. Find Staples if he's there, escort him back. Bring a good suit, in case there are photographers at the airport. If he's not there, then it's *no stone left unturned*, *no expense spared*, et cetera. Davis would stay here, be the public face of the operation.

"You've got Global in studio tomorrow," he said to her. "Seven a.m. Perky haircuts who will lob you softballs. Optics," Mellon said gravely, wrapping up. We left his office.

"Tell Global you're happy to talk," I said, "but you're busy catching villains. Get them to send a crew to the station. You want home field advantage. You don't think it's odd they want you in studio?"

"If I do it in the office I've got Toussaint and Pierce standing off camera doing a jerk-off pantomime."

It made sense for Davis to be the public face, and it almost made sense to send me to Kingston, if that intel was solid. And maybe it made sense to go on breakfast television and lay out the official line.

"Don't do the athlete speech," I said. "*We're giving 110 percent*... You need to be memorable and substantive."

"Substantive?"

"Maybe not substantive. Don't lie, don't tell the truth. Think grey area."

Davis had a double major in psychology and sociology as well as a master's degree in criminology. She'd done a stint in city hall, then took time to have a kid and get divorced. She had maybe two more years on the force. My guess would be politics.

FROM THE AIR, Kingston looked like paradise. Set between a natural harbour and the Blue Mountains, which rose from the northern suburbs in a wall the texture of velvet. The elegiac remains of the middle class spread out in a lush grid, fine neglected homes and gorgeous plants. Goats, and rusted, corrugated tin fences, and concrete buildings that looked like they'd been left by a previous civilization. The cab driver took me past Bob Marley's old house. I remembered sitting in someone's living room, smoking a joint, thirty years ago, listening to Marley on six-foot speakers.

I was staying at a chain hotel downtown that was surrounded by a ten-foot fence with razor wire on the top. A sign in the lobby read IF YOU ARE A STRANGER TO OUR CITY, *do not go out* WITHOUT CONSULTING A CLERK. I checked in, then took a cab to the police station. There were bullet holes in the concrete outside. It was early afternoon, maybe 35°C. I was meeting with a Detective Sprang.

He was sitting at a desk, white shirt, sleeves rolled up, fifties, a big man hunched over a laptop. He looked at me and got up heavily, like a bear coming out of hibernation. There were three other people in the small room. It was hot. A fan spun slowly overhead.

"Detective Abel," he said, his hand out.

"Jamieson," I said. "You're Augustus Sprang."

"I am. How can I help?"

"Any thoughts on where Delroy Staples is hiding would be a great help."

"We can talk to a few people." I followed him out to his car, a beat-up Rover. We drove through the streets, past skinny dogs, past a naked man walking on Hope Road, past the tangle of flowers and weeds that grew in real time. There were clouds coming in, luxurious, stately.

It was hard to gauge how Sprang felt. There was a polite but insistent diplomatic war going on between our two countries. Canada was trying to send Canadian/Jamaican criminals who had been born here back to the island, saying they had been criminalized here. Jamaica took the Audley Staples argument that they became criminals in Canada and so we should keep them. The nature/nurture argument between governments was basically political theatre—the bottom line was no one wanted the expense of incarceration, or to have to deal with them when they got out.

Sprang probably knew all this and was probably told to help me, though maybe not too much, and was probably resentful. Ideally, they would have caught Staples already and handed him over, giving them some diplomatic leverage. We drove in silence through the streets, then up into the Red Hills. The windshield was cloudy from smoke and dust and the world outside had soft edges, the city going by like an old movie where the print is damaged.

We came to a service station that looked like a Walker Evans photo, a rusted pump and a sign advertising Red Stripe beer. A goat was tethered to a stake. Five kids played with a soccer ball, red dust rising up in puffs.

We drove very slowly for two minutes, then pulled over and parked. There was a subtle opening in the bush at the side of the road. Sprang looked in, motioned for me to follow. A goat path that wound through the trees. We walked for forty minutes. The air got cooler as we climbed but there was no breeze and I was sweating heavily. We finally emerged from the jungle onto the spine of a hill. The hills to the north faded in blues and greens.

There was a row of houses along the spine, prim wooden bungalows, an ordered, unlikely settlement. The air was cool, fragrant, perfect. We walked to one of the houses. There was an old man sitting on the porch, small, wearing round sunglasses. His face had the expectant squint of the blind. In front of him were homemade weights made of welded car parts. Two chickens were in a coop.

"Who's that?" the man said.

"Augustus Sprang, Kingston police. Denham Town," Sprang said.

"You a ways from home, Augustus."

"I'm looking for someone who's a ways from home."

"Lord guide us home. Are you alone, Augustus."

A shape appeared behind the screen, large, bigger than Sprang. Stopped there. In the shadow I could only see the outline. Maybe 6′6″, a solid 260. A voice boomed, "He's not alone, Ludwick, he has a white man."

"A white man," Ludwick repeated.

The shape stepped out. The largest woman I'd ever seen. Maybe fifty. Her hair was plaited, streaked with grey. She stood on the porch with her feet apart, her head close to the ceiling. She was an inch taller than Sprang, maybe ten pounds heavier.

"Massie," Sprang said softly. "You're a vision."

"I'm a ghost, Augie. That's why you haven't seen me in fifteen years. Maybe too busy with ACID, knocking heads, feeding rude boys to the sharks."

"ACID is long ago, Massie. I'm a peaceable man now."

"There are no peaceable men. They just get too old and tired to ruin the world."

"The world was ruined before I came into it."

"And all that ruination was caused by men. Some of them men like you, Augustus. Now why did you drag a white man up into these hills? A live sacrifice to atone for your sins? You'll need more than one, I suspect, though it's a start."

There were a few other people on their porches now. This was as close to live theatre as they would get.

"Looking for a man, Massie, a bad man."

"Bad men down in Kingston. This is the Kingdom of the Good."

"He could have family up here. Staples."

"Staples." She rolled the name around in her mouth. "Barrel children and chicken thieves."

I wondered how Delroy could find this place. He'd been gone a decade. His mother disappeared, father and grandmother in Toronto. Who was here who would take him in?

"We send our angels," Massie said, "and they send us gangsters."

Sprang stared up at the complicated sky. "Abraham?" he asked.

"The Lord took him. A mercy. His grave is there you feel like praying, Augustus."

Sprang nodded.

"You still doing the Lord's work, Massie?" Sprang asked.

Massie's laugh was like a lion's roar, it resonated through the hills. "Someone has to," she said, "while the Lord drinking Red Stripe on the beach."

We stood out there in that sun and Sprang and Massie talked for another half hour, a combination of family catching up and the odd hint about the Staples clan. He didn't introduce me. We weren't invited to sit. I could feel the sun boring into my skull. My legs were sore. I could have used a glass of water but there wasn't any offered. It occurred to me that Sprang knew we wouldn't find Delroy Staples up here, that this was essentially theatre.

"I'm sorry for your troubles, Massie," Sprang finally said.

"My troubles were thrust upon me," Massie said. "You invited your troubles in for a drink and now they want to stay."

Sprang turned and left the way we came and I followed him. There were fifteen or so people on their porches watching us. They were mute, without expression, like a photograph.

On the way down the path, a violent thunderstorm hit. It was too loud to talk. We had some protection from the rain, but it was hard and persistent and the path got slippery and I fell hard three times before we finally emerged onto the road. I tried to clean some of the mud off before getting in the car, but Sprang waved it away and got in.

"Cousin?" I asked.

"Mother's side," Sprang said.

"Interesting woman."

"Her husband stuck a knife in her one night and she took the knife out and snapped his neck like a chicken. So, yes, interesting."

We drove the rest of the way in silence. It was a pleasant drive, the city fresh from the rain, the sun instantly hard. I had the feeling that I was being played, that Mellon or someone above him called someone they knew on the island, a cop, who gave Sprang the job of babysitting me, who was understandably resentful and took me on this snipe hunt to eat up the day. He dropped me at the hotel.

"You'll let me know if you hear anything," I said.

The sound he made might have been affirmative.

I went up to my room, took a shower, washed the mud off my clothes and hung them over a chair on the balcony.

It was after 5 but I looked through the phone book, then called the Justice Minister's office. I was surprised when a woman picked up. I asked to make an appointment with the minister, gave my name, said I was a Toronto detective here on official business, apologized for not calling earlier. She put me on hold, came back and said I could have twenty minutes at 9 a.m. the next day. Another surprise.

I took a nap, woke up an hour later, got dressed, and went down to the bar and ordered a beer. I had jerk chicken, rice, yams, another beer, and went upstairs and read *Island on Fire,* an account of the revolt that ended slavery in the British Empire. I slept, dreamless, for nine hours and woke in the sterile roar of air conditioning.

EPHRAIM LIGHTLY WAS about sixty, from his voice I'd guess educated in England, a veteran of two dozen global symposiums on race and crime and immigration. He was the Minister of Justice, wearing a grey linen chalk-stripe suit, a crisp white shirt, expensive loafers, no socks. We were in his office, a spare, tasteful room, sitting in leather club chairs. We each had a coffee.

I told him I was there looking for Delroy Staples, murder suspect in Toronto. Lightly had heard about the case.

"What makes you think he's on the island?"

I told him about the Miami intel.

Lightly shrugged. "Perhaps they are right," he said. "But you hold power on this island by having ears everywhere on the ground, and I haven't heard anything."

There was a small silence, then Lightly said, "No one is a criminal at the age of eleven. They go away, they think they are heading to the Promised Land. Then they are met with racism and alienation and marginalization and poverty and disillusionment. Their parents are cleaning offices at night, barely making enough to buy them winter clothes. Would that be fair to say, Mr Abel?"

"Something like that."

"Then they steal a bicycle, or they are found with a knife they are carrying for their own protection, and they become part of the "justice" system, and they walk down that path until they are jailed, then sent back here. We have become a dumping ground for the world's criminals. Let's take your Delroy Staples." A subtle emphasis on *your*. "He arrives in Toronto, has some trouble adjusting, is streamed into a vocational program. When you give school credits for working at a McDonald's, you are in effect creating a proletariat class. And the proletariat, at some point, history shows us, he rises up." Lightly had a specific knowledge of Toronto, either through briefing, or personal experience. I guessed the latter.

"You think that's what Delroy Staples was doing, rising up?"

"I can't say what he was doing, if he is, in fact, the guilty party. We can surmise that he is understandably frightened he won't get a fair trial."

"He'll get a fair trial."

"From your perspective, perhaps, they all look fair, Mr Abel. I can assure you it doesn't always look that way from the witness stand."

We talked for an hour; it was mostly a philosophical discussion. The coffee was very good. I shook hands and left and walked around Kingston. A naked man crossed the road ahead of me. He looked like the one I'd seen the day before. A big man, in good shape, with the stately gait of the mad. Lightly hadn't heard about Delroy being on the island. And he hadn't heard that I was coming to look for him, which meant this was purely cop to cop. I went back to the hotel and called the Miami police department and spent an unpleasant twenty minutes being routed through various communications people who didn't know anything about a Delroy Staples. I phoned the editor of *The Gleaner*, who agreed to meet me in the afternoon.

Willoughby James was late forties, balding, rumpled. We walked to a street tavern that seated about eight people, a small fan perched on the bar. He ordered beer for both of us. If Delroy Staples being on the island was a charade, he might know, might have heard something. Not enough for a story, but enough for a barroom anecdote.

"Is my guy on the island?" I asked.

He shrugged. "If the police know where he is, they'll wait until you're off the island before catching him. Don't want to make it look like the Mounties came down to solve our crimes."

"If he was here, would he be up in those hills?" I asked.

James shook his head: *No*. "More likely down in a scheme."

"A scheme?"

"Housing project. Governments build them to house their sufferers. The government falls, then the new government builds a scheme across the street to house theirs. It's like Belfast, man, you cross the street and you see the enemy."

"Kid's gone for years. Who takes him in?"

"We are a generous people, Mr Abel. Someone will take in the strays."

I listened to his lilting voice, which went up an octave when he was excited, then asked him to recommend a hotel. I wanted something a little more relaxed. He gave me the name of a place.

"Up on the hill," he said, and pointed. "Woman who owns it is named Charity, though why, no one knows." He laughed. "You say hello to Charity for me."

CHARITY'S HOTEL WAS called the Rebel Respite and was tucked into the hill. The road was a line of iron gates. I pressed the small buzzer at the front and waited. A woman came down the gravel roadway. She was somewhere between fifty and a hundred, diminutive, slim, a face that had done all the aging it intended, skin stretched tightly.

"Mr Abel," she said, unlocking the gate. "Welcome."

She let me in, locked the gate, and I followed her up the driveway. She had a dancer's walk, erect, gliding. The growth was dense. There was one car parked, which I assumed was hers. The hotel was a large house, I guessed maybe five rooms. It was white and spartan and clean. There was a table outside under an awning. I told her that Willoughby James at *The Gleaner* said hello.

"That fatuous shrivelled sand crab," she said. She showed me my room: small, white, functional. There was a ceiling fan. No air conditioning.

"Dinner is at seven," she said as if I had no choice, which I suppose I didn't.

I unpacked, laid down on the heavily starched sheets, got up for the sunset, a muted affair, sinking behind the hill. A few pale red streaks drifted up from the horizon. I went down for dinner, taking a place at the table outside. I wrote up my notes.

Charity brought me a beer. Twenty minutes later she brought two plates of jerk pork and a salad made of something I didn't recognize and sat down with me. I took a bite of the pork. It was so spicy my eyes watered. I had a long sip of beer.

"What brings you to paradise, Mr Abel?" she asked.

"Call me Jamieson. I'm here looking for someone."

"You're police."

"Toronto."

"How are those Maple Leaves of yours?"

"Still a symbol for failure. You know Toronto?"

"I was there in 1992. I went to bury my father."

I nodded sympathetically. I had a mouthful of the pork. Delicious but lethal.

She told me her father had gone to Toronto when he was seventeen to go to university. It was the early 1960s. There were so few Black people then that they said hello to one another on the subway. Her father was a lawyer who worked as a public prosecutor, a crusader who had a heart attack in the courtroom and whose last word was *guilty*. She flew up for the funeral, her mother didn't. We finished our dinners and Charity brought two more bottles of cold beer. She sat back. The air was cooling and fragrant. The setting was stunning. Charity took a joint out of her top pocket and lit it, inhaled deeply, then handed it to me.

"Join me, Jamieson," she said, extending the first vowel of my name. She had a hypnotic voice.

I stared at it for a moment. Charity smiled. I couldn't remember the last joint I smoked. Maybe that one thirty years ago, listening to "No Woman, No Cry." I took it and examined it and took a careful drag. I told her about basketball and policing and we smoked the whole thing and Charity brought out more cold beer and I was preposterously stoned. Her face shimmied in the light of the paper lanterns that hung in the garden. Lizards darted in my periphery, hundreds of them, stopping and starting like rush hour traffic. Her face was both new and ancient and her voice sounded like something coming out of the earth. She smiled and told me a story.

Port Royal was the wickedest city on earth. But first it was the most beautiful city on earth. Beauty is corrupted in nature, that is its role. The Spanish had it for 150 years, then the English. It was 1655 when the English took it, and piracy, then as now, was the most lucrative business. Do you know what the government called piracy—forced trade. Ha ha ha.

Everyone in Port Royal had their hand in privateering, every prostitute and barkeep, every politician and merchant. It was the Sodom of the New World. Strumpets would walk the streets naked for two pieces of eight. The animals and birds were drunk from the ale flowing in the streets. And the rum—Kill Devil rum—didn't kill the devil, it gave birth to him, and he wandered the streets rejoicing in what he had made. Only Boston was bigger in the New World, but this was the world's id, its blackness and debauchery on full display. There was no need to hide their sin from God as they did in Europe; they could copulate and drink and fire their muskets into the skulls of their slaves while sitting in the tavern. If you came to Port Royal, you signed a contract with the devil.

There was a pirate named Yardley whose vileness was without boundary. He boarded Spanish ships and took their gold and set fire to the vessels and cheered as the men sank with their ships. He mutilated prisoners and fed them to dogs and laid bets on who would be eaten last. He consumed more rum than ten men and whipped his slaves and murdered every prostitute he ever violated, wanting a clean slate, he said. But even Yardley, the most barbarous man on earth, had a weakness, the weakness that most men have: love.

He was in love with a prostitute named Queen Anne and because she did not love him he tied her naked to the whipping post in the town square and whipped her while she screamed for mercy and he sang an English folk ballad. She was scarlet ribbons slumped against the blood of a thousand unfortunates. But her screams woke her husband from his rum stupor and he saw his love tied to the whipping post and he roared and wept and brought down his broadsword on Yardley, cleaving him at the shoulder. While Yardley lay stunned and maimed on the stones, the husband cut off Yardley's leg at the knee and roasted it in the fire that always burned in the square to remind us the devil was never far. He ate from the roasted flesh as if it was the finest beef and danced a jig. Yardley was still alive, watching his own flesh consumed, understanding that the devil had finally come to claim him.

At that moment, all the parrots of the island lifted off their perches at once. A million strong, hovering in the air, their colours blotting the sun. A quiet tremble in the earth, a simple jolt. All of Port Royal stopped and looked down, then up at that multi-coloured sky. The adulterers and murderers and slaves and whores, the aiders and abettors, the loose and the looser, the landed gentry and those they landed on. And for one precious minute they felt God's respite and the world was still.

Then God came to his *senses and the earthquake hit.*

The city was built on sand. It liquefied, people and dogs and buildings and sin sucked straight down to hell. Geysers erupted, water sent by Satan himself, heated in the bowels of purgatory. Survivors were given an hour to think on their sins, the grief they had laid upon this earth. Then the tsunami hit. The entire cemetery where Captain Henry Morgan's casket lay was washed to sea, the newly dead mingling with those they had murdered.

And who was left?

The vilest and basest, who committed depredations and robberies and violence. The million parrots circled above, watching the animals from the jungle mix with the living who mixed with the dead until it was impossible to tell them apart.

It was 1692, June 7, still morning. God's Judgment come and gone.

That city is still down there. Divers go and find pieces of eight and the bricks of taverns and brothels and empty chests. The bones are the whitest on earth. There is a watch that was recovered, dated 1692, stopped at 11:43. The exact moment God quit and left this town to the devil.

I WOKE AT ten, the heat already in the air. The fan beat softly above me. My head was stuffed with rags. I showered and dressed and walked down to the garden and sat, my mind buzzing and vacant. The birdsong was deafening. Tiny lizards skittered across the gravel. The sun was high, punishing. The city, laid out below, in a haze, innocent from a distance, like all cities.

Charity came out with two coffees and a plate of pastries and fruit. She sat down.

"Are you a witch?" I asked.

She laughed, full-throated, vaguely sexual, a witch's laugh. "You can't come to Jamaica and leave without a ganja moment," she said.

"Did you tell me a fairy tale?"

"I told you the true history of this city. And I should know. I witnessed every moment of it."

WHEN I ARRIVED at the Toronto airport there was a photographer and two newspaper reporters and a film crew. They asked about Delroy. I was polite, evasive, said a search hadn't turned up anything and I couldn't comment any further because it was an ongoing investigation.

The next morning's headlines read TORONTO COP SEARCHES FOR JAMAICAN KILLER. There was a photograph of me. It had been a pure PR play. This would be someone above Mellon. The police chief or the mayor or both wanted to nail down the idea of imported crime in the public imagination, that we were looking for the Other. I had been played and it left a very sour taste.

FOUR

DAVIS AND I WERE in the station looking through Belisle's report on Infinity.

"So how was your holiday?"

"Pure PR. The Miami intel was horseshit, there was nothing in Kingston. It was a set-up."

"You think Mellon?"

"I'm guessing the chief or mayor or both. A political play: Polite society terrorized by violent outsider."

"So Delroy is still in town."

"He's not in Jamaica."

Infinity was Pierce and Toussaint's case, but we wanted to check for any connection to our girls. Unlikely, but.

"Belisle says the bruising's not consistent," Davis said. "Some pre-, some post-."

"So the killer hits her before strangling her."

"Scraping looks like a moving car, the way she caught that hard earth, the ruts from the heavy machinery."

"He thinks a tie is the murder weapon. Fibres are dark blue, almost black, mulberry silk, the most expensive silk in the world, and the reason it's so expensive is it comes from the *Bombyx mori* moth, which is raised in captivity in deepest China. The eggs are kept at 65–75 degrees Fahrenheit, then the larvae are fed mulberry leaves 24/7 by Buddhist priests." I looked up at Davis. "Christ, there's another whole page on this. Belisle's doctoral thesis. Bottom line, a tie made of mulberry silk can run $350."

"This is the shit Belisle lives for," Davis said.

"Says it's the strongest natural fibre on earth."

"I thought that was supposed to be spiderwebs. So who has $350 to drop on a tie and an affinity for sex workers?"

I knew of one possibility.

Toussaint and Pierce came in, Pierce doing an awkward sort-of-samba dance, singing, in a tortured accent, "Hey Mister Tallyman, did you get your banana tallied..."

Davis looked up, thought about saying something.

"How was your publicly funded wild goose chase to Montego Bay?" Pierce asked me. "Is it true they keep the best pot for themselves?"

Possibly. "You guys have the Infinity case," I said.

"To Infinity and beyond."

"You have anything yet?"

"Canvassed the strip. She was beloved et cetera. Few of her regulars we're checking out, though probably someone new, some rube, finds a dick, loses his mind."

I nodded. Pierce and Toussaint were my age, old school. They barely acknowledged Davis's existence.

"So what happened down there," Pierce asked. "You find anything or you just lay on the beach smoking weed."

"Pretty much the latter."

"No stone unturned," Pierce said. "Or was it *No turn unstoned*?" The two of them laughed and shuffled along, Pierce singing again.

"I need to check something," I said to Davis, getting up, putting on my jacket.

"Something."

"Back in an hour."

I DROVE INTO Rosedale, like arriving in Oz, the world suddenly green. The homes were set back from the quiet streets, the hush of money. A man in shorts walked a borzoi, the only visible pedestrian. Rosedale was just across a ravine from St. James Town. They were the city's starkest contrast. Every house here was north of $3 million, some of them went for 20 or more. I drove through streets that wound in concentric half-circles, a maze that followed the horse trails Mary Jarvis had ridden in the nineteenth century. She was the one who named it Rosedale, for all the wild roses that grew in the area. Her husband, William Jarvis, was sheriff of the Home District, and a supporter of the Family Compact, the network of humourless, quietly corrupt Tories who ran the province. He was the one who put down the 1837 rebellion led by William Lyon Mackenzie. In his newspaper, Mackenzie lamented that the country was in the hands of a few covetous men who had blurred politics and business. The sons of the privileged raided Mackenzie's offices and smashed his printing press. Five years after a slave revolt in Jamaica, Mackenzie gathered a group of unhappy farmers to deliver democracy to Toronto and they marched down Yonge Street, defiant, God on their side. All the colonies rebelling against Britain's palsied ownership, a country adept at acquiring colonies, less adept at managing them. All those pink countries on our school maps.

I got to the house. It took some finding. I hadn't been here in more than a decade. It was two storeys, stone, leaded windows, one of those architectural hybrids, vaguely Georgian with a little Arts and Crafts. The scale was a bit off. I guessed it would be north of $5 million. A gardener was working on a tree with an electric clipper. The grass was newly mown.

I rang the bell and he answered. His face hadn't changed much in ten years, heavier, the eyes weary. He'd be mid-seventies, a bit older maybe, a diminutive man who was rounding into a circle. He was wearing chinos, loafers, and a red cashmere sweater against the chill of the air conditioning. He didn't recognize me at first glance but he had a politician's gift for faces. He wasn't happy to see me, but his face brightened mechanically. He had been a politician for forty years and had been very good at it.

"Detective," he said.

"Titus."

TWELVE YEARS AGO, I'm cruising the night shift in the West End and see a limo parked in a dead-end street. It's 3 a.m. I pull up, blocking the exit. Routine check, knock on the glass, tinted, can't see anything. No one opens the window. I hammer hard, tell them to open up. I can hear things moving inside, sounds. I'm getting nervous. When a heavily tinted limo window goes down, you have no idea what you'll see: a pile of kids on prom night, a shotgun.

"Three seconds," I say, "or I smash the glass." I've got my stick out. Window goes down. There's a driver, kid maybe nineteen, wearing a black limo driver suit that doesn't fit. I tell him to open the back door or I'll come through the window. Kid's nervous as hell, unlocks the door, I open it, look inside.

Titus Bishop, West End city councillor, is sprawled, stoned. His pants aren't entirely pulled up. There's two sex workers, one on each side of him. The one nearest me is half dressed. She's high. Coke residue on the seat. She's wearing handcuffs, the kind that have pink fluffy padding to protect your wrists. There is a smear of blood on her face, from her lip, it looks like. The other one is naked except for heels, also in cuffs. She has bruises on her legs. The sex worker closest to me says, *Won't you join the party, Sunshine?* A bleak stoned smile. Her name's Violet. Her friend is Rose. Titus is a seven-time city councillor with a coke problem and a noted bagman for the Conservative party. This is the snapshot. The story behind it would be more complicated. I get the key to the cuffs, unlock the girls, ask them if they want to press charges, *No, just friends having a good time.* I tell the driver to drop them where they want, take Titus home, make sure he gets inside the back door. *Go home, pretend your summer job was painting houses.* I follow them, he drops the girls at a house in Leslieville, then drives to Titus's house, helps him inside. I drive back to the station, write up my notes, take them home, keep them in my desk.

I went back to Titus's house the next morning, rang the doorbell, talked to him, staring at his bleary face as it registered the debt. It was something I carried in my back pocket. Titus had a lot of juice. There could come a day when I needed him. Except I never did. But Titus was the only person I knew who had a taste for sex workers, some surprising kink, and could afford a $350 tie.

SO ALL THAT history hovered between the two of us on this pleasant summer morning.

"Please come in."

I followed him to his study. It had a bay window that looked out on the backyard. There was another gardener back there, trimming the forsythia. I thought it might be a little late for pruning. It would be his wife's money that paid for the house, unless he had skimmed a lot more than I imagined. Titus's shelves were lined with books. He had a mahogany desk with nothing on it. There were photographs on the wall of him posing with minor luminaries.

We chatted briefly. He knew the statute of limitations for favours had run out long ago. He was out of politics. I wasn't a real threat. His wife came in, a handsome woman who was a few years older. She had silver hair, a square masculine jaw, still fit-looking, wearing tan slacks, a black T-shirt, jewellery that was subtle but expensive. She was five inches taller than her husband, her face heavily lined. She had a regal bearing. They had married late, just before I'd found him in that limo. He was the longest-serving councillor in the city's history and the only one to represent two different wards He'd become the sitting member for Toronto Centre and retired a few years ago.

"This is Detective Abel," he said. "My wife, Dorothy."

Dorothy smiled. "A pleasure, Detective. I hope nothing tragic has happened."

"There's been a series of break-ins in the area," I said. "Just routine canvassing."

Dorothy gave a half smile. She knew that every house within a ten-block radius had an alarm system to rival the Vatican. And she probably knew some of her husband's netherworld and probably didn't know all of it.

"I hope that you punish the guilty party," she said pleasantly, and left. You see couples and wonder what kind of bargain they struck.

I told Titus about Infinity. I didn't mention the tie.

"Those poor women, standing outside in every kind of weather. I see them in the winter, shivering. It looks like the nineteenth century."

"Where is Sheriff Jarvis when we need him."

Titus wasn't going to offer anything—*Surely you don't think that I*...

"We are all of us prisoners, Detective Abel," he said slowly. "Imprisoned by need and appetite, and we weigh the consequences of escape. There was a time when those appetites went unchecked in the world. But now everyone has a phone, every life is a movie that shows on YouTube for six minutes, and in those minutes futures are destroyed, lives compromised. We are revealed for what we are, both victim and viewer. It's rarely an encouraging picture."

"No."

"So we do what we can to help the less fortunate, to bring balance to our world." He looked out the window. "The predations of age aren't all bad, Detective. There is comfort in a garden. In a quiet evening with a glass of wine and a good book."

We chatted a bit more and I got up to leave. His wife came in again.

"Has justice been done, Detective?" she asked.

"I hope so." Bishop probably still had appetites and some of them probably still found their way out of the cage. He had a taste for violence—that girl and her cut lip—but I doubted he was a killer. But I wanted to see his face. He wouldn't have the strength to strangle Infinity or dump her body. He would have needed a driver, an accomplice, which would be a liability he would be unlikely to take on. He probably had a mulberry silk tie, though.

I STOPPED ON Bloor and went into Holt Renfrew and asked for the most expensive tie they had. The saleswoman was late forties, slim, elegant, her hair expertly coloured. She had a kind face, though it may have been professionally kind. She assessed my clothes instantly without quite glancing down. She could see I wasn't the guy who buys a $350 tie.

"That's our only criteria?" she said with a small laugh.

"It needs to be mulberry silk." I showed her my badge. "Detective Abel. I'm wondering how big the market for $350 ties is."

"Bigger than you might think."

"How many are made with mulberry silk?"

"Some, certainly, though it's not always on the label. It's something you would have to know."

"You'd sell how many ties over $300?"

"In a year? Several hundred maybe. They are a handy gift at a price point that works for a lot of things."

"And they get the worm story."

"Sometimes."

"So the city, all stores..."

"We probably sell the most, but more than a thousand or so ties like that in a year, I would say."

"And how many of these are mulberry?"

"Is this a murder investigation?"

"Why would you ask that?"

"I'm guessing it's not a stolen tie we're looking at. Mulberry, maybe three hundred in the city, though this is more guess than anything."

I looked around the store. There were a handful of shoppers. A line of dark suits, a table filled with summer sweaters in the colours of a kid's crayons.

"I did have a customer who bought a bunch of them," she said.

"Mulberry?"

"Twenty-six of them, I think."

"Corporate gifts? Like for top-performing hedge fund managers or something."

"You'd need a lot more than a tie for hedge fund managers. They were Zegna. We needed to order them."

"How much were they?"

"If I remember correctly, $325 each."

"You remember the colour?"

"Midnight blue, I think."

"You have a record of this?"

"I'll have to check with the manager. I'm not clear on our policy regarding revealing client names."

I nodded.

"Now would be an excellent time to tell me if this is a murder investigation," she said.

THE MED SCHOOL kid's name was Marcel Paul and his lawyer was Charles Tait, a Black man in his sixties who wore a bow tie and who had spent enough time on high-profile cases to know how the media battle was fought.

On the evening news that night he tamped down his usual flamboyant style. He was sombre and articulate. He sensed this was a war that would play out over months, and his ground game was subtle and measured. No histrionics. "The police," he said, "are looking for a Black man because they need the killer to be Black. In their world, that is what makes sense. That is the narrative they understand. Let me ask you: What would happen if the police were rounding up white medical students and breaking their jaws? What does that narrative look like? Better to stick with what you know: *The city is under siege, we are being attacked by foreign elements.* That is what brings them comfort, and it brings fear to the public, and the next time the police chief goes to city hall and asks for an increase in their budget, this will be part of the reason. This is the most convenient narrative, the most profitable narrative." He talked about justice and race as though he were a cultural studies prof, keeping his powder dry.

THE FOLLOWING MORNING I called a friend who taught art at the Ontario College of Art and Design. Miriam O'Neill had wild dark hair, a collection of stuffed animals, and a volcanic Irish temper. We'd gone on a few dates five years ago. She was married now, I'd heard. She agreed to meet me at a cafe around the corner from OCAD.

"Is this stolen art, Jamieson?" she asked. "That would be exciting."

"No. I want you to take a look at something with me. Street art. Kid known as Maestro did it. A series of murals in St. James Town. I want you to tell me what you see in them and if you recognize anything in this kid's style."

"You mean a student?"

"Could be."

We drove to St. James Town and started with the sheep.

"Remember," I said, "kid has maybe twenty minutes with this."

Miriam nodded. She looked at it from a few different angles, touched the black lines and looked at her fingers.

"He has confidence," she said. "He probably did this as a drawing, worked it out on a small canvas and brought it with him. Sometimes that makes the artist more careful, the result looks a bit controlled, sterile. But there's an exuberance in these strokes." She took a few steps back and read the caption, LAMBS TO THE SLAUGHTER.

"It's from Jeremiah," I said. I took out my notebook and read, "'But I was like a gentle lamb led to the slaughter; And I did not know that they had devised plots against me, saying, Let us destroy the tree with its fruit, And let us cut him off from the land of the living, That his name be remembered no more.'"

Miriam digested this. "There's more of these?"

I took her to the one I'd been looking at when Ambrose Fortier tried to jack me. Miriam looked at the large C, bright red.

"There's a little Robert Indiana in here," she said. She bent down and looked at the Egyptian figures. She stood up and took a step back and gave a half smile.

"Red C, Red Sea," she said. "Moses leading the Israelites out of Egypt."

"God closes the sea up on the Egyptians, they all drown." My two years of Sunday school at the United church.

"Bit on the nose."

"So who are the Egyptians?"

ST. JAMES TOWN was the largest high-rise community in the country, with nineteen buildings that ranged in height from fourteen to thirty-two stories, each tower named after a different Canadian city. The towers were built in the 1960s and more than eighteen thousand people now lived in them, making St. James Town the most densely populated community in the country. It had been built for the middle class, who would be working downtown, and was based loosely on Le Corbusier's Towers in the Park concept. Except the middle class wanted to live in the suburbs and have lawns and cars, and St. James Town was roughly two-thirds immigrants and was designated as one of thirteen economically deprived areas in the city. It housed what had once been the world's tallest mural, a phoenix rising, a symbol of hope, the kind of thing the government commissions while it's cutting welfare payments by 20 percent.

In the last three months the crime rate in St. James Town was six times higher than it had been a decade ago during this same period. The rest of the city was stable: falling in some categories, but St. James Town was an anomaly.

St. James was the patron saint of pilgrims, one of only three people invited by Jesus to witness his transfiguration, and one of the few to witness Jairus's daughter being raised from the dead. He was also the first apostle to be martyred, sentenced to death by Herod, beheaded. His remains were taken to Spain, where he had been spreading the Word, apparently transported in a rudderless ship with no sail, and buried in the church in Santiago de Compostela, where he still listens to people's prayers and makes them come true.

The prayer of St. James begins:

O glorious apostle,
St. James, who by reason of thy fervent and generous heart
wast chosen by Jesus to be a witness of his glory on Mount Tabor,
and of his agony in Gethsemane;
thou, whose very name is a symbol of warfare and victory:
obtain for us strength and consolation in the unending warfare
of this life.

It was the last two lines that resonated with me.

I WENT TO Ambrose Fortier's trial date hearing. He was wearing a suit that he didn't look comfortable in and a tie the lawyer probably gave him and he sat there, impassive. Devin Nunes was speaking on his behalf. His suit was expensive. Fortier was a thug. He'd been cool as jazz, had done it fifty times. That's probably why he'd gotten complacent with me. His band, White Lives Madder, had a website, filled with crude lyrics, some grainy footage of the band that sounded like the Sex Pistols gargling kerosene, and an address to send donations to "help stop black domination of the music industry." Now he was sitting there being defended by a Black lawyer who made more in a week than Fortier made in a year, a pre-emptive move against his racist past floating to the surface. Fortier looked over at me. I gave him a mechanical wave. Trial scheduled for whenever, free on bail.

AT 8:30 P.M. I was sitting in my condo. I would walk to a Jays game if they would spend a little money on the bullpen. I made a second martini and took out some sesame crackers and hummus that I'd made two days ago. There was a hummus war going on, centuries of debate over who had invented it, who made the best. There was no point in buying the commercial version, which tended to be smooth and lifeless. I liked it coarser, garlicy, a bit sharper, more lemon. The idea that five simple ingredients—chickpeas, tahini, lemon, garlic and salt—could produce so many variations and such lasting arguments was testament to the power of food. It brought people together, brought them to the table, where they spent four hours arguing over who made the best hummus or the most authentic chili—an argument over chili in Texas had resulted in the shooting deaths of two chili apostates. I nibbled on the hummus and started a semi-elaborate salad from the recipe in the magazine they give out free at the liquor store. Technically it was supposed to have edible flowers, but you have to draw the line somewhere. I tossed together black beans, Kalamata olives, a sharp cheddar that had been aged for eight years, red pepper, and arugula, then made a dressing with olive oil, lime, jalapenos, and cumin.

The television was on, all news. I looked at the screen. It was black and white, like a home movie. The sound was garbled. I turned it up. There was our mayor, his mouth on a crack pipe, eyes lit by madness. The video had been shot on someone's phone, looked like a basement maybe. He took a hit, did his Jamaican impression. The only audible word was *mon*. A quick cut back to the anchor, a pleasant-looking woman who said the response from the mayor's office was that this was a doctored tape put together by his many elite enemies to discredit the extraordinary work he was doing for the People. She read, *It is unfortunate but not surprising that my enemies have sunk to such depths, but it is a reflection of the times in which we live.*

FIVE

BRITAIN CREATED COLONIES IN its own image, carved Tudor architecture out of the wilderness, paved streets that would one day host a dark Rolls convertible carrying helpless royals mechanically waving to a cheering crowd. At its centre would be Tory rectitude and the rule of law and a hierarchy that would remain as rigid as Britain's. The Family Compact worked hard and worshipped regularly and kept themselves to themselves. But cities start as one idea then become another.

To the south of St. James Town was Regent Park, which had started as a Dickensian ghetto for Irish immigrants who walked to the stinking tanneries and worked like mules and stopped at the tavern on the way home and drank and fought and then went home and fought. For the ruling class, this part of town offered a handy object lesson about Us and Them and you could take your children to witness the moral abyss, ethnic deficiencies, and financial ruin that lurked on the wrong side of the tracks. More importantly, Regent Park was comprehensible. These were the slums that you saw in London or Dublin; the ruling class recognized the people and their weaknesses and their inherent utility and *the poor will always be with us*.

While it was true that the residue of the Family Compact still wielded a disproportionate amount of power, it was also true that that power was eroding, that the defences had been breached and every exclusive neighbourhood in the city had the complexion of a Gap ad. The shape of money was changing and what was emerging was a new, invisible hierarchy that gave off a high-pitched sound only bankers could hear.

There were still lapsed Methodists who had clout, but real estate was the city's one true religion. In the core, empty churches were being turned into condos. The real God wasn't above us, but beneath our feet.

WE WERE SITTING at a restaurant on Harbord, on the patio, drinking wine. It was a date. I had been on three dates in two years, all arranged through an online dating service I had very reluctantly joined, but I was 52 years old and didn't meet many women who weren't criminals, so. All three women had lied on their profiles. They weren't 49, 47, and 45, respectively. My quick background check yielded 56, 51, 49. I didn't care about the ages, but I cared about the lying. Two lied about what they did, one lied about how many kids she had. When you're a cop you are lied to every day by people who don't have a clue how the drugs got there, don't know where the knife came from, didn't see the stop sign. I had had twenty years of lies. I would put the number at roughly a hundred per year, so two thousand, career. Cops lie too: *Kid had a gun, I don't have a racist bone in my body, I became a cop because I wanted to make a difference*. Being a cop is choosing the lies you can live with.

"So have you ever shot anyone?" she asked. Helen, the woman from Holt's. I'd gone back to get the info on the mulberry tie guy, then asked if she'd like to go for dinner. She stood and assessed me, didn't say anything for four very long seconds, during which I felt deficient in a way I couldn't identify. *Why not*, she finally said.

I told her the majority of cops never fire their gun in the course of their career.

"That's probably a good thing," she said. "It's also not an answer."

"I haven't shot anyone."

I asked her about her work, about the men who bought $8,000 suits.

She told me there was a clothing hierarchy. Young billionaires came in wearing a hoodie and motorcycle boots, bought a few things, chatted casually, like they were in Dollarama buying Scotch tape. They'd gone beyond money. Old money bought Ralph Lauren, wore it until it frayed. They bought sturdy $500 brogues and wore them for twenty years. They wanted to deflect the fact that they had money, had always had money, would always have money. But the guy who came in for an $8,000 suit was only money. He needed the suit to say something he couldn't. He needed you to think his money was fascinating and that you'd touched the hem of Jesus's garment.

We ordered and Helen leaned across the table. "Okay," she said, "you have to tell me a story about what really goes on in this city."

"A gruesome cop story that no one would know."

"Exactly!"

I wondered if this was the only reason she'd agreed to go to dinner with me. I mentally went through my Rolodex of horror stories—assaults, overdoses, domestic homicide, an abusive husband beaten to death with a meat-tenderizing mallet. "First year on the force, I'm a rookie cop, working in the West End. I get a call that multiple shots have been fired. I'm in the vicinity, drive to the house. One of these goofy infill McMansions, maybe ten thousand square feet, some contractor's idea of Regency England combined with the Taj Mahal. My partner is this beanbag, three months from retirement, just wants to ride it out. The call says more than ten shots fired so we're thinking some kind of gunfight in there.

"There's a woman standing on the lawn, screaming. My partner says he'll go around the back, sends me in the front. I go past the screaming woman, the door's open."

"You're scared."

"I'm scared. Inside it's got a large, winding staircase. There's more screaming coming from upstairs. I go up, slowly, weapon out, the first time it's been out of my holster. In the hallway, there's a body, male, fifties. His face, he's been shot in the face multiple times—there's one in his chest, the rest in his head, looks like close range; there's powder burns on what's left of his face." I paused. "You sure you want to hear all this?"

"All ears, Detective."

"The screaming is coming from a bedroom down the hall. I creep along the wall, look in. There are two women, three kids, all of them screaming. I go to the end of the hall, to the master bedroom. The door's open a bit.

"I look inside. There's a woman on the floor, naked, blood spreading out. It looks like she's been shot multiple times. A guy is hunched over, sobbing. He has a gun in his hand. He looks up at me. I recognize him. He's a cop, a detective, maybe fifty years old. I've got my gun on him, tell him to drop his weapon. He has this look, hard to describe, like he's in a different world than I'm in. His face is this tortured mask. Wet, contorted.

"I tell him again to drop the gun. He doesn't drop it. He bends over the woman again, he's keening, making this sound I've never heard. I figured he probably killed the guy in the hall.

"By this time, backup has arrived, four cops. Everyone's got their guns pointed at him. One of the cops knows him. 'Jefferson, man . . .' he says.

"Jefferson looks up, doesn't recognize the guy, these sounds still coming from him. Then his face suddenly changes, like he's just walked into our world, sees five cops pointing their weapons at him. He puts his own gun to his head."

I paused, let the story hang for a second, took a sip of wine.

"And..."

"So now there are six guns pointed at this guy, five of us and him. The cop who knows him says, 'Jeff, don't do it, man.' Jefferson looks down at the dead woman, looks back up at us, his face has this look, like he's already somewhere else."

"He pulls the trigger."

I nodded.

"So what happened?"

"What happened is, Jefferson's working a case in North York, some guy who's running a sweatshop in a warehouse up there. He brings in kids from Karachi, they work and live in the warehouse, sixty of them, making clothes, paid nothing. He's the dead guy in the hallway. Jefferson was following him around, but the guy's very careful. So Jefferson starts tailing the wife, figures maybe she's part of it. But then he gets this thing for her. She shows up one day with a black eye, Jefferson confronts her, says he's a cop, asks her what happened, ran into a door, et cetera. Anyway, they end up having an affair. Jefferson's close to getting what he needs on the husband. He's going to bust the husband, rescue the damsel, carry her off, a white knight. He's watching the house. Hears shots, kicks the door in, alarm goes off, he finds the husband in the hallway, holding a pistol. He can see the wife lying on the floor behind him in the bedroom. Husband shot her twelve times, emptied the clip. Jefferson shoots him in the chest, fires six more in his face at close range, goes to the bedroom and collapses over his lover, takes himself out."

Helen looked at me. "A man in love."

I didn't tell her that some of the kids were as young as ten, working twelve-hour days in squalor. I never found out what happened to them. For two years I woke up with their faces in my dreams. And I didn't tell her that maybe Jefferson and the wife weren't actually lovers, that he may have been an obsessive middle-aged cop with mental health issues who created this whole thing in his head and died for a mirage.

It was a nice dinner. Helen was wonderful company, open, lively, a deep laugh, soft brown eyes. But I had the feeling I might be a novelty date, someone to tell her friends about over a drink.

After dinner we walked. She wanted to know about the mulberry tie murder and I told her I couldn't talk about it because it was still under investigation, which was technically true. The air had cooled a bit. I wondered if we should be holding hands. We walked for forty minutes, talking, then she said it was late. I flagged a cab and she gave me a quick kiss and got in. I watched the cab disappear. I thought about that laugh, the way her hands moved when she described something. I walked back to my condo, a pleasant twenty-minute stroll.

I lied to Helen about never shooting anyone.

THE VIGIL FOR Dashika and Angela at Queen's Park had started on a sombre note. Dashika's mother said a few words. Angela Blair's mother wasn't there. Charles Tait, the lawyer for Marcel Paul, told the crowd that the time had come to say no: no to systemic racism, no to senseless death, no to innocent lives disappearing. I watched the clips on the news. Tait was a gifted speaker and he had the crowd.

The numbers were difficult to judge. The next day, the official department estimate was three thousand. The newspapers ranged from two to five. No one is a genius at estimating crowd size. A handful of white supremacists agitated on the periphery. There was a jumpy video taken on a cell phone, faces distorted by hate.

DAVIS SPENT MOST of the morning at a meeting of the Jamaican Canadian Association. I lingered at the back, watching her. There was an undercurrent of hostility in the room. She gave a short talk, then moved among the crowd, answering questions, assuaging fears, connecting. I left and drove toward St. James Town. A call came in about an overdose in a crack house on Sherbourne. I was fifty metres away and took the call. It was one of those three-storey Second Empire houses, painted light green, likely built by a wealthy church-going Tory 150 years ago and now home to roughly twenty crack ghosts who were lined up like a receiving line leading to a bedroom on the second floor, where a woman was lying on a stained mattress, dead. I checked for vital signs, asked the congregated what she'd taken, waited for Belisle to arrive and tell me what I already knew.

"Who owns this place?" I asked no one in particular. There were eight people standing there, eyes cloudy and dim, wasted. Nobody knew. Nobody knew anything.

Belisle arrived, confirmed the overdose. Could be fentanyl.

Back at the station I looked up the ownership of the house. It was owned by a numbered company. I did a title search on ten more properties on the street, going north and south of the crack house, all within a few blocks of St. James Town. They were owned by three different companies, all numbered.

LATE AFTERNOON, MELLON called Davis and me into his office. He paced while we waited for the obvious. Most of Mellon's management style came from television. He was six months from retirement and had one foot on the golf course, but he knew this case would define him. He paced and ranted about how the whole city could go up, how we don't sleep, we don't eat until we bring this guy in. Some of this, I guessed, was parroted from the speech the city chief had given him.

"We bring this guy in, we shut this down. The mayor is leaning very, very, did I mention *very* hard on this and you two are not delivering. Do I need to find some team that is prepared do whatever is necessary to end this fucking nightmare?"

He'd already brought in Lloyd and Max, who were certainly prepared to do whatever was necessary. I assessed his office. There were six framed photos of Mellon wearing a golf shirt and standing beside someone semi-recognizable. There was another photo of him in front of what looked to be a 1967 GTO. It didn't matter if Staples was the killer. If we brought him in, it bought everyone time. It would be a few months before the trial started, another six before it ended. The papers would take a break. Right now, there were two stories every day, stories about the girls, about St. James Town, about corruption in our division, about police relations and visible minorities, about how we would have already found the killer if the girls had been lying on a floor in Rosedale.

"We need Staples. That is the bottom line," Mellon emphasized.

"The bottom line," I said, "is that we're not delivering because you sent me to Kingston on a three-day PR exercise that was designed to cement the idea in the public's mind that this is a Jamaican problem and you've got Davis doing three interviews a day because the only other female officer of colour in our division quit six months ago and is suing the city alleging racist, sexist, and Islamophobic behaviour, all of which is true and all of which was conducted in the division you allegedly run in a part of the city that is 76 percent visible minorities. The mayor's home movie is being played on the news of every western democracy and right now we are being held up as a shining example of what happens when you let the lunatics run the asylum. We live in a city of seven million that is allegedly the most multicultural in the world and has fewer murders than Lubbock, Texas, and right now we're living in a Spike Lee film and you need to widen your fucking perspective."

Mellon stood there, mute, mulling. He could suspend me. But he'd put my picture in the paper, and he couldn't afford to lose Davis, his strongest link to anything approaching a humane picture of a force that had come under increasing pressure to deal with systemic racism. Some of this was waddling through his head as we sat in that lull. He should have retired last year. He was tired and lost. We were probably a year apart in age.

"Find him," Mellon said tersely, and turned away.

We left and walked in silence, then Davis said, "I'd appreciate it if you let me make my own enemies."

"He needs you. You're the face of this investigation. Anyway, he's gone in six months."

"But for the next six months, I've got him as an enemy. Courtesy of you. You seem to like making enemies. You have a natural talent for it. But if I'm going to make an enemy, I'll do it on my own terms. I don't need to inherit yours. A lot can happen in six months."

Davis walked off to her desk. She was right; a lot could happen in six months.

SIX

POLICE DIVISIONS ARE ESSENTIALLY a version of high school where you have harmless lifers, earnest young bicycle cops with sociology degrees, the head-cracking cohort, a group that hasn't found a niche, and the psychopaths on the fringe. One of the jobs of the superintendent is to determine which of these groups represents the Cool Kids. We were the first and only division to stage a wildcat strike. It happened forty years ago and that residual militancy was the office culture that Mellon inherited, and under his gelatinous leadership, it had survived more or less intact. Police actions aren't based on a set of formal rules but on shared mythologies. We act on impulse, out of survival, and those stories are shaped into a narrative afterward, then circulated as myth, and out of that we fashion good and evil.

I DID A quick background check on the numbered companies buying real estate around St. James Town. Technically, the company owner's name doesn't have to appear anywhere. The listed officers are often just beards, a few stooges from the law firm that set it up. It can be strictly legit, or dirty money, or offshore money that wants to find a way in. I wondered what this was. The Chinese were big into the condo market, apparently. This could be a new play for them. Build them instead of just buying them. The first numbered company had been set up two years ago. There were two officers listed. One of them was a lawyer named Wachevsky. I looked him up and found he was with Delaney Hutch. The other officer was Ambrose Fortier.

THE TWENTY-SIX MIDNIGHT blue mulberry ties had been bought by a real estate company called Heaven Home. They specialized in the condo market and their office was on the west side of town, not far from my condo. The area had mushroomed in the last decade, two dozen new glass condo developments, live/work, niche retail, restaurants with clever names filled with millennials in tight sports jackets.

It was the third day of a heatwave, the point where people were getting jittery. The streets were bright and dead. Twenty-four hours had passed and I still hadn't been suspended. My guess was I probably wouldn't be. Mellon didn't want to open that mess up, especially with his world currently on fire. But his dislike of me would no longer have the polite veneer it had had for the last decade. I wondered what he would tell his guys in the division. I wondered, if I got into a jam and called for backup, who would arrive, and when.

I pulled up at Heaven Home and parked in front of one of those remodelled warehouses. Inside there were open ceilings and exposed ducts and sandblasted wooden pillars and new blonde oak floors. A dozen people moved around the office, uniformly fit-looking, wearing expensive, well-cut clothes. It looked like there was a dress code, maybe even a body-type code. I asked to see Germain Porter.

"Is he expecting you?" the receptionist asked.

"No." I showed her my badge. "I just have a few questions for Mr Porter. It's important."

She put in the call, waved me in.

Germain Porter was early forties, a gym-built body in a very well-tailored summer suit. He had a subtle tan, bleached teeth, an expensive watch that didn't call attention to itself.

"What can I help you with, Detective?" He motioned for me to sit on one of the Breuer chairs.

"You bought some ties at Holt's, twenty-six of them."

"Ties?"

"Midnight blue, Zegna, $327 each, with tax $369.52." I checked my notebook. "This would be May 3."

Porter looked genuinely puzzled, then made a connection. "Ties. Right. Jenny ordered them. We had a thing, a client thing, in May, I wanted to present a sense of team, uniformity."

I nodded. The team looked pretty uniform already. "How is the condo market these days?" I asked. "I hear it's softening. Market saturated."

"Hard to saturate a market that is bringing in eighty thousand immigrants every year, not all of whom have a five-hundred-grand down payment for a cramped million-dollar semi in Leslieville that needs eighty grand in upgrades to make it livable. Add to that mix millennials who have a decade in the gig economy and would rather saw their heads off than commute from a distant suburb—basically the only housing they can afford—to get to their downtown tech job ..." Porter recited this, a speech he'd delivered dozens of times. "Condos are still king."

"How many are offshore buyers looking for an investment?"

"Less than people think."

The rumour was three in ten condos bought in the last decade in the downtown core were owned by offshore investors.

"How many of those are Chinese?"

"Again, less than you'd think. Bit of an urban myth."

There were estimates that there were 65,000 empty condos owned by foreign buyers parking their money, the majority Chinese, though real estate stats were notoriously unreliable. There might have been fourteen thousand conversations about real estate going on at exactly the same moment in the city, people talking about crazy prices, saying they couldn't afford to buy the house they're living in now, wondering how kids will ever be able to own. Real estate was the civic religion, offering salvation, hiding our sins. I told him I'd need the names of all the people who had the blue ties.

"It's a crime to wear Zegna?"

"Hopefully not."

I told Porter it was part of an investigation, he said he'd get me the names. I left and sat in my car, let the AC take hold, and sent an email to Helen asking her to let me know if anyone came in and paid cash for a blue Zegna mulberry silk tie in the next few days. I'd sent her an email after our date, thanking her for a lovely evening, and as I pressed send I'd thought I should have phoned instead, but wondered what I would say after thanking her for the evening, and if there would be an awkward silence, and what

I would fill that silence with, and I wondered if I had somehow been jettisoned back to high school in a time machine.

AT 5 P.M., the mayor called a press conference where he revealed that he had a problem, a surprise to virtually no one, and the first step was to admit to having a problem, and it took a lot of courage to get up in front of the world and admit to addiction issues, but it was a disease, and he was seeking treatment, and his family was standing by him during this difficult time. The tears appeared to be genuine.

I met with Davis at the station and walked her through the pieces that were orbiting around St. James Town.

"We have a crime rate that is through the roof," I said. "We have a small-time white supremacist thug who is being represented by a Bay Street firm. We have neighbouring real estate being bought up by numbered companies, one of which lists our thug as an officer. We have a dead sex worker who was strangled by a tie made of mulberry silk that could match the fibres of a tie bought by a real estate firm."

Davis gave me a cold look. "This is ... Look, Abel, maybe your unifying theory will yield all the secrets of the universe, but right now we still have two brilliant girls who have been murdered, two grieving mothers, an entire city that wants closure. Let's start with that and work outward, take the shortest route to solving the murders. Then we can take a walk through your conspiracy."

This was delivered in an aggressive whisper. "This station is a shithole," she continued, "and half the squad thinks I'm invisible and the other half thinks I'm Little Miss Diversity and at the moment I don't give a shit. One thing that that weak-ass, cowardly sack of shit is right about is: we need to keep our eyes on the prize."

I suspected that neither of us was long for this division. Mellon wanted me gone. Whoever took over his job might feel the same way. Davis would take the next strategic step, maybe run for city councillor. I'd always felt we'd been paired to cancel one another out—put the progressive woman of colour with the guy who doesn't fit in anywhere. I looked like the head-cracking cohort but sounded like a diversity hire with a psychology degree and excellent cycling skills. I was essentially stranded between office cultures. Maybe that's why Davis and I had never really gotten close; we each saw the other as a sort of reprimand.

"Maybe it's a badge of honour not having any friends on the force after, what, twenty years," she said, "given the sick options. But still..."

"You understand we're being played," I said.

"You think I don't know that? My picture is out there, my *face*. We don't solve the crime, I take the heat. We do solve it and it will be the work of a dedicated force that pulled together in the city's time of whatever...The mayor and chief will step into the spotlight and I'll become a backup singer."

"Mary Wilson."

"What."

"Backup singer in The Supremes. Diana Ross..."

"I know who the fucking Supremes are."

Davis stared up at the ceiling. I could see her counting the months until she was out of this shitshow.

"I talked to this girl," she said. "Esme, friend of Angela's. Kind of off and on friendship. Felt maybe she'd been put on the shelf after Angela started hanging with Dashika. She remembers Delroy. Says she got the sense that him and Dash were sort of a couple, but like one of those movies where there's a teen couple and one of them has cancer or something, like a permanent sadness, but that they both kind of embraced it. They both knew that Dash was going away to a new life and that there wouldn't be any room for Delroy in this new life. Anyway, she said she's downtown one day, sees Delroy, he's with this guy, white guy, cornrows, talks like 50 Cent, kind of skeezy, she says. She's pretty sure his name was Pete, but when Delroy introduced him as Pete, the guy says, 'Call me Lord Yo.'"

"Lord Yo."

"That's it."

"So let's see if we can find Lord Yo."

"WHAT MADE YOU think of him?"

"I was on a date, a woman I met, and she asked me for a story about the city's underbelly. That's the story I told her."

My therapist's name was June Godfrey. She was roughly my age. She'd once been the go-to therapist for cops with PTSD, on a city retainer. She looked like a suspect: average height, average weight, no distinguishing features, hair an indeterminate colour between blonde and grey. I had gone to see her after Jefferson shot himself, mandated by the chief, and I'd seen her a few times over the years. You have to be careful about therapist visits. Cops are encouraged to see them and when you do it's held against you, a sign of weakness.

"What is it about Jefferson that has stayed with you all this time?" she asked.

"I don't know. When I told this story to Helen—my date—she said, 'A man in love.'"

Godfrey waited. This was her MO.

"Jefferson's a guy who was my age now, early fifties. I don't know his story, but I'm guessing divorced, like two-thirds of the cops in the world. Sees this woman, she's beautiful, in distress. He spends days, maybe weeks observing her. So maybe he kind of creates this relationship in his head before there is an actual relationship. And maybe there wasn't an actual relationship. He's just imagining one, like how he's going to rescue her, put her husband in prison, take her away, keep her safe. When he looked up at me, when I had my gun on him, his face had this look. It's like he wasn't living in the same world that I was."

"What world do you think that was?"

"I don't know. Maybe Helen was right. The world of a man in love. It's not always the real world."

"Are you going to see Helen again?"

"I sent her an email—thanks for the lovely evening, et cetera. She sent back a thank you, but sort of perfunctory, like the minimum that etiquette requires in these things. I had the feeling I might be a kind of novelty date. You know, you date someone way out of your normal social world, bit exotic, tell your friends about it, like I'm the dating equivalent of Afghanistan."

Godfrey waited.

"I lied to her."

"To Helen. What did you lie about?"

"She asked me if I'd ever shot anyone."

"You said no."

I nodded.

"You're afraid she'll think you're a violent man."

Violence is unexplored territory for most people. It's like those fifteenth-century maps of the world with dragons at the edges. They look at violence from a distance and they form ideas based on television or video games. But when you're in it, it's like a Jackson Pollock painting. You don't make conscious decisions, you react. The myth is that cops have been trained to react a certain way. We have been trained, but what we've been trained to do is testify in court afterward. On the street, under threat, something limbic kicks in, and we react because that's who we are, then we create a story around it afterward.

Godfrey's office was like her, shades of beige, neutral, soothing. She had a non-judgmental expression, one she may have worked at early in her career but that now came naturally. I talked for another thirty minutes, then got up and left.

OUR DIVISION USED to be housed in a dingy building in the heart of Regent Park. It was cramped, with green institutional paint that was peeling, and it was thankfully part of the second razing of Regent Park, that time to make way for $12 billion worth of condos. Our new headquarters was at the western edge of the division, in a renovated heritage building. The striking brick facade was intact, but it had been gutted and the interior looked like a spread from *Architectural Digest*.

Pierce walked up. "So what's the deal with you and Davis," he said. He mimed fucking, hands holding imaginary hips.

His eyes were lit up, the face of a malevolent leprechaun.

"You know the only thing worse than fucking your female partner," he said, "is not fucking your female partner. Or maybe she's on the soccer team."

"You geniuses making any progress with Infinity?" I asked.

"You have a law degree, Abel," Pierce said. "Why the fuck are you at this desk?"

"Two-thirds of a law degree."

"Two-thirds lawyer, one-third asshole. Which, if my math is keerect, makes you 100 percent asshole."

Mad Max walked up, stood on the periphery. I stared at him, which was like staring at a snake in the zoo. He should have a sign around his neck: DO NOT TAP ON THE GLASS.

"You saw Belisle's report—the tie, mulberry silk," I said to Pierce. "You running that down?"

"The guy who did it, 90 percent chance he's from out of town, dental convention, doesn't know it's the trans strip..."

"How many dentists discover there is more than one dick in the car, then strangle her with a $350 tie."

"Look, Abel. No one gives a shit about a dead hooker other than other hookers who worry they're next and who don't vote and don't pay taxes. What the city's fine citizens *do* give a shit about are two girls of endless fucking promise cut down in their prime, et cetera, and right now you've got four-fifths of fuck all."

He was right. We didn't have anything. Didn't have Delroy, and I wasn't sure Delroy was our man.

"What's your success rate with those assaults and robberies in St. James Town, Pierce?" I asked. I knew the answer, had looked it up: in the last three years, he and Toussaint had followed up on 254 complaints and resolved fifteen of them.

Pierce stared up at the ceiling. "Mellonhead is gone in six months, probably less. Who do you think is going to be the next division super? Who has the seniority, the understanding of this division to step up?"

"You're a born leader, Pierce. I'd take a bullet for you."

"Good to know," he said. "Good hunting out there, Abel. Lot of dangerous animals in the jungle."

Mellon had gotten the message out; I was on my way out. Likely after this case was solved, or not solved. No one had to pretend to get along with me anymore. Max had what might have been the beginnings of a smile.

I WAS SITTING in the box opposite Ambrose Fortier and his lawyer, Devin Nunes, both of them expressionless.

I had checked out the post office box number on the White Lives Madder website, which was tied to a woman named Lisa Hendricks, whose address was on Sherbourne, an apartment in one of the houses that had been bought by a numbered company. I ran her name. Four charges of soliciting, two shoplifting, one drug possession. At dusk, close to 9, I'd parked outside her place and waited. Less than an hour goes by and Fortier shows up. He stands outside, gets on his phone, puts his phone away, goes around the back. She comes out, very white, very skinny, halter top, short shorts, heels. She does her sex-worker stroll on the sidewalk, on the passenger side of passing cars, so the john has to lean across the seat to talk to her. A Honda stops and she leans in, her breasts almost out of the top. Ambrose steps out from behind a parked car on the other side of the street, reaches in the driver's side window, grabs the keys out of the ignition, shows the knife. I'm out of the car, come up on Ambrose, have him spread against the car, cuff him, phone it in. The Honda guy is shitting himself. Lisa takes off, those skinny legs, her clumpy high heels clacking on the sidewalk.

Now we were sitting in the box. "Loved your last album," I said to Ambrose. "It reminded me of Marvin Gaye, that soulful sound."

Ambrose stared straight ahead. Nunes looked like his mind was elsewhere.

"Ambrose," I said. "Second time in less than two weeks you've been run in after jacking someone with a knife. Getting to be a habit."

Neither of them said anything.

"I'm familiar with your knife work, Ambrose." I said. "What I'd like to know more about is your job as an officer of Ontario company...." I checked my notebook and read out the numbers. "Anyone can tell you're executive material. Four charges on your sheet, a suspect in hate crimes, a beloved recording artist. The kind of guy every company wants representing their brand."

"Are you charging my client with a crime?" Nunes asked, almost bored.

"I guess this is one of those cases they warned you about in first-year law school, Mr Nunes, when they explained how in a democratic society everyone deserves a fair trial and you have to leave your personal bias in your briefcase and defend that Nazi to the best of your ability or otherwise our legal system cannot be seen to be just."

Nunes just sat, waiting.

I recited two lines from one of Ambrose's songs. "'I am the wolf, head of the pack / you are prey, one dead black.' Ring a bell, Ambrose?" I asked. I turned to Nunes.

"Assault with a weapon."

"He was defending a Ms Lisa Hendricks..."

"Who was just brought in on a soliciting charge."

"Which does not change the fact that Mr Fortier saw a woman being attacked and intervened."

"Which does not change the fact that there were two reliable witnesses and one of them is a police detective and the only attack involved your client with a brand-new knife."

"There was no bodily harm, Detective."

Nunes probably had instructions to spring this guy if possible. But that would be hard this time. And if they couldn't spring him, he was dead weight. The way Nunes pursued the next step would indicate which way they were going to jump.

THE NEXT DAY, I asked to visit with Fortier. He sat down, told me he wanted his lawyer. Fortier still had his dead-eyed con face. "The thing is, Ambrose, your lawyer doesn't want you." I didn't actually know this for a fact.

"I'm paying him $900 an hour, and he does whatever the fuck I *tell* him to do." Ambrose stabbed his index finger into the table.

"I don't know who's paying him but it sure as hell isn't you, Ambrose. Whatever purpose you served for Mr Nunes and his colleagues, they don't need it anymore. So what was your purpose, Ambrose?"

He sat there, his hands splayed on the table, then stared up at me. "Do you have any idea who I am?" he said evenly.

You occasionally hear this from people, a guy who gets caught going through a stop sign in a Porsche, went to a fundraiser for the mayor, thinks he's big time. But you don't hear it from guys like Ambrose Fortier.

"I know exactly who you are, Ambrose. You are a white supremacist low life who is getting paid to be a white supremacist low life, except they cut you loose and now you're back to being a freelance Nazi nitwit who can't sing." Ambrose didn't blink. "Did you kill those girls, Ambrose?"

Fortier pointed an index finger at me, thumb cocked, then put the hammer down and laughed. "You're on the bubble, Abel," he said. Then he shut up.

I WAS ON the bubble, though not for the reasons that Fortier thought. Any day I might be offered a quietly insistent, disappointingly modest buyout, and the union would encourage me to take it, and there would be a non-disclosure agreement that would prevent me from even saying there had been a buyout. They needed Davis, but they didn't need me. And maybe Davis needed them. She'd been on the evening news and told the camera that the tragedy of Dashika and Angela's deaths was helping to move the department to greater transparency and accountability. "I understand that we have a ways to go," she said. "But we are on the right path." I'd seen a few of her TV appearances, had seen her deliver speeches to three different neighbourhood associations. She walked a very fine line, appealing to them as a visible minority, reassuring them as a cop. There was something else though: she was offering a vision for the city that was political in scope. The department was using her to deflect their sins, but Davis was subtly distancing herself from the department. She might be distancing herself from me as well. She understood the power she held and she knew how to use it to her advantage. Davis understood power, how it moves, its fleeting life.

SEVEN

ON SUNDAY, I READ the *New York Times,* did the crossword, drank three espressos, ate two of the heavenly croissants from the French bakery on the next block. There was a woman who was always there, maybe the owner, late forties, slim despite all that temptation. She always looked overheated, a wisp of hair out of place on her forehead. She had an accent that produced an odd longing in me. I engaged her in conversation just to hear that voice. She told me that most Canadian butter capped the amount of fat at 82 percent. But you needed at least 83 percent to produce brilliant croissants, so she bought New Zealand butter. The butter cartel, she said, was responsible for countless pastry crimes. In France, they would all be hung.

I walked to the local market and bought fresh artichokes, an onion, celery, carrots, fresh thyme, parsley, and navy beans, then went to the Italian grocer for infornata olives. I stopped at the fishmonger and bought a shockingly expensive halibut fillet. It was hotter now, the real force of summer. I went home, watched the Jays lose on TV, and mixed a martini at 5:30. I made a stock with the celery, carrots, onion, and thyme. I heated oil in a heavy pan, added a diced onion, garlic, and a cup of artichoke hearts, then sautéed them for seven minutes. I added the stock and simmered for ten minutes, then put it all in the blender. I seasoned the halibut with salt and pepper, sautéed it for three minutes a side, removed it from the pan, added shallots and garlic and sautéed those for another three minutes. I put the halibut back along with the stock for another two minutes, then arranged the navy beans on a plate with three artichoke hearts, placed the halibut on top of the beans, drizzled the sauce over it all, and sprinkled parsley and ground coarse pepper over it. I sat on the couch and watched a subtitled movie about the agonies of adolescence and ate my dinner. I mixed another martini, watched the sun disappear behind the building across the street. I read two chapters of a book about a serial killer in Chicago during the 1893 World's Fair.

It had been almost three weeks and we didn't have anything. The papers hadn't let up. They were using the case to push for police reform, to call for a commission to investigate racism on the force, calling for Mellon's resignation, the police chief's resignation, calling for the mayor to resign. The mayor was calling for a moratorium on immigration in what could be an early testing of the waters for a run at national politics.

I went to bed at 10 p.m. and fell asleep to the sound of helicopters and dreamt of a hockey game. The ice on the river was endless, bare trees on the banks. A flat, empty light, the sun gone, a pale moon. There were hundreds of players on each side, vicious, armed, twisted faces, not entirely human, a Fellini landscape of grotesques. I had the puck. They were on me.

EIGHT

I DROVE TO St. James Town. It was hot, people leaning into the shade. The kind of June heat that got people very worried about July and August. There were six murals that looked like they'd been done by Maestro, all with a biblical theme. Exodus played a part in some of them: the Israelites fleeing slavery, Moses parting the sea, the Egyptians following and drowning, every man in Pharaoh's army dead. Though no sign of the Israelites getting to the Promised Land.

The city had a graffiti squad that operated like hieroglyphists, identifying tags, removing tags, catching taggers and hiring them to do legitimate murals, giving talks to underprivileged communities about the power of art. One of the cops on the squad was Mary Binetti, who'd come to our station to talk about graffiti. I called her and asked about Maestro.

"We don't know that there is a Maestro," she said. "It might be a collective."

"A crew?"

"Maybe not even a crew, really. It could be more of an idea. Like a terrorist organization with cells that don't know the identity of other cells. We thought at first that Maestro was a person who spawned imitators. Now I'm not so sure."

"This is political, you think?"

"It didn't seem so much at first, but they have been getting more political. Or at least more obviously political. Maestro uses a lot of biblical imagery. The scale is ambitious—there's one on the viaduct that would have required harnesses and probably support crew. It's more than a hundred square feet."

I hadn't seen it. "What's on it?"

"It's Moses, wearing a police hat, a police badge, holding a tablet. The Sixth Commandment."

"Thou shalt not..."

"Thou shalt not murder. Except it says, 'Thou shalt murder.'"

"You have any sense of what this collective looks like? Who we're looking for?"

"Our guess at this point, and it's more guess than anything hard, and not something we'd ever say out loud, is a Black male, someone who spent time in church as a child and has some art school training. The slavery theme runs through quite a few of them."

"You checked OCAD? The art schools?"

"We did. We showed them photos of the work. It didn't ring any bells with any instructors."

"You haven't brought anyone in?

"We've had a few people we thought may have been involved, but it didn't go anywhere. You have to basically catch them in the act. At this point, there are people who aren't involved but who would like to claim to be involved. So it's complicated. There is a level of sophistication we haven't run into before."

She quickly walked me through the hierarchy of graffiti artists—writers, as they were called. From tags, to bombs, to throw-ups, to burners, to pieces. Pieces were the most ambitious. Maestro only did pieces, and the scale and ambition had sparked copycats.

I thanked Mary and drove to the station. There were two phone messages and three emails from a *Star* reporter, Tanya Willing. *Just want the police perspective*, she said, as a counterpoint to all the noise that was out there. Suggested a ride-along, so her readers could see how hard the force was working to catch the killer. She'd written three pieces on the case, mildly inciting. She was attractive, a bit ruthless on the page. She said she may have something that could help me; maybe we could help each other. She knew she was supposed to go through communications even to get boilerplate quotes. Even sending her an email saying I couldn't talk about an ongoing case would be dangerous—it would either be the start of a communication or end up in the paper as part of her next piece.

I suspected that Pierce and Toussaint weren't going to follow up on anything in the Infinity case, weren't going to check out the mulberry ties. Something was hovering over this case, something large and corrupt and ill-defined. I didn't have enough to convince Davis or anyone else I should be spending time on it. I hadn't entirely convinced myself. I called Porter at Heaven Home and asked if he could send out a memo for all twenty-six of the recipients to arrive at work on Thursday wearing the mulberry tie. He could have said no, called his lawyer, but he didn't. Maybe he felt it was an event, a team-building thing. Maybe he was worried there was a murderer in his crew.

Helen hadn't responded to my email asking about anyone buying a tie. I phoned and asked her if they'd sold any midnight blue mulberry ties in the last week, someone paying cash, probably wearing a hoodie and sunglasses.

"Is this connected to those girls in St. James Town," she asked.

"Possibly, and please don't ask me how."

"You're not sure yourself." This was half a question. "I'll check on the tie. Though he could probably find one online."

"Online might leave more of a trail than cash at a store."

"Hmm."

If someone needed that tie, they might come in before the line-up. "Can you keep an eye out for our tie-buyer today right through to Thursday morning?"

"Are we closing in on something here?"

"Too early for that. It's just a hunch, Helen."

"A gut feeling? Isn't that how they always say it on the cop shows?"

I wanted to ask her out to dinner again but it seemed too calculating. We chatted for a few minutes, then she had to get back to the floor.

I RESEARCHED DELANEY Hutch, the law firm that employed Devin Nunes. I did an internet search on Heaven Home. I watched a video online of Bobby Dale giving a speech at a large backyard barbecue in Don Mills. He talked about family values and the city he grew up in, and how that city was being taken away. He reminded the crowd that Don Mills was the first suburb in the country, an oasis of full employment, low crime, wives who could cook, kids who stayed out of trouble. He talked about the Leafs winning the Cup in '67, with players like Bobby Baun, guys who had heart. Dale could connect with these people. He had a shambolic charm. He looked like them, sounded like them. Memory is a fragile thing—he was creating memories for many of these people, of a time when a poorly educated white male could still be king of some small kingdom, before progress and globalism and multiculturalism and all the other *-isms* nudged him toward the off-ramp. They applauded and he raised his glass in response, the farewell salute of a dying species.

I checked the Jays score, called Davis for an update, and had a staring contest with Mad Max, who was sitting at his desk fifty feet away. Max was one of those people who genuinely enjoyed violence, the kind of guy that made other cops say *It's a good thing he's on our side*. But Max wasn't on our side. He wasn't even on his own side. He was nature: indifferent and bloody, simple animal impulse in a shitty suit. I stood up, grabbed my jacket, walked out to my car and drove to the viaduct to look at Moses.

NINE

THERE WERE A FEW reasons I had pretty much failed to connect with anyone on the force. One of them had to do with a police league hockey game seventeen years ago. I had gone to Wisconsin on a hockey scholarship. I was 6′2″, 190, a rushing defenceman who could skate. We won the Big Ten championship two of the years I was there. I had a cup of coffee with the Detroit Red Wings. Hockey is essentially two games. There is the elegant Olympic version, on a wide ice surface, that prizes speed and brilliant passing. And there is the small-town, minor league version of enforcers and brawls, where finesse is suspect and often punished. The annual police hockey tournament was firmly in the latter camp.

The tournament never started that way. It was all fellowship and friendly insults and blustery testosterone, but on the ice, veneers are stripped away. *The ice is where you discover yourself*, my Wisconsin coach used to say.

I had felt guilty leaving my mother to go to university but rationalized it with the hockey scholarship. I would have had to take on a lot of debt to pay for my own tuition. It was my first time away from home, living in a dorm at first and then a crappy apartment with one of the hockey guys. In my fourth year, I lived with a girl named Kate Sibeleski in a flat in a ramshackle house. She was from Oak Park, a long-limbed, auburn-haired Chicago girl who occupied the world as if it had been created for her. She had come to Wisconsin to spite her parents and distance herself from childhood friends, most of whom had gone east for college. My friends were mostly guys from the hockey team, but in my last year, I cocooned with Kate, skipping the beer-soaked team celebrations and after-practice bar marathons, the chugging contests and arm wrestling and fighting with the locals. It was with Kate that I took up cooking. We bought three cookbooks—*The Joy of Cooking, The Moosewood Cookbook,* and Julia Child's *Mastering the Art of French Cooking.* After two earnest, healthy *Moosewood* recipes, Kate gave the book to a shaggy mystic in her poli sci class. *The Joy of Cooking* was used mostly as a doorstop. But we plugged away through Julia, burning bechamel, undercooking duck, making things where we were short five ingredients. Neither of us ever mastered French cooking. We drank wine and pronounced on its qualities ironically. We watched foreign movies, studied together, and devoured each other at night. She was shockingly carnal and I felt like a sexual hick. Our furniture was scrounged and overstuffed and faded. The only new thing we had was the bright red Fiat Spider her father had bought her for her eighteenth birthday. We raced out of town and drove to the surrounding lakes and had elaborate picnics and made love and napped and drove home.

It was the happiest I'd ever been. I realized with Kate that my previous experience with happiness had been incredibly limited.

I was hard-pressed for happy childhood memories; they were largely erased by my father's enigmatic death and my mother's sad decline. I was happy playing hockey, but Kate was celestial, a different magnitude. I felt like an explorer who had found another world.

It had never occurred to me that it would end. After our last exams, she said she had been accepted at USC. I hadn't known she'd applied. She was going to do a master's in marine biology. I imagined driving down there with her, along the fabled Pacific Coast Highway. She often wore tortoiseshell Ray-Bans and a headscarf, like someone in a French film. We would find a cool apartment. I'd get a master's degree or play defence for the Los Angeles Kings.

She told me she was going there alone, starting *a new chapter*. We were standing under the marquee at a French film festival when she delivered this news. *The 400 Blows* was playing. I thought my legs might give out. I knew instinctively and immediately that there was no argument I could make that would change anything. She had a Midwestern pragmatism. We walked home, drank too much, went to bed, made love, and cried. She fell asleep and I stayed awake, looking at her, memorizing every detail of her face and body. The next day she loaded two suitcases into her car and drove away, wearing the headscarf and Ray-Bans. I was eviscerated.

That night I went out with some guys from the hockey team, a last pub crawl before most of us disappeared from one another's lives though we all swore that night we would stay in touch forever, the brilliant championship team. But we didn't—at least I didn't. I never saw any of them again.

It was close to midnight and four of us were weaving down the street, in search of one more bar, singing drunkenly. A police car shot by us and locked up its brakes and went into a skid.

Another cop car came from the other direction and squealed to a stop. Four cops jumped out and ran to a point half a block ahead of us. A figure was flushed out, like a game bird. He must have been crouching between parked cars. He ran and was tackled and the cops were on him, their sticks out, hammering away like they were building something. We got closer and I saw it was a Black kid, maybe fifteen, on the ground, his face bloody, his lip torn. I thought they were going to kill him, beat him to death. I yelled for them to stop it, then started toward them. One of the guys on the team tackled me and then Pachenko sat on me, saying, *Stay out of it man, seriously, stay the fuck out of this.* One of the cops came over and said it would be a real good idea if we all just went home, got a good sleep. My face was just off the pavement. I could see the Black kid, his pulpy ruined face, head pressed to the sidewalk. I could see his eyes, those of a child, uncomprehending.

IF YOU TOOK hockcy and married it to the law, its offspring might be the police force. After the death of my mother, I viewed the law as a kind of death, cloistered with paper and precedents in an airless office. I needed something more visceral. I could have played minor league hockey somewhere, but decided on the force instead. I may have been seeking some of the camaraderie that I'd found on hockey teams, but I never found it.

We played 52 Division in the first game of the police tournament. I was a strong skater, had good puck-handling skills, but my greatest strength, unglimpsed by NHL scouts, was my ability to see how the game was unfolding, where it was headed. I had a minor in history and I saw each game rise and fall as empires did, Rome extending itself too far, then collapsing, the American century spreading across the globe, then eaten from within. Russia expanding and contracting like the machine-forced breathing of a hospital patient. I shared these thoughts in the dressing room to understandable ridicule.

Fifty-Two Division had a guy named Wallace, nicknamed The White Whale: big, pale, said he'd played Junior A, which probably wasn't true, but he had some skills. He never shut up, yelling insults from the player's box. *Who's a pussy. Who wants it.* He had a city-wide reputation for violence; a suspect had died in his custody. He was a dirty player, and he took one of our guys out with a hard elbow to the face behind the play, breaking three facial bones, giving him a concussion. I could feel that familiar heat moving through me. The Whale was playing defence, imposing but slow. I carried the puck up the ice, rushed straight at him, made a simple, well-timed deke that he bought and he was left stranded, exposed. I scored, five-hole, skated around the net, and said *Beached Whale* as I skated by him. We collided a few times during the third period, exchanged words. He managed a slash that left a welt on my calf. The heat was building up, something red and unaccountable that obscured most of the world. When we finally squared off, I landed a solid punch that took him down. His helmet flew off. I was on him and got in six hard, very fast shots before I was pulled off. Wallace had a broken nose, a broken jaw, and a concussion that kept him in a dark room for six weeks. He needed eighteen stitches for the wound on the back of his head. I had a broken metacarpal in my hand. I refused to apologize afterward and was threatened with disciplinary action. I thought about that day, guys from both teams grabbing for my arms, pulling on my jersey, yelling, the words an angry, meaningless collage of fear and hate. His blood on the ice, his face ghostly, without expression. The adrenaline ricocheting around my system, my breath coming hard, in another world.

I'd been at 22 Division but a week later, I was transferred to 51. It was still called the Punishment Station then, where bad cops from around the city were sent. I was paired with Benny Singletary, early fifties, a year away from retirement. Each night Benny would tell me about the epic shortcomings of all three of his ex-wives. I scanned the streets, hoping for a crime in progress just to save me from Benny's monologues. He didn't make it to retirement. I went into a late-night Vietnamese place for takeout and came back to the car and he was dead. I checked for a pulse, nothing. I drove him to the hospital. It was odd, him sitting in the passenger seat, quiet for the first time. The autopsy showed a massive coronary. He was fifty-three. None of his ex-wives attended the funeral service.

TEN

I WENT TO DELROY'S old school, asked to see the yearbook from his year, checking to see how many Petes were in his grade or the grades above and below. Maybe Lord Yo had been a classmate, someone from the school he'd hung with. There were three Peters. Everyone looks innocent in their high school yearbook. I spent an hour tracking them down: one away at college, one working in the family dry cleaning business. Neither of them promising candidates for Lord Yo. I talked to the mother of Peter Manning, the last one. She didn't know where he was.

"Does Peter still look like his school photo?" I asked.

She laughed. "I wish," she said. "He looks like what's-his-name..."

I waited.

"Snoopy."

Snoopy. "Snoop Dogg?" One of three rap artists I could name.

"That's the one. Where he got that from..."

I drove to Ms Manning's house, a small yellow and white bungalow that could have used some paint. The front yard was unkempt, the grass yellow and brown. She answered the door, a short woman with grey streaks in her brown hair. Her face held a weariness. I introduced myself.

"Why don't you go around the back," she said, "and I'll meet you there. The house is an *oven.* We can sit in the backyard."

I walked around the back. Her sidewalk was buckled, weeds coming through the cracks. The backyard was yellow grass that had been hammered into dirt in places. A small dog was tethered to a cinder block. Ms Manning was standing in the shade. There were two lawn chairs and a round metal table.

"We can sit here," she said. She took out a pack of cigarettes and offered me one. I shook my head and she lit one and tilted her head back and exhaled. The large metal ashtray was overflowing.

She told me Peter was basically a good kid who ran with the wrong crowd. She hadn't seen him in more than a year. He might be living downtown with a woman. Going through a phase.

"They're exposed to everything these days," Ms Manning said. We stared out at the yard. There were a few dry flowers in a small garden. A chicken wire fence. The dog was asleep or dead.

I asked about her husband. Divorced ten years ago, she said. Peter lived with her until he was an adolescent, then moved in with his father. Was getting to be too much for her, she said. "He needed a father at that point," she said. "He needed discipline in his life."

She checked her phone and gave me the number for her ex-husband, Ed.

“I’m the only one living here and I come outside to smoke,” she said. “It’s crazy, isn’t it. The times we live in.”

I DROVE BACK to Lord Yo’s school and talked to the principal. She didn’t remember him. She put me in touch with three teachers who might recall something. Two of them didn’t remember Peter Manning, but the third did, a geography teacher who said she thought Peter was one of those students who was hiding something. There were kids in school, she said, they had things going on at home, kids who’d been abused, kids who’d come from a place of violence and weren’t quite sure how to adapt. She thought Peter Manning was one of those. It was just a feeling, she said. She couldn’t give me an example of anything.

I PHONED PETER Manning’s father and left a message, then ran Ed Manning’s name—two assaults, petty theft, one armed robbery conviction where he’d done two years. I drove to the address that matched the phone number. The house was in Leslieville on a dead-end street. Most of the houses looked like they’d been renovated. The neighbourhood was being taken over by the young and hip, by gay couples who gutted the small Victorians, or contractors who bought the row houses that had once been filled with labourers who worked in the tanneries and hog rendering plants. You didn’t have to walk far to get a nice espresso. From the outside, Manning’s house looked like one of the unrenovated ones. The steps were unpainted wood, rotting, sloping to one side. The small porch was jammed with junk and two wooden chairs. There was aluminum foil on the window upstairs, a blanket stretched across the picture window. I rang the bell, waited, rang again. I heard voices inside. A woman opened the door, small, wiry, wearing a singlet, dark hair plastered to her head, suspicious eyes, mid-forties. Behind her I could see part of a man's body: shorts, a meaty thigh, no shirt, sprawled on a couch. There was the sound of daytime television.

I introduced myself. The woman repeated my name over her shoulder to the guy on the couch.

"You can't come in here," she said. "You need a warrant. I know the law."

"Personal experience?"

"You ain't got a warrant and you ain't got a right," she said. Her mouth was a thin slash.

"I'm just here to ask Mr Manning about his son."

"He don't live here."

"But he did at one point, didn't he?"

"Whatever he done, it's nothing on us."

"I don't know that he's done anything. Mr Manning," I said, my voice louder, talking to the figure on the couch. "I'm just looking for a little background information on your son Peter."

Sounds came from Manning, blending with the television.

"Far as we're concerned," the woman said, "he can fucking stay in the background." She shut the door. I heard it lock. I stood on the porch and looked at the street. A couple with a stroller had stopped, was looking at me. The houses behind them had had the brick pressure-washed and tuck-pointed. They had pristine porches with thin, horizontal cedar fencing, the yards filled with tall exotic grasses suffering in the heat.

I CALLED DAVIS, told her about Lord Yo a.k.a. Pete Manning.

"Both parents East End?" she said. "You talked to them both."

"Yeah, father did some time. I'm guessing not a happy relationship there. Mother said he fell in with a bad crowd."

"The 'bad crowd,' source of all evil."

"What time is the Mellon thing?"

"Seven, I think. Prepare to be inspired."

IT WAS DAVIS and me, Lloyd and Max, and some uniforms. We were in the big boardroom. It was all glass, part of the force's push to greater transparency. It had a table that sat thirty or so. There were eighteen of us. Mellon was standing at the head, leaning, his hands on the table. He looked tired.

"I know, as leader of this division, that there are ..." He paused, searching. "Rifts. There are things that divide us." He made a point of looking at Davis and me. "But we need to come together on this thing. This thing is bigger than our differences."

This sounded cribbed from somewhere, a politician's speech. Most of what came out of Mellon's mouth felt like it came from somewhere else. He wanted to know everything we knew.

I told the assembled that we had a lead on a guy, Peter Manning, a.k.a. Lord Yo, a known associate of Delroy Staples, passed the photograph around.

"These two knew each other in school," I said. "May have reconnected. Manning may know where Delroy is. They were East End, but maybe downtown or West End at this point, away from the streets where he might be recognized."

"What have you and Max got," Mellon asked Lloyd.

Lloyd said they had heard from a CI that Delroy could be in Parkdale, had some of the local guys looking at rooming houses, canvassing convenience stores, fast food places, needle/haystack territory.

"This kid is in hiding," Mellon said, "he thinks we'll eventually stop looking, he'll be able to come out of hiding. We make it clear we're never going to stop so he gets itchier than hell. So he knows this is his whole life and he's going to want to get a peek at the world."

I could see Davis had doubts about this approach but didn't think it was worth raising the issue. The uniforms didn't say anything. Max didn't say anything. Max never said anything. Mellon said we had one more week with this and then heads would start rolling.

It was after 8 p.m. by the time we wrapped. Davis and I walked to the Distillery District to have dinner and debrief. The air had cooled a bit. She called home while we walked, talked to the sitter, talked to her daughter, told her she didn't shoot anyone today and to stop asking her that question. We went to an oyster place and ordered twenty-four Malpeques and sweet potato fries and a citrusy New Zealand white.

"What did the mother say?" Davis asked.

"Basically a good kid who lost his way. I'm guessing it's a bit more complicated. After the divorce, he lived with her until he got too much to handle. Then over to the ex-con father."

"You think Lloyd's intel is solid?"

"Who knows. It makes a certain amount of sense. It would be the right neighbourhood to hide out—high density, lot of rooming houses, other side of town. He might be able to move around a little, even."

"You're still not convinced Delroy's our guy."

"I think he's just the best candidate in a very thin field. For all we know, it was Ambrose Fortier and we have the killer in custody."

"You really think he's an option?"

"A racist with a knife who works the area…"

"Can we sweat him a bit?"

"Not as long as he has Delaney Hutch on retainer."

"What the hell is that, anyway?"

"I don't know. Has to be something there. If they cut him loose, we may get something."

The oysters were good. There was a freshness to the white wine. It was approaching magic hour, the sepia light descending. We were sitting outside. The air was soft. People walked by on the cobblestones, going to the theatre, holding hands, looking at menus. When Davis and I were first partnered up, I wondered if it would lead to anything, but the age gap was too big, and Davis had her eye on a goal that was in the middle distance and she viewed me as something between an ally and a speed bump from the beginning. I wasn't sure how she saw me now. But sitting with her, having a nice dinner, drinking wine—it was a glimpse of what could have been.

"Are Lloyd and Max still taking people down to Cherry Beach for 'questioning,'?" Davis asked, her hands forming the quotation marks.

"I doubt it." Cherry Beach had taken on the quality of mythology. It was where bad cops used to take suspects for beatings, sex workers for *favours*. There was a song about it—"The Cherry Beach Express." It held an outsized place in the civic imagination and hadn't been much use as a practical site for more than a decade.

We had a pleasant dinner. We shared a dessert and talked about life outside the station. Her daughter was doing well in school. Davis would take time off after this case, take her somewhere, do something, make up the time. Davis was still doing interviews. She was good on camera, adept at handling the sometimes hostile questions, at appearing to give the public something substantial without actually giving them much. She'd gone around the city, speaking to different community groups. I told her I thought she was doing a great job with the PR. I didn't tell her that it was starting to look like a campaign.

DELANEY HUTCH WAS a large law firm, founded eighty years ago, mostly corporate, a lot of real estate work. They had a criminal firm on retainer that mostly dealt with their corporate clients. There was no longer anyone named Delaney or Hutch. Very well connected, both locally and internationally. They had helped broker an attempt by a Chinese firm to buy a Canadian mining company, a deal that was vetoed by the federal government for vaguely stated security reasons. Two years ago there was an Ontario Securities Commission investigation, something the firm may have done with some client's stock, something that was ongoing. The OSC was an investigative body that was notoriously light on investigation. Delaney Hutch was linked to the numbered companies through one of their lawyers—Wachevsky. And Ambrose Fortier.

I could try talking to Wachevsky, but talking to lawyers was usually a waste of time. Fortier was probably the best way into this, though he could simply be a useful idiot that the firm was using for the reason I suspected they were using him: to foment crime and the fear of crime and make it easier to tear down the buildings, an old-style slum clearance.

I called the prison, asked to talk to Fortier.

"You can't talk to him," the duty manager said.

"And why is that?"

"He's dead."

"When?"

"Stabbed this morning."

"Stabbed."

"Eleven times."

I hung up and drove to the prison and confirmed what the guy on the phone had told me, then called Davis, told her Fortier was dead.

"Fortier said you were on the bubble?" Davis said. I'd told her about my meeting with him.

"Yeah. He had to have some juice somewhere to have a lawyer like Nunes represent him. Hard to see Fortier calling any shots though."

"And now he's dead."

"Prison beef, stabbed eleven times with a short-blade shiv."

"You think it was a hit?"

"I do. I think whoever was paying Devin Nunes $900 an hour decided to cut him loose and didn't want the loose end."

"We can't bring Nunes in."

"No."

"And the guy who stabbed him?"

"A lifer named Mullins. Hard-ass, fifties, said it was self-defence, said Fortier attacked him, said they were having an argument over whether professional wrestling was fake."

"Has a sense of humour at least."

"Mullins has another six years to serve, so maybe someone is holding the money for him, but maybe he has someone on the outside, a kid, wife, someone who gets the fee."

"Very slender, Abel. And it doesn't bring us any closer to the killer."

She was right. It didn't bring us any closer.

I ARRANGED TO talk to Randy Mullins. He wanted his lawyer present, he said. He was represented by a Legal Aid lawyer named Lilly Tam. I introduced myself, sat down across from them. The paint on the steel table was chipped. Under the harsh lights, everyone looked like Halloween. Mullins had a lifer's face, nose pushed in, those lazy reptile eyes that take in everything. He had rough skin and homemade ink, arms that came from the prison gym. Lilly Tam was maybe 115 pounds, a white shirt, blue jacket, blue bow, sitting with her back straight like a schoolgirl.

"Mr Mullins," I said. "You had an argument with Mr Fortier, I understand."

Mullins barely nodded.

"He threatened you."

Another almost nod.

"Mr Fortier told you he was connected, that he was the kind of guy who could have you killed with one phone call."

This got Mullins's attention.

"Guy was all mouth. He's here a week thinks he owns the joint. If he hadn't of come at me, someone else would have taken him out."

"He wasn't protected by the white supremacist group?"

"Didn't really have time to mingle," Mullins said.

“Eleven times though. Crime of passion.”

“You don’t have to answer that, Randy,” Tam said.

“It wasn’t a question,” I said.

Mullins shrugged. “Short blade. With self-defence, you want to make sure.” He smiled. He was missing a few teeth on one side.

“You married, Mr Mullins?” I asked.

“Still looking for the right girl.” He turned to Lilly. “What are you doing with the rest of your life, darling?” He had an ugly laugh.

Tam looked at me. “Do you have any more questions for my client, Detective Abel?”

“No.” I did have more questions, but I could see that I wouldn’t get any answers from Mullins. It was odd that he’d requested a lawyer and she’d showed up so quickly. He was a veteran thug, the kind of guy who could handle himself in an interview with a cop.

On the way out, I checked with the warden’s office and asked for any communication between Mullins and the outside world, any letters, any taped phone calls, visitor logs. They said they’d round up everything they had and give me a call.

I got in my car, drove across town. It was hot and would get hotter, air moving in from the parched west, dry air coming in across dead fields and picking up humidity over the Great Lakes as it arrived in the east. The heat got into everything. It got into apartments and you couldn’t get it out. It got into your system and you walked around, carrying that heat. People got irritable, traffic got meaner. Everything on a knife edge.

ELEVEN

I WAS SCHEDULED TO look at the mulberry tie line-up at 11:30 a.m. I was working from my condo in the morning to save driving across town twice. I made a third espresso because I'd read that caffeine helped ward off heart disease and diabetes and I embraced every dubious scientific report that supported my current diet—dark chocolate was healthy, red wine was good for the heart. Espresso, blueberries, kale, and three servings of fish a week and you could live forever. I sat in front of the computer, scrolling through searches for Titus Bishop. At 10:15 I got a call from Helen.

"Guess what?" she said.

"We got a bite?"

"This morning, literally the *minute* after we opened, this man came in, looking for a tie, had to be midnight blue, he said.

"He say mulberry?"

"No, just midnight blue. Had to be Zegna. Said he was a Zegna man."

"And this guy..."

"White-male-late-forties-five-ten-one-sixty-brown-hair-starting-to-recede-blond-highlights-blue eyes." This came as a quick recitation. She may have been reading it. "His nose was kind of... not right for his face somehow. Hard to describe. He told me he was a Zegna man, but he wasn't wearing Zegna."

"You sold him a tie."

"You could congratulate me on my detective skills."

"Thank you, Miss Marple."

"I did sell him a tie. Midnight blue."

"He paid cash."

"He did. There's one more thing." She waited a beat. "The tie isn't Zegna." She waited for me to say something, then said, "I told him we were out, but I could order one."

"But you weren't out."

"No! Now you have to admit that is good detective work."

It was. "That was brilliant, Helen. So what is our guy wearing?"

"Our guy is wearing Armani. I told him no one could tell the difference, that they used the same Italian mill, run by the same family for more than a century, that was nestled in the hills outside Milan."

I thanked her, finished my espresso, read a puffy magazine profile of Titus Bishop from eleven years ago titled "Between Two Worlds" where he was described as someone who was *giving back*. No mention of what he may have taken.

I drove to Heaven Home through choked streets, the heat coming through the windshield. Horns and death threats echoed through the stalled traffic. I checked in with the receptionist and she motioned to one of the expensive chairs, said I could take a seat, asked if she could get me anything, pressed a button on her phone, announced me to Porter. He came out a few minutes later, wearing a beautifully tailored sports jacket, polo shirt, no socks, suede loafers, his hand extended, his realtor smile.

"Detective," he said, "I've got the whole crew waiting for you in the boardroom. I feel like we're in one of those Agatha Christie mysteries. You know, they get everyone in the drawing room and the detective runs through all the reasons that everyone in the room basically wanted the guy *dead* and then points to the killer. And it's never the guy you think it is."

"If only it worked that way," I said.

The glassed-in boardroom was in the middle of an open plan. The table would have seated forty or so. There were twenty-six people lined up, seven of them women, a few of them wearing their ties, most just holding them. The dark tie was a bit sombre for daytime, too heavy for summer.

"This is Detective Abel, everyone," Porter said. "He is a homicide detective and you are now officially part of his investigation. One of you killed Colonel Mustard in the library with the candlestick." Porter laughed and his crew chuckled dutifully. He motioned to the ties. "Twenty-six mulberry silk ties that cost me an arm and a leg." I saw my guy; Helen's description had been pretty good. He was one of the guys wearing his tie. I scanned the crowd. A few of them were resentful they had to participate in this, a few of them were happy to be there—it gave them a story to tell at a dinner party. My guy was near the middle, strategically trying to get lost. I scanned the crowd, acknowledged their ties, apologized for the inconvenience, thanked them for their time. We filed out and some of the people went back to their desks, others headed out. Even though it was an open-plan office, they had a fair amount of space between the cubicles. I watched my guy go back to his desk, sit down, take out his cell, his fingers working.

I thanked Porter, apologized again. He excused himself, said he had someone waiting in his office, said he hoped I'd solve the case, whatever the case was. I walked over to my guy. He looked up at me, trying to stay steady. Right now his senses were taking sensory information and turning chemical and nerve signals into electrical signals, which were activating the adrenal gland, creating adrenaline. His amygdala was trying to catalogue his fear: Was it new? Was it familiar? The hypothalamus was deciding between fight and flight, except he couldn't really do either. The pituitary gland was starting to churn out a physical response while his hippocampus was sorting through pertinent memories and singling out which of them to deeply, deeply regret. The body can release more than thirty hormones and chemicals when it is fearful or anxious and I guessed this guy had almost all of them going. So beneath his blond highlights was a switching station of guilt, impulses crashing through his system.

"It's a beautiful tie," I said softly.

He struggled for a response. I leaned down, lightly grasped his tie in my right hand, stroked the silk with my thumb. "That silk," I said. I turned it over and saw the Armani name in elegant script. "Why don't we go for a walk," I said. His face was panicked, sweating. I had a hard time making him for Infinity's killer, but it is always dangerous to make judgments. "You can follow me out or I can cuff you." All this was said in an intimate whisper that couldn't be heard in the nearest cubicle. We got up and strolled through the open plan, past the receptionist, out into the midday heat.

"What's your name?"

"I haven't done anything..."

"I'm guessing you've done something. The question is whether it's a crime or not. What's your name?"

"Christian. Christian Dekker."

We walked to my car. I told Christian to get in.

"I want a lawyer," he said weakly.

"You can have one. We'll go to the station, you can call your lawyer, we'll book an interview room."

"You have to charge me with something."

"Is that what you want, Christian?"

"No...I mean, but you have to, don't you, to take me in?"

I shook my head no. Christian got in the car.

"Tell me about Infinity, Christian," I said.

His face twisted a bit then collapsed and he burst into tears, both hands up to his face, sobs that shook him. He tried to catch his breath, like a baby crying and you get that moment of silence as they take in air then start wailing again. I took the slow route to the station, though every route was the slow route these days.

"It's not a crime," he said.

"Bill C-36," I said. "It is illegal to purchase sexual services."

Christian wiped his eyes. "It wasn't like that."

"What was it like?"

Christian stared out the window. We were stuck behind a streetcar. The guy behind me was on his horn. A cyclist hammered on the side of a Buick that had edged into the bike lane and the driver got out and screamed a death threat. The heat moved like water, seeking any opening.

"She's gone," Christian finally said.

"Did you kill her, Christian?"

"God no." He started to sob again.

"She was strangled with a blue tie, mulberry silk. You were given a blue mulberry silk tie as a gift. You no longer have that tie and had to buy a replacement at Holt's this morning at 10:01 a.m. and your missing tie was used to kill Infinity."

Christian was crying uncontrollably. I turned south to get away from the paralyzing traffic and ran into new paralyzing traffic. There was construction up ahead, men in orange safety vests smoking in the shade.

"I feel like it was my fault," he finally said.

"If you strangled her with the tie, it was your fault."

"I *gave* her the tie," Christian said, trying to compose himself. "I wore it one night and she thought it was beautiful. I told her the story, the mulberry silk story, those moths."

"*Bombyx mori,*" I said.

"Do you know why they're called that?"

I hadn't gotten that far into Belisle's dissertation.

"The silkworms are born," he said, "then fed mulberry leaves by Chinese monks, or it used to be monks anyway, and kept in a strict temperature-controlled environment. But they aren't allowed to become moths because if they do, they ruin the silk cocoon they've made. So they are drowned before they can turn into moths. That's where the *mori* comes in. And Audrey...Infinity, she thought this was heartbreaking and beautiful and she felt like she could identify with them somehow."

"The silkworms?"

"They're born into captivity, they make something beautiful, then they die young. Murdered actually. Audrey didn't have an easy life. She was very brave, you have *no idea* how brave," he said with surprising force.

It would take courage to grow up where she did, and it took courage to stand out there, waiting for the next john, who could be anyone.

"How did you meet?" I asked.

"She was working. But it wasn't like you think. We fell in love."

I wondered if Infinity had been in love.

"You don't believe me," he said.

What does love look like? A prism that reflects the vulnerable heart.

"Sometimes we just went out for dinner, or we would just talk. We talked for *hours*."

"You paid her."

"Not like that. I make a good living. Most years anyway. She never had money. It just disappeared with her. I wanted her to move in, but she wouldn't."

"You understand that could be viewed as a motive, Christian." If he couldn't have her, no one could.

The city crawled by. The blare of noon on the sidewalks. People scurried out of the light like cockroaches. I saw a dozen parasols. We finally got to the station. I booked Christian for purchasing sex, which was enough to hold him until his lawyer arrived. It took a certain physicality to strangle someone and I didn't think Christian had the physical force or the temperament, but I could be wrong and he could be a very convincing psychopath.

I called Davis, told her I had the owner of the tie that killed Infinity.

"You have the *murderer*?"

"I don't think he's our guy, but I think it was his tie and I'm holding him on a john bust just in case."

"So this doesn't get us any closer with Moore and Blair."

It didn't, no. Generally, cases got simpler as you got deeper. You eliminated suspects, gathered evidence pointing to the guilty party, but this was going in the opposite direction. Every day brought more complications.

I MET HELEN for a quick lunch. She was working and only had an hour. We went to a French bistro a block away and sat at an outside patio. She ordered a salad and I ordered an omelette and we both settled for water.

"So?" she said, her face opened up in expectation.

"The tie?"

"Yes, the tie. Did I sell a tie to a murderer? Did you catch him? Will the city give me some kind of commendation, you know, a medal or something?"

"I would say no, no, and no."

"What happened? And you can't tell me you can't talk about it because it's an ongoing case."

I told her part of the story and told her she couldn't tell anyone. She was in the sun and I was in the shade. I'd offered to trade but she said that, working inside all year, she needed a little vitamin D. Her hair was lit by the sun. She was wearing a cotton dress with a bright oversized floral pattern, part of a deep red orchid taking up half the dress. Her salad was messy but she didn't mind, dabbing at her mouth with each large mouthful. We talked about police work and the passive aggressive relationship among commissioned salespeople. She had grown up in the Maritimes, her father a cod fisherman turned hardware store employee after the cod disappeared. She came to Toronto, worked in retail. She liked people. She thought it would take her somewhere else, but it never did. She was engaged once, but it blew up. Small pieces of her life emerged.

We each had an espresso, then I walked her back to the store. She gave me a quick kiss on the cheek and disappeared and I wondered if I had been downgraded from the quick kiss on the lips of our dinner date, or maybe it was because it was where she worked and maybe the semiotics weren't as complicated as I thought and I should stop analyzing things like a moonstruck middle-schooler.

TWELVE

I DROVE TO THE strip, parked, got out. There were always new faces, hesitant, self-conscious, girls who'd come from small towns, from shitty lives, where they'd sat in their bedrooms and listened to the sick thumps of their parents' fights. They found community here, the shared fears, living on the bright edge of something. I approached Natasha, who I'd known for three years. I'd helped her out once, a difficult date. Natasha always checked the ID of her clients, looking at drivers' licences, looking for an address while they were in the bathroom. I'd gone to his house to have a talk. He was having dinner, a downtrodden-looking wife, two kids at the table looking at me, his face desperate, his eyes pleading.

Natasha was tall and blonde and sometimes had a Russian accent. With her heels, she was an inch taller than me. She was wearing a bikini top that barely contained her breasts. She had on white shorts with the top button open, the zipper down two inches. A tasteful purse, a Kate Spade knockoff.

"Business or pleasure, Detective?" she asked, smiling her professional smile.

"You look bewitching, Natasha," I said.

"That's the general idea."

"You knew Infinity."

Natasha's mood changed suddenly. "Have you found him yet?"

I shook my head. Natasha nodded. "Are you *going* to find him? Are you even *looking*?"

"I was hoping you could help me look, Natasha."

Her expression was a combination of anger and weariness.

"I understand that blowing cops is the price of doing business," she said with some heat. "But lines need to be drawn. In return, we need something at least *resembling* protection. Instead, we get the opposite."

"You've had trouble? Recently?"

"You're serious about finding Infinity's killer." She had a hard stare.

"Did a couple of detectives canvas the strip last week?" I asked.

"Canvas? Is that what we're calling it now?"

Natasha looked in her purse, took out her phone, scrolled through some names. "I'm going to give you an address," she said. "You go there, *alone,* you don't tell anyone you went there, that you talked to her. She isn't filing a complaint, I don't want you leaning on her to 'come forward' or to 'do the right thing.' You talk to her, you figure it out. But she's not part of this. Understood?"

I nodded.

Natasha assessed me. She read off the address. "You need to see this and you need to forget you saw it and never forget you saw it and you need to douse that station in gasoline and light a fucking match." She hissed the last words.

I got in my car and drove to the address. It was a Victorian house south of St. James Town. The house was in reasonable shape, probably three rental units. The address Natasha had given me was number 3, so the third floor. I guessed that Natasha had phoned to tell her to let me in. I rang the bell. I knew it would take a minute to get down the two flights of stairs. I waited. A woman answered the door, my age, grey hair, sturdy. She looked familiar but I couldn't place her.

"Jenny," she said wearily, standing in the doorway, assessing me. "I'm with Guiding Light." An advocacy group for sex workers, providing legal help, moral support, a pathway out of the life.

"Jamieson," I said. We didn't shake hands. I followed her up the stairs, which sloped to the right, the 120-year-old joists sagging in the middle. The air in the stairway was stale, the carpet worn. The door of the apartment opened to a tiny kitchen. Jenny led me to a cramped living room. There wasn't much light and the furniture was dark and too large for the space. There was a girl on the couch, sitting on one side, her knees drawn up. Her face was battered, a mess of purple, her nose broken, lip split, one eye swelled shut. Bandages on her head, a steel splint on two fingers. I thought she might be sixteen. She was terrified.

"One of your people," Jenny said.

"You're sure?"

Jenny wasn't sure if she could trust me. The girl was sure she couldn't. She was shaking. I didn't want to ask her what happened, she'd never get through it. I didn't think she could get through a description.

"His eyes," I said. "What colour were his eyes."

The girl sat on the couch, rocking slightly. A tear formed and slid down one cheek. Her voice was a little girl's.

"Dead," she said.

IT WAS FRIDAY morning. The traffic was surly, the heat building, the sun already a punishment. I did an internet search on the ownership of St. James Town. Most of it was still owned by the original developers, Fairlane Properties. Five years ago there had been a fire in one of the buildings that had resulted in two deaths. Complaints about the elevators not being safe, lack of maintenance, air conditioners that didn't work. At this point in their lifespan, most of those buildings were held together by duct tape.

Six of the buildings were owned by the provincial government and operated as subsidized housing. Another developer—Skyfield Development—owned some of the remaining Victorian houses on the property. Ten years ago, Skyfield had been part of an attempt to almost double the size of St. James Town, expanding south, razing the Victorian houses and building another twenty towers. It had been opposed by the mayor at the time, and also by Titus Bishop.

I looked up Skyfield Development, which appeared to be dormant. They had made that ambitious, failed gambit. Since then, they'd done a few small developments. Nothing in the last three years that I could see.

THERE WAS A message from the jail; they had a package of Mullins's recent communication with the outside. There wasn't much. He'd spent most of his adult life behind bars. He'd received six letters over the course of eleven years. He'd made calls to the outside twice in the last year, one of them in the last week. He'd had one visitor in eighteen months, also last week. I listened to the most recent recording.

"So you got my message," a voice said, not Randy's.

"Yeah."

"It's win-win."

Randy's unfortunate laugh. "Inside, there's always a loser."

"Yeah, well that's the idea, isn't it, Randall."

A silence long enough that I thought the call might be over.

"You're a team player," the voice said.

"Been a while since I had a team."

"I'm sensing yes."

Another silence.

"Listen, if it's yes, don't say anything else."

Silence.

I checked the number. It belonged to a guy named Bradley Weeks who had done two years of a five-year jolt for aggravated assault, article 268, one who "wounds, maims, disfigures or endangers the life of the complainant." If Delaney Hutch wanted Ambrose Fortier dead, they would use a cut-out, a guy like Weeks, to get in touch with a guy like Mullins. I wondered if it would be worth getting a warrant for Weeks's phone records, but they would have likely done everything in person or used a burner phone so there wouldn't be a trail. Weeks had been Mullins's lone visitor last week.

I ran a check, got Bradley Weeks's car registration, a 2008 Cadillac CTS, red. I drove to the address that matched the phone number. It was a high-rise on the edge of Regent Park, one of the places that hadn't been razed in the massive urban renewal plan next door. I waited for a resident to open the basement garage door with his fob, then followed the car into the underground parking lot, looking for a red Cadillac, found it, checked the licence number, and parked my car right behind it. I walked to the foyer. It had chipped green paint, cloudy glass, the smell of urine. I took the elevator up to the twelfth floor, knocked hard on 1253, stood outside the range of the tiny glass viewer.

"Mr Weeks. Police. Detective Abel. Open the door."

I stood outside for a minute. I didn't hear anything inside. I imagined Weeks walking stealthily up to the fisheye viewer in the door. I knocked hard again, waited another minute, then took the elevator down to the parkade and waited behind an SUV that gave me a clear look at my car and Weeks's Cadillac. Weeks came down ten minutes later, saw his car was pinned. There was a beat before he put it together, but I was out of the shadows, holding my badge.

"You're under arrest."

He stared up at the crumbling concrete of the ceiling. "You don't have anything on me," he said.

That could prove to be true, but I hoped there was enough to hold him.

"What's the bullshit charge?"

"Conspiracy to commit murder," I said, "punishable by fourteen deeply fulfilling years in prison."

I brought Weeks in, booked him, drove home. I poured a glass of a Cotes du Rhone that had been recommended by the wine columnist. It was under $20, a bargain. I was trying to save money on wine and had decided that I could spend an average of $25 a bottle, which meant if I could find a decent $17 bottle and had four of them, I could splurge on a $57 bottle and stay on budget. I wasn't sure I had a palette that went much past $40 but there was a sense of anticipation that came with a $57 bottle of wine.

I turned on the television. I wasn't in the mood to make dinner. I took out some crackers and truffled Crotonese cheese, sliced some soppressata, and put some antipasto from the Italian grocer on a plate. Davis was on the news, giving an update on where we were with Moore and Blair, a speech about how they hadn't been forgotten, would never be forgotten. "The department needs to change and I am a part of that change," she said. The camera loved her.

THIRTEEN

I DIDN'T TELL DAVIS about the sixteen-year-old girl with the battered face. We had talked about Dekker though and I sensed that Davis wanted some distance from him. If it turned out that he was the one who had, in fact, killed Infinity and we had had him in custody and let him go, it would be Keystone Cops headlines for two weeks and all of it would land on me. Davis and I had split up for most of the investigation, partly because of her PR duties, and partly to cover more ground. The plan was to liaise on a regular basis, compare notes, but we were drifting a bit. I felt like we should be having a talk about our relationship.

I went into an interview room where Bradley Weeks was waiting with his lawyer, who turned out to be Lilly Tam. Once more, she was wearing a blue suit and a blouse with a bow. I nodded hello. Lilly started in right away with a precise recitation of the reasons we didn't have enough to hold her client. It occurred to me that she was much tougher than she looked.

"We have a phone call..." I started.

"Which contains no incriminating evidence,"Tam said.

"Which could be interpreted as accepting a job, said job being the knifing of another prisoner."

"Mr Mullins has pleaded self-defence. There are three witnesses who have testified that Mr Fortier attacked Mr Mullins with a knife."

If there was one thing that Ambrose Fortier understood, it was knives. If he had attacked Mullins, he probably would have finished the job.

"Three prisoners," I said. "Those are your witnesses."

"Those would generally be the kind of witnesses you find in a prison,"Tam said. She had an assured, matter-of-fact delivery.

"We have Weeks visiting Mullins a week before Fortier is killed." I knew how weak this was.

"They are friends. They had a friendly visit. And there is no connection between Mr Fortier and my client. There is no motive."

I looked at Weeks. He had black hair slicked back, heavy through the shoulders, large hands, dark eyes.

"I'm a friendly guy,"Weeks said, his hands opening up. "I like to stay in touch."

"Hopefully we can arrange that, Brad," I said. "You and Mullins were close?"

"We're just two guys."

"In eleven years, Mullins received six letters."

"Hence,"Weeks said, "the need to reach out to a lonely soul."

"Because you know what it's like in jail, right?"

"There are worse things than jail,"Weeks said.

"Like getting stabbed eleven times," I said. "That would be worse."

"Guy was a piece of shit, apparently," Weeks said. "You should buy Randy a steak dinner and a stripper."

Ambrose was a piece of shit. Mullins and Weeks were pieces of shit. Weeks was going to say something but Tam clamped him shut.

This was a familiar, infuriating position, knowing a guy was dirty but also knowing there wasn't enough to prove it. After an hour of unhelpful conversation where Weeks said he'd never heard of Delaney Hutch, didn't know Fortier from Adam, had only stayed in touch with an old friend because it can get lonely in the joint, et cetera, there wasn't much choice; I had to cut Weeks loose.

I went to my desk, scrolled through emails, looked up to see Max staring at me. Dekker was sprung, and for all I knew he could be a killer, and Weeks was sprung and I was convinced he was involved in Fortier's murder, and I suspected it was dead-eyed Max who had almost beaten that girl to death and I couldn't prove anything. This was the walking definition of a Very Very Shitty Cop Morning.

I stared back at Max. My head was filling with that redness, like mercury rising, crowding out rational thought, crowding out logic and reason and God's golden light.

FOURTEEN

THE SECOND WEEK OF July saw record heat—eighteen people, mostly seniors in long-term care facilities, dead of heat-related causes. There was a fire in one of the towers in St. James Town that killed four people. Eight hundred and twenty-one people had to be evacuated and find somewhere else to stay. Maestro put up two new pieces. Bobby Dale announced that he would run for mayor again in four months; the city needed him at this crucial juncture. Helen called a few times, feeling she was now part of the case. I had asked her out, to see a play, and she'd said she'd love to but was up north visiting her sister on the weekend. I told her enough about the case to keep her interested, but not enough so I'd be in violation. I felt I was being played, but I wanted to keep some kind of connection with her and so let myself be played a little and felt shitty about all of it.

It was early afternoon, the air heavy with exhaust, threatening to rain but not raining, an ugly day. I was sitting at my desk when Davis brought in Lord Yo. She'd been working a girl from Dash and Angela's school, a girl who connected her to another girl who then connected her to another girl, and Davis had followed the dismal trail of Yo's unhappy lovers, all of whom he had tried to turn out, and finally found the former Peter Manning in a rooming house filled with empty takeout containers, empty beer cans, and cockroaches. He was nodded out on some combination of street drugs. It was impressive police work, especially given the time she had spent talking to reporters and community groups, and had the added benefit of seriously pissing off Lloyd and Max, who had been looking for him in the same neighbourhood.

And now Pete/Lord Yo was in interview room 4, twitchy and pale, half sprawled in the uncomfortable chair. He was big, more of his father than his mother, over 6′, 210 pounds. Davis was seated across from him. I watched from behind the glass. Davis had him on possession of illegal substances, human trafficking. The idea was to make a deal for Delroy's whereabouts.

"Peter, you understand what kind of trouble you're in," Davis said.

"I want a lawyer."

"Your lawyer is on his way."

"I want a girl."

"A girl."

"Girl lawyer."

Davis stared at him, his cornrows, the heavy, fake gold chains, the T-shirt that said THE FUCK YOU WANT? with a faded portrait of a rapper. "You want to choose your lawyer," Davis said, "then you'll probably need a $10,000 retainer. Or you can wait for whoever they assign to you. In the meantime, we can chat."

Pete stared up at the acoustic tile ceiling.

"We're looking for Delroy Staples. You know him."

"Everyone looking for Delroy the Boy." His speech had a laboured musicality.

"Peter, we have you on possession, human trafficking."

"That bitch won't roll on me."

"We dig a little deeper, Peter, and I'm going to bet we'll find trafficking a minor. That's real time. You're what, twenty-two years old? You get out when you're thirty-two. Except you won't be thirty-two, because prison years are like dog years, and when you get out in ten years, you'll be sixty-two."

"Ain't none of them bitches roll on Lord Yo."

It was hard to tell how much of Manning's breezy, disturbing confidence was an act. Most of his adult life was an act.

"How long have you known Delroy Staples?"

Manning rolled his shoulders, weaving slightly in his chair, building to a response, shrugging. "Five years, give or take."

"You met in high school."

Manning gave a noncommittal nod.

"He made quite an impression on you, Peter."

Manning slowly processed this as an insult.

"When was the last time you saw him?"

"Last time I saw him was the last time I saw him."

"Where was this?"

Manning shifted in his chair, found a new contemptuous slump posture, waved one hand around vaguely. Davis tried another tack.

"Your father is Eddy Manning."

Manning looked at her. "What that motherfucker got to do with shit."

"He did time." Davis looked at her notepad. "Little more than two years for aggravated assault."

Davis sensed an opening.

"He beat you, Peter." It was half question, half statement.

"I kick his bitch ass he even *look* at me."

"When was the last time he looked at you, Peter."

"Fuck this. My man going to speak for me, motherfucking mouthpiece."

Ten minutes later, his lawyer arrived, a sad sack in a beige suit that didn't fit. The conversation got more formal. Davis wasn't making a lot of progress and finally cut off the questioning. Better to let Pete spend a night in jail, get a sense of what he was in for. Wait for him to get twitchier, to want to talk.

I thought about Ambrose Fortier and wondered what Mullins had gotten for the hit. Money must have changed hands. Someone would hold it for him. Follow the money. My cell rang. I looked at the display. Mary Binetti.

"Abel."

"Jamieson, hi, it's Mary Binetti, graffiti squad. I've got someone here you might want to talk to."

"Maestro?"

"No, but she may be an associate. She was at one of the murals, had paint that matched. We picked her up. Maybe she can help you."

"Arrested?"

"No, just detained, and we can't keep her for long, but she may answer a few questions."

"There in twenty."

I drove to their station. The rush hour traffic was murderous. The streets were dusty and angry. It hadn't rained in three weeks.

Blue clouds threatened in the west, but they had threatened before and then drifted north. Pedestrians were exhausted; they moved heavily along the sidewalk like circus elephants, grey and plodding. I parked at the station, went in and asked for Binetti. The desk cop pointed down the hall. "First left," he said, "then right."

I found Binetti in a room with a woman, early thirties, mixed race, maybe Filipino and Black. She was slim but muscular, wild hair, dark eyes filled with resentment.

"This is Detective Abel," Binetti said. "This is Angelique. Detective Abel has some questions for you. I'm going to leave you two alone."

"Shall we talk about my *rights*," she said.

"I'd rather talk about your art." They were detaining her as a potential witness, a grey area that took advantage of the fact she didn't have a lawyer.

"Art isn't something you explain," she said. "Like Edward Hopper said, if you could put it into words, you wouldn't need to paint it."

"Those pieces in St. James Town..."

Angelique cocked her head slightly.

"The sheep with the whip," I said, "The big red C..."

"Yeah, I know them."

"I'm asking your professional opinion."

She thought about it, a half smile. "I would say the artist shows promise."

"I'm sure Maestro would be happy to hear he shows promise."

Angelique laughed, a genuine laugh. It changed her face completely. "You people so *hot* on this Maestro. You don't know who the fuck he is and you were the ones created him."

"Like God."

Angelique laughed again. "'For man looks at the outward appearance, but the *Lord* looks at the heart.'"

"You spent time in church, Angelique."

"You can walk with God or you can walk with the ways of the world, but you can't do both. It is a *narrow* path and few can walk there."

"Are you quoting scripture, Angelique, or making it up."

She smiled, a small gap between her two front teeth. "You should have stayed in Sunday school," she said.

She laughed again. She said it was just a gig. She'd gotten it online. Fill in some mural. She got the address, the colours they wanted her to use, very specific instructions.

"They paid $300," she said, shrugging.

"How'd they pay."

"Bitcoin."

I nodded. I didn't understand bitcoin despite having had it explained to me more than once and left it alone.

"You've worked for these people before?"

"These people?" she said with a smile. "Who knows. This is the modern world, you do work you don't understand for people you can't identify and get paid in currency you can't see."

"Brave new world."

"Except the brave part. Everyone hiding, sneaking around online like sheep-killing dogs."

"While you're out there painting."

"Hard to find work as an artist these days."

"It's dangerous work."

Angelique shrugged.

“You hang from a harness? How do you paint the side of a bridge?”

“Very carefully.”

It was hot in the interview room. The back of my shirt was damp. There was a sheen of perspiration on Angelique’s forehead but she didn’t seem to mind. She sat, composed, her hands in her lap. We chatted pleasantly about art and God for twenty minutes. There was the dull drone of air conditioning.

“Who is your favourite artist?” I asked her.

“Damien Hirst.”

“Hirst? Really?” All I knew of Hirst was the shark, which I’d remembered as more of a parlour trick than a work of art. “Why?”

“He made the most money.”

FIFTEEN

THE LANGUAGES SPOKEN IN St. James Town in descending order of percentage are: English, Tagalog, Tamil, Unspecified Chinese, Mandarin, Korean, Spanish, Russian, Serbian, Bengali, Urdu, French, and Other. I was reading the stats on my phone, standing in front of another biblical mural, this one with a burning city. Sodom? Our vengeful God rained fire and brimstone down on a few towns. There had been eight fires in the night, three of them still going. Two deaths, three firemen in hospital. The streets were parched. It was 11 a.m. and the sun was a dim aureole behind a sick yellow haze. The air was thick. The city smelled like a killing floor.

I called Binetti.

"Have you ever had taggers who were being paid to put things up? Like commissioned pieces?"

"Well, we commission pieces, quite a few. It's part of the outreach program. We try and steer them toward something productive, more aesthetically...pleasing."

"And they buy into that?"

"Some do. Some of them feel it's selling out, of course."

"But no one else commissioning a piece, like hiring them to deface a rival's business, something like that."

"It happens. We've had complaints. But nothing that's easily proven. How did you do with Angelique?"

"We talked about God and money."

"They're often confused for one another."

I thanked her and hung up.

I walked to the tower that had had the fire. I wondered where they had all gone. More than eight hundred people. It was on the books as arson, and the four deaths as homicides. One of Maestro's works was on the north side of the building, undisturbed by the fire. It showed Jesus on the cross, wearing a loincloth and an orange sports jacket. Behind him, more than a dozen crosses receding into the background, each with a FOR SALE sign hung on it, the blurry name of realty companies below. I took a photo with my phone.

I DID A deeper dive on the properties around St. James Town; six had been bought by three numbered companies. The department had a forensic accountant on retainer, a guy named Clement Ton, and I called and left a message.

Max was at his desk. I walked over. He swivelled to face me.

"Great detective work on the Lord Yo thing," I said. "You and Lloyd spent, what, three weeks over there, Davis walks in, eats your lunch."

"Fuck off, Abel."

"Makes you wonder what the fuck you guys were doing the whole time."

Max just kept up his stare. I had one hand in my pocket. I was trying to look casual.

"That murder in St. James Town, Infinity," I said. "Apparently a psychological profile narrowed it down—guy who's afraid of his own sexuality, kind of a self-loathing thing, only he externalizes, right, takes it out on the sex worker. So basically a crime of passion, in a sick, complicated way." Max's face tightened a bit. It was already tight, and now it looked like it could split open. "You can do sick in your sleep, Max. Complicated might be a bit of a stretch, but people grow."

What Does Justice Look Like? My first-year law professor had written those words on the blackboard on our first day, then waited until it sank in. We spent the next seventy-five minutes discussing it without coming up with a hard answer.

Max's face was dark, one hand on his desk. His brain chemistry right now looked like a wolverine on meth. There was a sick electricity in the air between us. I turned and slowly walked back to my desk, adrenaline shooting through me. I sat down, took three deep yoga breaths, or what I thought might be yoga breaths, then called Jenny at Guiding Light and told her to move that girl out of that apartment, just to be safe, to do it now.

I looked at emails—four more requests for interviews, all of them promising a balanced look at a station under siege. Clement Ton, the forensic accountant, returned my call and we talked a bit about offshore corporations. I told him what I wanted him to look into.

"So I should invoice the department?"

"What do you charge?"

"Two-fifty an hour."

I thought about that for a few seconds. "Can you get it done in two hours."

Accountant silence at the other end.

"It was a joke," I said. "Let me know when you've got something." I hadn't cleared this with anyone, had no authorization to spend that money. But everyone wanted results. Less expensive than my PR skate through Jamaica.

I left, got in my car, drove to Lisa Hendricks' place, Ambrose Fortier's former girlfriend. She lived on the second floor of a house that needed paint, the yard dead, a Confederate flag in one window. She was home, not happy to see me. She had on boxer shorts and a singlet. Her place had two small fans going and was stifling. I invited myself in, sat on a green chair and sagged down. She sat on the worn couch, pulled her legs up to one side. I asked her about Ambrose, what he was like with her.

"He was different," she said. She said he was on the verge of something big. He'd taken her with him to look at Lincoln Navigators but they wouldn't let them out on a test drive. He told her he'd come back, find the same dickhead salesman, take out seventy-six grand in cash, peel off the bills, stuff them in his mouth and drive out of there.

We talked for half an hour about Ambrose and his plans. She had a cat that curled up on the couch. Her furniture was shabby but the place was relatively neat. Without any make-up, she looked like any teenager. Ambrose was an easy guy to read and Delaney Hutch would have led him to believe that he was a key piece of something and that he would be rewarded. They'd take him to an expensive steakhouse, red banquettes and $80 T-bones, order a bottle of champagne, show him he's going to be a player. It would be easy to pull his strings. But to what end? He was small-time, jacking the locals. It didn't make sense.

SIXTEEN

A CITY ON FIRE

TANYA WILLING | Constable Mike Meredith has a sociology degree. His hobbies are cycling, hiking and birding. He grew up on a farm. His wife is a nutritionist. His five-year-old daughter is cute as a bug. I know this because he showed me the photo of her he keeps in his wallet. Meredith has a nice smile, blue eyes, a calm demeanour. He is Mister Rogers with a gun (which has never been out of its holster). In the good cop/bad cop sweepstakes, Meredith is the good cop, perhaps the best cop in 51 Division. He's the one who takes journalists like me out for tours of the neighbourhood and shows us that police are just like the rest of us, only nicer, and our city is the safest, bestest place in the whole wide world.

Except our city is burning. And our mayor is fiddling while it burns. And our police force is corrupt.

When I went out cycling with Mike Meredith (on the crappy second-hand mountain bike I bought after three previous, much nicer, bikes were stolen) we stopped and had breezy conversations with sex workers. He knew their names, asked about their kids. He knew the name of the guy at the ice cream place, asked how his university classes were going. People waved at Meredith while we ate our cones. Mothers smiled. The sun shone. He knew the names of birds. He told me he had always wanted to be a police officer, had wanted to make a difference.

Two weeks ago, I had a much different ride-along, as they are called. This one was with Adele Murkee, the twenty-nine-year-old Muslim officer who is suing the city and the police force, alleging sexism, racism and Islamophobia. There were no ice cream shops on this tour. The sun didn't shine. We sat in the living room of her one-bedroom apartment while she gave me a tour of her career. She, too, had always wanted to be a police officer, had wanted to make a difference.

But maybe there was too much difference.

Let's start with the crude drawings of her having sex with what were supposed to be terrorists that appeared on the bulletin board a week after she joined the force. Her nickname (unprintable), the sexual innuendo, the intimidation, the exclusion, the Muslim jokes (What's the difference between a Muslim girl and a hippie girl? The hippie girl gets stoned before sex).

Fifty-One Division serves a population that is more than 70 percent people of colour. There is a significant Muslim component, and women accounted for 67 percent of the demographic in the last census. So you would think having a female Muslim police officer of colour would be an advantage. Residents would see someone Who Looked Like Them.

That was certainly the idea when the division recruited Murkee. And that was why she joined. Now she's applying to law school. Win or lose, however her lawsuit goes, she isn't coming back to the force. And the details that will come out during the course of her court case, which will be reported here and elsewhere with varying degrees of glee and doubt, will likely have a chilling effect on any Muslim women who, like, Adele, thought they could make a difference.

Years ago, I interviewed a University of Toronto criminology professor who was near retirement and, therefore, unusually candid. He told me that policing was the Great Liberal Lie.

Most people in western society, he said, know that police have to bend the rules in order to do their job. And by most people, I include the snowflakes and libtards and vegans who walk among us. It isn't spoken out loud. We don't talk about it over lattes or chardonnay or any of the other drinks that liberals are regularly accused of sipping (I'm more of an espresso/Bordeaux gal). It's more of a collective consciousness thing.

We watch TV and we see cops who rough up some witness in order to catch the rapist. They dangle people they know are guilty out of eight-story windows. They are prepared to administer rough justice when the courts fail us.

And we cheer them on.

We also don't want hypodermic needles on our lawns, we don't want gangs terrorizing our schools. We don't want sex workers in our driveways. We want the cops to deal with it, to do whatever they need to do, but we don't necessarily want to see them doing it. We don't want to see cops beat a suspected burglar with their batons.

Right up until we've been burgled ourselves. The goal posts are always shifting.

The Wise Cop knows this dichotomy exists, both in society and within individuals, and understands where the line is drawn and when it moves. At any given moment, they can do x, but can't do y.

But the line is a blurry one, and getting blurrier. Who can you intimidate, maybe assault? Well, someone who is selling fentanyl to middle school kids. That probably works for many of us.

But the kid who is high and who calls a cop a fat, brain-dead Wiggum (the name of the police chief on "The Simpsons") as Riley Cutler, age 15, allegedly did before he was allegedly kneecapped by said Wiggum with a baton? Well, not too sure about that one.

The line that defines the Great Liberal Lie is determined by leadership. We elected an actual school bully as mayor (Bobby Dale used to beat up kids at John A Macdonald Collegiate—an earlier investigation found nine of them willing to reminisce). Mayor Dale and his followers are fond of plain speaking. Well, here is some Plainspeak: Mr Dale is a misogynist, racist, alcoholic, crack-using halfwit. But we, the people, elected him. What does that say about us?

That we feel marginalized, that we are angry and fearful, and not always exactly sure what we're fearful about. It says we are easily misled and we don't have a firm grasp of recent history (or any history, really). It says we wanted to blow things up.

Where else to look for leadership? The police chief is flailing and the division superintendent at 51 is a spineless lump with one foot on the golf course.

So where does that leave us? In a bit of a pickle. And how do we get out of it? We won't be rescued by politicians, certainly. And we can rule out the police. Journalists aren't going to ride to the rescue because they rarely do. We need to look to ourselves.

But first we need to look *at* ourselves.

I chatted happily and easily with Mike Meredith on the ride-along. We both pretended that we were friends after six hours of cycling around the city. He said he hoped we could get together again. We both said we had a better understanding of what the other did for a living. He told me that the bird I heard was a sora—*Porzana carolina*—quite rare.

I empathized with Adele Murkee. Try working in a male-dominated world with the last name Willing. How many sexual puns do you think you would hear? (roughly 100 and counting). And when you're young and just starting out, it's a different time, sort of, and maybe you go along with it, laugh along with the hyenas, make a joke yourself, try to become a member of the club. Then you start hating yourself for going along with it. Then you start hating them for making you hate yourself.

So I empathized with Adele. But I also empathized with her because that's what journalists do to get the story. *I feel your pain.* Sometimes we do feel their pain. Sometimes what we feel is a deadline.

Humans aren't always a wonderful species. We are tribal, given to dark thoughts, dark urges. Society stifles those urges and allows just enough of them to get out so we don't build up too much pressure and explode.

But now the city is exploding.

Maybe the city was always on the verge of exploding. Maybe all cities are. That's the nature of urban life. Maybe it was on the verge of exploding 100 years ago, when it was a lily-white Protestant hick town that ran on righteousness, overcooked roast beef and coal. Maybe those

Methodists spent 90 percent of their waking hours trying not to have impure thoughts about that woman in the next pew showing a bit of ankle. Maybe the women were all simmering with resentment over the spectacular dullness of their lives, the sanctimonious sandbox they all sat in—arid as the Gobi Desert. Maybe they secretly wanted to stick their dinner knife in the eye of their smug husband as he explained politics to them as if he were talking to a golden retriever.

Whatever.

The city got more interesting. It became the entry point for a million immigrants and we suddenly (well, over a generation suddenly) had foreign languages, unfamiliar customs, better restaurants (way better restaurants). And most of us thought this was fine.

But the immigrants didn't stop coming.

And one day, we woke up and that white supermajority had become a minority and was getting smaller. And people started wishing for a long-ago time when we had full employment and women who knew how to cook and the suburbs were paradise.

Except we never had full employment and the suburbs were never paradise. But you can't beat the power of a seductive narrative, can you? Just ask Bobby Dale. We have a million people believing that something they never had is somehow being taken away.

It took roughly two generations for Toronto to go from having just enough visible minorities to field a football team and give liberals something to feel smug about to being the most multicultural city on earth. The most recent census showed: Whites, 48.5 percent; Visible (former) Minorities, 51.5 percent, and if you count Indigenous people as visible minorities, which Statistics Canada doesn't, the number is probably closer to 55 percent. And this news arrived with the subtle message that the gap would increase. And there was a part of the new white minority who weren't thrilled with this trend, guys like Bobby Dale, who remembered a childhood as white as Wayne Gretzky's Christmas. And there was a part of the new visible majority who wondered why everything still felt the same.

So now we've got a narrative problem, a police problem, a leadership problem and a racism problem.

Add to that wonderful recipe the murders of two promising, innocent girls. Add Dashika and Angela, one Black, one white. Stir, occasionally whip up, then put it all in the hot oven of July. What do you get?

What you get is the summer of our discontent.

We have towers burning in St. James Town. Who set those fires? Maybe the same guy(s) who murdered Dashika and Angela. And maybe the police just cracked the case this morning using a combination of handsome bicycle cops who have studied control theory at university, head-cracking psychos (who only crack heads that deserve cracking, mind you) and the kind of cool forensics we see on TV. It will all be in tomorrow's paper with a grim mugshot of the perp and we will all breathe a collective sigh of relief and go back to the business of being the most multicultural city in the world.

Except they haven't cracked the case. Instead, the case is cracking us, pointing out all those fault lines that we very cleverly keep hidden every time the UN comes by for an inspection.

The city is unravelling. I'm starting to unravel along with it.

SEVENTEEN

IT WASN'T A SURPRISE that Mellon thought I was Tanya Willing's source inside the division. He had gone through my emails on the office computer, found two from her requesting interviews. I hadn't responded, but Mellon didn't care. The contact was enough. Mellon looked like hell. He normally looked like hell, but now there was a cadaverous quality to his skin, the hint of a palsy. He wasn't sleeping. He was just wishing this would all get wrapped up. The "spineless lump" description was fair. He was already being referred to as SL in the station and it had barely been twenty-four hours.

I had booked a room to question Lord Yo. Davis was going to be lead, but she wasn't picking up and I didn't know where she was. I decided to go ahead without her. I went into the box. Lord Yo was nowhere to be seen. In his place was Peter Manning, the cornrows replaced by short, neatly combed hair, his jewellery gone, his fuck-you T-shirt replaced by a white button-down and a shitty green tie. The sad sack lawyer who had been with him when Davis questioned him had been replaced by the ubiquitous

Lilly Tam. She was wearing a different outfit today, a very plain brown skirt and jacket.

"Ms Tam," I said. "An unexpected pleasure."

"Detective Abel."

"Peter," I said. "The makeover looks good on you. Very *Brady Bunch.*" He was wearing glasses that may or may not have been prescription. He didn't know who the Brady Bunch were. "When was the last time you saw Delroy Staples?"

Manning thought for a moment.

"I think it was, like, a year ago?"

His voice was different. Gone were the ersatz rap rhythms. His hands were folded on the table instead of moving in swirling semicircles.

"You two were friends."

"For a while, yeah."

"You're still friends."

Peter looked at Tam, maybe trying to remember her instructions. "The thing is, Delroy had a temper, man. You never knew when he was going to blow. He did some bad shit and I got tired of waiting for the bomb to go off, you know."

"You were afraid of him. Big guy like you."

"No. Well, yeah, I guess. I mean he could really lose his shit, man."

I didn't think he was afraid of Delroy, and I didn't think he'd tell me if he was. But he was afraid of something. He had it under control, but I could smell it.

"Were you and Delroy together the night Dashika and Angela were murdered?"

"Don't answer that," Tam said to him. "My client just said he hasn't seen Delroy for a year."

"Were you there, Peter, in that apartment, when those girls were murdered? Is that you on the security footage?"

"Detective Abel," Tam said, "there is no image of my client on any security footage. I suggest you play by the rules. Which I shouldn't need to remind you are very clear when it comes to evidence."

I nodded. Except there weren't really any rules. I could use whatever tricks I had to trip up Manning. "Have you ever been to that apartment?"

"No."

"Did you know those girls? Ever meet Dashika or Angela?"

"No."

"But you were friends with Delroy. He was dating Dashika. You would have met her."

He shrugged. "Delroy dated a lot of women. I met some of them. She might have been one of them."

"Where were you that night?"

"Out, you know, driving around with my crew, just..."

"I'll need the names of your crew."

"I'll get those to you, Detective Abel," Tam said.

"Tell me, Peter, at what point did you start acting like the illegitimate son of 50 Cent and Lil Wayne?"

"Don't answer that, Peter." Tam had her hand up.

I leaned in. "Does the name Delaney Hutch mean anything to you?" I was asking Manning but watching Tam.

"This interview is over," Tam said.

"She a porn star maybe," Manning said.

Tam didn't have any reaction. She stood up, picked up her briefcase. There were Legal Aid lawyers who took money under the table, and I wondered if Lilly Tam was one of them. It couldn't be coincidence that this was our third encounter. The two of them left, Manning looking at the one-way glass.

DAVIS CAME IN twenty minutes later and was extremely pissed that I'd gone ahead without her.

"I couldn't get hold of you."

"I *brought* him in." She stared up at the ceiling. "What did he say?"

"Blowing smoke mostly. Has a new look for the courtroom. I doubt he knows where Delroy is. Something about him though, something a bit off."

"Like how."

"Like he's searching for a genuine personality and he's not having much luck. Trying on different personas like you try on jeans."

"You should have waited." That cold stare of hers.

"You were talking to some community group? I know the department needs you as their poster girl but…"

"I am out there *connecting* with people, Abel. You, *you* create distance…" Her arms went up, indicating the entire world. "*I* brought him in, *I'm* the one who connected the dots…"

It was possible that we were both right: she was spending too much time "connecting" and I had a gift for creating distance. But she had brought him in and we left it at that.

Davis looked at her phone, then left. She didn't say where.

I drove to St. James Town. I'd gone through some of the case files from the last year, the several hundred unsolved crimes that had been allegedly investigated by Toussaint and Pierce. There might not be any connection between any of these crimes and the two murders, but this was starting to look like one of those cases where you have to get lucky, some random piece of the puzzle that doesn't seem related.

I parked and looked at my phone. There was an email from Tanya Willing on my personal account. I wondered how she'd gotten it. *Everyone probably thinks you're my source inside the division so you may as well meet me for a drink. We can help each other. How is Ursuline at 6?* Her twisted journalist logic. I put my phone away.

I had taken a look at the St. James Town crime stats for the past four months, looking for a pattern. Of the eighty-two robberies and assaults that had involved a dangerous weapon, none had been solved. Seventeen rapes were unsolved, as well as four arson cases. What had been solved was a stolen bike ring and three domestic assault cases. No graffiti busts, but there rarely were.

It was possible that Ambrose Fortier had committed many of the robberies and assaults. A few statements I had looked at had a description that matched Fortier. There were quite a few that had vague descriptions—average height, average weight, between twenty and thirty, wearing a hoodie, didn't get a good look, et cetera. Not specifying race, but the semiotics were clear. I knocked on the doors of three people who had made statements. Two of them reluctantly gave me a little more, most of it pointing to Fortier. I knocked on a fourth door, the address that was on the file, home to Berezat and Ashofta Nawaz. A man opened the door. Mid-thirties. His wife stood six feet behind him. He was thin, with a paunch, thinning hair, wearing a white singlet. She was sturdy, nervous, wearing a patterned turquoise dress.

I identified myself, showed them the badge. "Mr Nawaz?"

"Yes."

"I'd like to talk to you about the crime you reported."

Berezat stared at me blankly. "Crime?"

"You reported a robbery. June 4. The robber had a knife. He took your phone and wallet, threatened you."

"I didn't report a robbery."

I looked at him, looked at his wife. They were both nervous. Many of the people in St. James Town had a fear of authority in whatever form it came in—the brutal version they'd left behind, or the unknown version they'd found here. So maybe he wanted a little distance from the statement he'd made.

"You didn't make a statement to a Detective Pierce on June 4?"

Berezat stared.

"Average height. Thin. May have been with a big guy, inch taller than me, thirty pounds heavier."

Berezat was trying to calculate what answer would put him and his wife in the least amount of danger.

"But you were robbed on June 4," I said.

He shook his head. "No."

"Mr Nawaz, I can understand that you may be fearful that this statement might put you in some kind of danger. It won't. The perpetrator is dead. This is a just a routine follow up. Police policy."

I showed him the file. He saw his name, looked up at me.

"We don't want to make any trouble," he said. His wife was visibly scared.

"You're not in any trouble, Mr Nawaz," I said. "I can assure you, this is just routine. Nothing to concern yourself with."

But they were concerned. They would remain concerned. I had ruined their day, their month. It was possible that the Nawazs regretted reporting the crime. Maybe thinking whoever robbed them was part of an organization that would seek vengeance. But it was also possible he was telling the truth, that he was never robbed, that he hadn't filed a report.

In the course of the afternoon, I encountered nine others who said they hadn't reported a crime, hadn't filed a statement. I read the statements back to them. No one recognized the statement, or the crime. Which made them even more suspicious of me. I went through the statements more carefully, noticed certain similarities, grammatical tics, stylistic quirks. They were signed by Pierce. Did he make them up? Whatever the hell was happening was on a large scale and the only person I could trust was my partner, and I wasn't sure she trusted me.

It was after six and I drove home, parked, and walked down King toward the grocery store. I passed a dozen restaurants, people sitting on outdoor patios, talking, drinking wine. I saw Helen. She was wearing a sleeveless beige summer dress, sitting with a well-dressed man who looked to be in his late forties. Summer suit, no socks, expensive shoes. Likely a customer of hers. Some guy who was shopping for a new suit and they flirted a bit. He tried on more suits than he needed to just to keep that conversation going. Maybe bought one that was more expensive than he would have liked, just to make an impression. I stopped for a second. They were holding wine glasses, both laughing. Her hand touched his forearm, an intimate gesture. I hurried on and studied that photograph in my head for too long and felt slightly nauseous.

I went back to my condo and mechanically started assembling a one-pan Japanese chicken dish, sprinkling flour on the chicken thighs, mincing garlic and ginger, squeezing the limes. I was surprised at the effect seeing Helen had on me. I felt like I'd been punched. We'd only gone out on one date, two if you included lunch. There had been a chaste kiss, my only kiss in more than two years. By any modern definition, we didn't have a romantic relationship. Maybe the only thing holding us together was the Nancy Drew aspect of those mulberry ties. She looked like she was having fun with that guy. I wasn't fun. But she was, and that's part of what had attracted me to her. More than I realized, clearly. In the stubborn photograph in my head, she was laughing at something the guy said, her eyes slightly closed. The gut punch of a failed romance was something I hadn't experienced in decades. But I remembered it now, that all-consuming longing. A sickness.

I melted butter in the heavy, expensive frying pan I'd bought at the upscale kitchen store. I'd gone in three times, picking it up, testing its surprising weight, looking at the price tag, hoping there was a sale before finally paying full price. I added the chicken thighs and browned them on both sides and took them out and put them on a plate, then added the onion to the pan, followed by the Madras curry powder I'd had to go to Little India to find, then the garlic, ginger, and nutmeg. I added more butter, stirred, turned the oven on to 350°F. I opened a $72 Saint-Émilion premier cru that was my reward for six discount Cotes du Rhones and poured a large glass and swirled it around and breathed it in and imagined I knew a lot about wine.

I rinsed the rice until the water ran clear and added it to the pan, added carrots and white wine. The recipe called for a dash of Worcestershire sauce, a sauce I inherently distrusted and left out. I put the chicken back in, brought it all to a simmer, then covered the pan and put it in the oven and sat down and turned on the news.

Bobby Dale had left rehab and driven his SUV into a war memorial along Lakeshore Boulevard. This was the big news. He had minor injuries. There was footage of the black SUV nestled against the memorial honouring Our Glorious Dead, the front crumpled slightly.

After twenty minutes I took the chicken out of the oven, took the lid off the pan, and put it back in the oven. I poured another glass of wine. It filled me with a soothing warmth. The sun was behind the buildings. There was a pink glow that reflected up onto the clouds that hovered, giving a warm, diffuse light. A romantic sunset.

I pictured Helen at the restaurant. He would have asked her out for a drink, then they'd had a second drink and he suggested dinner, sitting outside in that soft air, exchanging intimacies, stories about their childhood, leaning in.

I checked my emails. There was an email from Facebook to wish happy birthday to a poet who had been dead for twenty years. There was a message from Tanya Willing. *I have something for you.* I wrote back: *Ursuline tomorrow. 6 p.m. off the record.*

I took the chicken out of the oven, put it on the stove. I placed it on a plate and composed it and compared it to the photograph in the cookbook, then carried it to the sofa and sat in front of the television. The weather guy issued a solemn storm warning, something about the lake effect. We could get up to four inches of rain. "Thank you, Noah," the anchor said and looked at the camera and told me not to wash my car.

EIGHTEEN

TANYA WILLING WAS FORTY-NINE. She had dark hair that had been coloured, with faint auburn highlights, and there was a slight fox-like quality to her features, the way her nose turned up. Her undergraduate degree was in political science and women's studies and she had a master's in journalism from Columbia. In the last decade she had had six speeding tickets, forty-one parking tickets, and had run a stop sign. She drove a blue Volvo that was seven years old. She was sitting at a table for two, wearing a sage green dress and heels, and stood up when I approached, her hand extended.

"Detective Abel," she said. "Thank you for coming."

"We are off the record."

"Understood."

I waited.

"You want me to actually say it?"

I nodded.

"Our conversation is off the record."

"And you're not recording it."

"I'm not recording it."

The history of the Ursuline Sisters was posted on the wall behind her in an antique font. Founded in 1572 under the patronage of St. Ursula, who died, along with 11,000 other virgins, in 383 CE in Cologne, Germany. Most of the virgins were beheaded, but Ursula was shot with an arrow from a barbarian's bow. This story, like so many, could stand a bit more investigation. How did 11,000 virgins end up in a town that probably had a few hundred people in the fourth century? How do we know they were all virgins? If whoever was telling the story had said a hundred virgins, maybe I'd have gone along with it. Stories are what get us in trouble.

"Curious name for a bar," I said.

"Kind of fits, though," she said. "A cloistered room cut off from the world, filled with sexual frustration, loneliness, and doubt."

"You're Catholic."

"Not lately."

Tanya had a glass of white wine in front of her. The waiter came by and I ordered a generic Malbec.

"How long has Mellon got?" she asked.

"I thought you had something for me."

"I do, but I thought we could trade, Detective. Mellon doesn't have control of the division. They can't afford to keep him there until retirement even though it's only months away. Do they bring someone in from the outside, promote from within? Who moves up?"

"Well, it won't be me." Under normal circumstances, they would bring in someone from outside. There would be a press conference about increased transparency, a new culture, et cetera.

But we were in emergency mode and they didn't have the luxury of that kind of transition. They needed someone on the inside, at least on an interim basis. They could put Jimmy Lloyd at the helm, God help us.

"Didn't Mike Meredith give you a few possibilities?" I asked.

"Mike's a sweetheart. Kind of a professional sweetheart that they pull out for the ride-alongs, still."

It was unlikely that Meredith was her source. He was a straight shooter.

"Jimmy Lloyd might get a tap on the shoulder," I said. "Father and uncle were cops. Blue bloodline. The optics would work." As long as no one talked to him for more than ten minutes and as long as Mad Max wasn't lurking in his shadow. I took a sip of the Malbec. A bit underwhelming. "So what is it you have for me, Tanya?"

She looked around the room. "It's your partner. Davis. She's making a run for mayor."

This shouldn't have been surprising, yet it was.

"She's going to officially declare in a few weeks."

"And you know this…"

"I know this because I know this. She's got a law firm bankrolling her campaign. Most of the early campaign money will be coming from them."

I felt a sudden jolt. "Which law firm?"

"That I can't tell you."

If it was Delaney Hutch, then I had just lost the closest thing to a friend I had on the force and Davis was much more complicated than I thought. "Can't tell me because you don't know?"

"Can't tell you because I can't tell you."

"You can tell me who it isn't though."

Her expression was noncommittal, weighing the slightly weaselly ethics.

"The initials aren't DH. The law firm."

She looked at me, calculating my future worth as a source.

"No," she said.

Davis was her source in the division. Davis was cultivating her, lining up good press before her run for the mayor's job.

"If you've got Davis feeding you on the inside, what do you need me for?"

"I don't reveal sources, Detective."

We talked for more than an hour without telling each other much. I wondered how long ago Davis had made a move. She would have put out feelers, sat down with potential donors. Her visibility and her effectiveness in front of the camera would have gotten a pledge. There wouldn't be any actual money at this point—they would have to file a Notice of Registration with the city clerk. Davis would have to formally declare. Neither party would want her candidacy on the record at this point. She probably had a handshake deal, one the law firm could get out of if things didn't work out. So Davis had her own pressures to solve this case: her candidacy was essentially linked to it.

Tanya and I shared small plates of charred brussels sprouts and grilled calamari, ordered a second glass of wine. We talked about the Ursuline Sisters, what their darkest thoughts might be.

THE NEXT DAY Mellon was gone. No office party with beer and backslapping, sharing funny stories about ol' Mellon, no speeches or tears or applause. Vanished without a trace. His office had been cleaned out, the photos all gone. In his office was Jimmy Lloyd, sitting there with his unfortunate smile. I poked my head in.

"You going to congratulate me, Abel?"

"Break a leg."

I walked to my desk, sat down, scrolled through emails, called Davis, left a message that sounded like a boyfriend who didn't understand why we were breaking up. I checked the weekly recipe from the cooking app I subscribed to. Crispy smoked eel with beetroot crème fraiche. It was time-consuming—normally a plus, but I wasn't sure about eel. Wasn't sure where I'd find them, or if I wanted to find them.

I did some research on Fairlane, the company that owned most of St. James Town. It was a family business currently owned by a man named Ludlow Luckworth, a reclusive, belligerent man who was largely estranged from his family—an ex-wife and a son and daughter. Fairlane was number two on a website titled "Toronto's Worst Landlords." There were faulty elevators, bedbugs, cockroach complaints, fires.

The houses in the surrounding area were mostly late-nineteenth-century, early-twentieth-century, a collection of Victorian and Second Empire, many of them grand but deteriorated. They were within walking distance of downtown, bordered to the north by the calm of Rosedale, to the east by the Don Valley, and to the south by the cool enclave of Cabbagetown, once a working-class Irish ghetto, now filled with architects, broadcasters, and solar panels.

Someone was buying property and whoever it was had gone to great lengths to drive the price down by implementing a crime spree, one that was ignored/abetted by at least two cops in 51 Division. It was unlikely Mellon was part of this. Whoever was behind it would have viewed him as too dim and/or weak. But now Jimmy Lloyd was running the show.

Whether the murders of Dashika and Angela and Infinity were part of it was unclear. I didn't tell Davis because it was one more theory that didn't illuminate, only clouded an already cloudy picture.

I drove to Heaven Home and parked outside and dialled their number and asked to speak to Christian Dekker.

"I'm outside, Christian," I said. "Come out and take a ride with me."

"I don't have to come out, and I'm not taking a ride with you." There was a forced certainty in his voice.

"You don't have to take a ride, Christian. I can come in and we can have a loud conversation about your connection to the murder of a sex worker."

I could feel Christian weighing his options.

"I'm looking for your real estate expertise," I said. "An hour of your time. This may help find Infinity's killer."

His grunt was vaguely affirmative. He appeared outside three minutes later. We drove to St. James Town and I pulled over on Parliament.

"What do you see," I asked, gesturing to the towers.

"The end of an era."

"These towers come down, what would you put up here?"

Dekker thought for a moment. "Before they came down, you'd need to get control of as much land around here as possible. Once someone figures out what you're up to, the price goes up dramatically."

"You'd put condos here?"

"Probably. Not all high-rise, though. Some mid-rise. Change up the scale, try and make it look like it wasn't a planned community, like it grew organically into one of the most desirable locations in town."

"All luxury?"

"Mix it up a bit. A few that are within reach. The aspirational class."

"How hard is it to get whatever zoning you need?"

"This part is already zoned. And despite what they say, city council is essentially pro-development."

"How big a hurdle is the provincial government?"

Dekker smiled. "If the government veers left, then you'd need to put in some affordable units. Otherwise..."

We drove back to Dekker's office and talked about real estate. Everyone talked about real estate. It was practically an official language. When we pulled up to his building, he stared straight ahead. "How close are you?"

"Close?"

"To catching her killer."

"I have a theory."

Dekker nodded and got out of the car, closing the door with more force than necessary.

I drove back to the station and looked through the files of the St. James Town crimes that Toussaint and Pierce had solved, the fifteen out of 254 they had closed. They didn't have anything on Infinity's murder. I put the files in my backpack and stood up. On my way out, Mad Max was standing by the door. He had a half smile, which made him look even more sinister.

"New sheriff in town," he said. He pulled two imaginary six-shooters out of imaginary holsters and fired at me, then holstered his weapons. If I wasn't fired or transferred within the next week or so it meant Lloyd was keeping me here for a reason, and that reason couldn't be anything good.

Max was wearing one of his ill-fitting sports jackets, an unsubtle plaid that mixed green and orange, tan pants, and a light blue shirt with the collar open.

"You know what you need, Max," I said to him.

"Tell me what I need, Abel." Every sentence from Max sounded like a death threat.

"A tie would really pull that whole outfit together. Maybe something in a midnight blue."

NINETEEN

SATURDAY WAS OVERCAST, A mercy. I made an espresso, read the paper, made another espresso, ate a blueberry scone. Bobby Dale's approval ratings had gone up after his drunken car accident and emotional public apology. I scrolled through my emails, sent another ironic note to Davis: *You don't write, you don't call.* I ran a search of property transfers to see if anything had happened in the last few days. Nothing registered, but I noticed there was a property—most likely a house—surrounded by four properties that had been bought by numbered companies. The owner was listed as P. Bannich. Whoever had bought the surrounding properties would have approached P. Bannich, offered to buy theirs, so they could consolidate it with the ones they already held and build whatever they were planning on building. He/she hadn't sold, clearly. They would have offered more. I made a note of the address.

I scrolled through the recipes from my subscription service and settled, finally, on marmalade-glazed duck. I printed out the ingredients, went out to my car, and drove to St. James Town. It was muggy. The grey sky made the city look dirtier. I drove to the address of the holdout. It was a large Second Empire house, the trim painted purple but chipped and faded. The rest of the house was peeling yellow, the ancient wood visible in places. Two windows on the top floor had aluminum foil in them. There was cardboard blocking another window. The porch sagged southward and was filled with dead appliances.

I rang the doorbell but couldn't hear a bell inside. I knocked loudly and waited, knocked again, hammering this time. It was a full two minutes later that the door opened a few inches. A woman's face appeared. It was heavily lined, a face that could hold a spring rain, as my mother might have said. Her eyes were dull. Her thick grey hair was cut short. It looked like she had cut it herself. It was dark in the house.

"Ms Bannich?"

She didn't say anything.

"Ms Bannich, I'm Detective Abel." I took out my badge and showed it to her. "May I come in and talk to you?"

She examined me closely, looked at the badge.

"I want to talk to you about the people who are trying to buy your house."

"It's my house," she said. Her teeth were dark, untended.

"That's what I want to talk to you about."

She nodded, opened the door a bit more and turned and started walking. It appeared to be an invitation. I followed her down a hallway. It was perpetual twilight in the house. It hadn't been renovated in the last century. These were the original floors, the original plaster, remnants of the original wallpaper. The living room was filled with boxes and piled floor to ceiling with stacks of newspapers, blocking most of the light. The kitchen was small but got some light from the back window. The yard was filled with small crosses planted in the dirt, a few patches of grass. She motioned for me to sit down. There was a red vinyl chair with a slash and white stuffing coming out and a small Formica table with aluminum trim. The refrigerator was rounded and small, seventy years old. I didn't want to see what was in there.

She filled a kettle with water and put it on the stove, put a lit match to the gas. She took out two mismatched china teacups, chipped at the edges. She took a cigarette out of a tin and lit it. She looked a bit like the poet W. H. Auden.

"Who wants to buy your house, Ms Bannich?" I asked.

She shrugged. "A man," she said. "Always a man."

She had the ghost of an accent, eastern European or Russian.

"They made an offer, you refused to sell. They made another offer."

She held up three fingers.

"They made three offers?"

She nodded.

"But you still refused."

She nodded again. "This is my house."

She took the kettle off the stove, poured some into a teapot, and placed the pot on the table. She put two saucers and two cups on the table and tipped her ash into a large, overfilled ashtray.

"They offered you a lot of money."

She shrugged again.

"They must want your house very badly."

"Not as badly as I want it."

"How long have you been here?"

"Sixty-eight years." She didn't need to calculate. They'd probably asked her the same question a few days ago.

I looked out to the backyard, to the crosses. I counted nine. "Those are graves."

She nodded. "Sasha, Pasha, Kitcha..." She trailed off.

"Cats?"

"Cats, dogs." She shrugged.

"They offered to move you to a new place?"

She nodded again. She told me her father had bought the house. He'd been a doctor in Russia, St. Petersburg. Her mother died in childbirth. She and her father came here. He died suddenly, she said, pointing to the basement door as if this explained his death. She'd been living in the house on her own all this time. She looked to be in her early eighties. The first man who'd come to buy the house had been young, very charming, she said. The second was from the same mould. The third wasn't charming, though. He was older, bigger, said this was the final offer, told her that living alone wasn't healthy, that people die alone in houses like this and their bodies aren't found for weeks. He walked around the house like he already owned it, she said. That was why she'd let me in. Something about that last guy, the implied threat.

She poured tea for us, lit another cigarette. The tea was dark, brackish, with black flakes in it. It tasted like tree bark. We talked for half an hour. She might have been grateful for the company but didn't want to admit it to herself. It was hot in her kitchen.

"These men," I said, "did they leave a business card?"

She nodded, got up heavily and looked in a drawer. I heard cutlery moving. She picked out a card and handed it to me. It read BRENT LAKEFIELD, SUNSET HOMES. There was a phone number.

"Which of the men gave you this card?" I asked.

"All of them."

"Three cards? All with the same name?"

She nodded, exhaled a cloud of smoke.

I stood up, thanked her for the awful tea, said I had to be going. She followed me to the door.

"It's my house," she repeated.

"It is, Ms Bannich."

I drove to the wine store and bought a bottle of Sancerre and a Bordeaux that had a score of 92 plastered to it, then drove to the market. I bought a duck, asparagus, English marmalade, and freshly squeezed orange juice. I bought a peameal bacon sandwich and ate it while I walked around and surveyed octopus and langoustines and halibut behind glass. The market was a comforting place, filled with possibility. Those possibilities were partly individual—the chef imagining all he can do with this—and partly communal, everyone gathered to break bread, to feast on the result.

I drove home, unloaded my groceries, googled Sunset Homes. There wasn't anything, at least not in town. I ran Brent Lakefield through the police database and came up empty.

I picked up my backpack, walked down the stairs, and turned to go uptown along Spadina, then through the campus, which was quiet. It took thirty-five minutes to get to Bloor and my back was wet against the pack. As a kid, Saturday was the best day. Sunday was marred by church, and everything was still closed back then. The weekdays were school. But Saturday was golden. In winter, we played hockey. There were shinny games that lasted all day, evolving games that at any given time might have a six-year age range—nine-year-olds playing with fifteen-year-olds, the young kids just happy to be on the ice with the big kids, to get an unexpected pass, to feel like they were in the big time. There could be ten guys on each side, a rugby game on ice. At dinner, that number could fall to three on each side. I was usually one of those last remaining guys. Shinny was where we got creative, where we imitated what we'd seen on TV. We hogged the puck, tried blind drop passes, skated with abandon. The weekly practices and games were where we worked on fundamentals, but shinny was where we soared. There were no referees, no adults. We called out our own heroics in the voices of announcers—*And Abel has tied this defence in knots, folks, and now he is deking out their stunned goalie, the crowd is on its feet.* There were fights, injuries, Johnny Gardner sliding into the post, his face hitting the steel, his teeth scattering on the ice, the game stopping to look for the white teeth on the white ice. At school two days later, he showed everyone the gap, stopping and exhibiting a rictus grin a dozen times, celebrating his wound.

In summer, we played ball hockey and rode our bikes into the ravines that snake through the city, the largest urban ravine system in the world, covering 110 square kilometres. It held forests and rivers and trails. Mostly it held mystery; it was where the city kept all its secrets. We saw deer, coyotes, racoons, snakes. Deeper into the trees we found a circle of stones, evidence of a fire, an old blanket, discarded condoms, an empty bottle, signs of an unknown civilization. We intuitively understood that the ravines were where bad things happened. Biking with two friends one day, we walked our bikes twenty metres off the trail, into the woods, laid them down, covered them with leaves to protect them from thieves and walked deeper into the woods. The trees were closely spaced. The trunks rose high, with few lower branches; the leaves were nearer the top, seeking the light. There were trees that were twisted and gnarled, trying to find the sun. The forest floor was spongy and there was deadfall everywhere, scattered at odd angles like pick-up sticks.

We spoke in whispers as we walked, convinced that something was in these woods, something dangerous. This turned out to be true. Deep into the woods we saw a blue nylon tarp strung across deadfall. There were other tarps, different colours, different materials: a dozen crude shelters that were joined into a sort of village. We could smell woodsmoke. Two men emerged from one of the tents, bearded, ragged. Then two more appeared. There was something on a stick they were putting over the fire. We all stopped breathing. I looked around slowly and saw a fifth man, to our right, maybe twenty feet away. He was watching us watching the other men. He was lean, had a beard, a checked shirt, dirty jeans that were held up with rope. His eyes were dark, his face as impassive as stone. This was where boys disappeared. This was why the Brothers Grimm had collected all those tales: to keep children from venturing into the woods where the witches and trolls dwelled. I yelled *Run!* and we all took off through the forest, running as only a frightened child can, hurtling, darting, running at full speed, past the endurance of those small limbs and undeveloped lungs. We ran until we hit the trail and it was impossible to run any more, then stopped, panting, bent over, an exhaustion that had a heaving violence. Before we had recovered we walked quickly along the trail, then up out of the ravine.

But our bikes were back there. I had a red CCM, cool, coveted. Bicycles were freedom. *We have to go back*, I said, *we have to get our bikes*. *No way*, they said, almost in unison. We talked about it, discussed the pros and cons. Going back risked death, or worse. We quickly constructed a narrative: a group of escaped prisoners were living in the ravine, killing and eating deer, rabbits, squirrels, occasionally children—essentially cannibals. We'd seen five, but that grew to ten, then twenty, a small army of savages that obeyed no laws of man or nature. If we went to the police, they would just escape again and hunt us down. That's how these things worked. We couldn't tell our parents. My friends decided to tell their parents their bikes had been stolen. They walked home.

I went back down into the ravine. When I got off the trail I took my jackknife out and opened it. I moved slowly, stealthily. A rabbit flushed. I heard crows above me, an aggressive symphony, a warning. There was little sunlight on the forest floor. It took twenty very slow, tense minutes to find my bike. I picked the leaves off so they wouldn't rustle and betray my position. My heart pounded so loudly I was afraid those men would hear it, track me through the trees, following that sound, a sound they would be familiar with, the sound of fear. When I got to the trail I got on my bike and pedalled as fast as I could and took the first path out of the ravine. When I emerged from the ravine, into the sun, I felt like a veteran of some kind of war.

Saturdays were no longer filled with possibility. Now they were a rebuke. Filling them was a Sisyphean task; as fast as I filled, they emptied. I walked to the Varsity Cinema on Bloor and stood in front of the marquee and chose a movie based on its title and start time, then went in. I settled into the comfortable seat in the dark and was grateful for the anticipation. The movie started strong and slowly slid off the rails. I went to another theatre and watched the last hour of a dark film about betrayal.

On the way home, I stopped at a shop that specialized in olive oil. The woman behind the counter had a pile of wiry black hair, a dark complexion. She was wearing heels and a black dress and looked like she was in an Italian movie from the 1950s. I wandered the store a bit and she came over, a purposeful stride, and delivered a soliloquy on cold-pressed extra virgin olive oil and how it was an ongoing scam and that most commercial olive oils were fraudulent, that the COLD PRESSED, EXTRA VIRGIN label was meaningless, that 80 percent of what was on supermarket shelves was either a lower grade of olive oil, or soybean oil, or technically rancid. Her story picked up steam, wound through the hills of Sicily, up into Tuscany, to Spain and Greece, and an anger built up in her as she outlined the subterfuge, the corruption in the olive oil world. "These bottles you see when you walk in the supermarket," she said, "they are lying about their virginity. All of them. They are whores."

Anything labelled *light* was even worse. *Cold pressed* didn't mean anything; most olive oils weren't pressed these days but made in a centrifuge. She said most commercial brands should be used as motor oil, and they were without the health benefits of real olive oil, the monosaturated fat, the antioxidants. She had dark eyes that were brittle with anger, but they immediately softened and she poured an ounce of olive oil into a small ceramic bowl. "Look at the colour," she said. It was a beautiful green. Though this wasn't, by itself, she warned me, an indication of quality. But the green oils tended to be sharper, more peppery, the gold oils more buttery. She dipped her finger into the olive oil and put it in my mouth and looked me in the eye.

"This is what a virgin tastes like," she said. She withdrew her finger and held my gaze.

I stared back, speechless.

She nodded perfunctorily and I left with a very small $52 bottle of olive oil that was an intriguing green. I thought of her as I walked back, created a backstory for her, inserted myself into her life—I retired and we moved to Tuscany, into a farmhouse that needed some work but had a large kitchen with a stone floor and white sheets on the bed upstairs where we made wild impossible love, then napped on those white sheets each afternoon. It was after six by the time I got home.

I took the duck out of the refrigerator, turned the oven to 350°F. I mixed salt and pepper together in a small bowl and cut the duck in half along the breastbone using a pair of shears, removed the wings and discarded them. I rubbed salt and pepper on the breasts and heated oil in a pan and seared them. I put orange juice, marmalade, and soy sauce into a small pan over medium heat until it reduced, then spooned a third of it over the duck along with the rendered fat and put it in the oven.

I turned on the news. There were more fires. The Jays dropped a squeaker, 12-3. Housing prices continued to climb. In international news, everyone was unhappy about something. I found a documentary about mushrooms and watched how fungi had changed the world. A sonorous voice told me that fungi were thallophytic plant-like organisms of low organization, bereft of chlorophyll, asexual, neither plant nor animal, really. He might be talking about humans.

After fifteen minutes I took the duck out and brushed it with more glaze, then put it back in the oven. I took out the iron stove-top grill and brushed oil on it, then took a handful of asparagus stalks and broke them at the joint and washed them, coated them in oil and balsamic vinegar and salt and pepper.

After another fifteen minutes I took the duck out and brushed on the rest of the glaze and put it back in the oven.

The fungi were connected in an internet-like underground maze that linked them to all of nature, an implied consciousness that monitored the deteriorating environment and did what it could to save the world. Fungi could feed us, kill us, heal us, get us high. They were mysterious and hopeful.

I turned the oven off, turned on the stove element, and turned on the broiler. I waited until the grill was hot, then put the asparagus on, then put the duck under the broiler for four minutes. I moved the asparagus around, then opened the oven and took a look at the duck. I wanted the skin to be crispy and a shade darker than golden brown. I turned off everything, let it sit for a moment, though not as a long as the recipe called for. I put one of the duck breasts on a plate, arranged the asparagus, poured another glass of the Bordeaux and sat down to find out what mushrooms could teach me about life.

TWENTY

SUNDAY MORNING, THE CITY woke up slowly, regretting its sins. The station was quiet. There had been another fire near St. James Town. I looked at the address. It was Bannich's house. I checked the preliminary report: an unexplained blaze, possibly an electrical fire from the ancient wiring, maybe arson, too soon to tell. The house was unsalvageable and would have to be razed. It was filled with old, dry paper, which accelerated the fire. I called the name on the bottom of the report. He didn't pick up and I left a message.

I drove to Bannich's house. There were still firefighters on the scene. The fire had scorched the neighbouring house but had been contained. Bannich's house was blackened and hollowed, the roof sagging, the windows gone. It was still smouldering. There was yellow tape around the scene. A dozen people stood on the sidewalk, taking pictures with their phones, selfies with the house as a backdrop. I showed my badge to the firefighter standing in the front yard and walked to the back. There were three firefighters there as well as Belisle, who was hunched over something.

"Anyone in there?" I asked one of the firefighters.

"One inside, one outside," she said.

"Outside?"

She pointed to Belisle, who looked up.

"What do you have?" I asked.

"Nothing good." He stood up. He'd been hunched over a set of bones. It looked to be an infant.

"Jesus. One of the graves?"

Belisle nodded. "The rest appear to be animals. Dogs, cats."

"And inside?"

"A woman, late seventies maybe."

I turned to the firefighter. "You think it was arson."

"There won't be a report for a week or so," she said.

"I know. I'm asking what do you think."

Belisle gave her a cold look. He wasn't big on opinions.

The firefighter cocked her head. "My guess, it was torched. Started in the basement, maybe an accelerant, maybe she just has twenty old cans of turpentine, rubbing alcohol, whatever, down there. But it hits the main floor and all that paper, that old wallpaper, the wood dried out." She shook her head. "No smoke alarms."

"This look like a professional job?" I asked.

"Hard to say. The less we find, the more professional it was."

The set of bones belonged to a baby, a few months old. I guessed whoever it was had been buried decades ago. The bones were heartbreakingly tiny and fragile, the small rounded skull. I felt a gothic chill and a deep sadness. Something terrible had happened. Her father had died here, she'd said, and that may have been her child. I didn't want to do any grim cop math.

"How long have those bones been in the ground?" I asked Belisle, though I already knew his answer.

"I'll have a better idea in a few days." He went back to his examination.

The air was acrid. All that P. Bannich was and all that she owned had been consumed, all those papers, records of something, all that wallpaper and furniture and memories and pain, all the chemicals and toxic shit that make up every modern life. Though her life hadn't been modern. It was a solitary life from another century, decades that accumulated like a dead weight. I wondered about that child, and the grief she'd held inside those walls for decades.

I walked to St. James Town and took another look at the mural that Maestro had made, the one with the crucified real estate agents and Jesus wearing an orange sports jacket. On one of the crosses there was a series of numbers I hadn't noticed before, small enough that I had to squint to make them out. I checked my notes, looking through my less-than-optimal filing system, and finally found the numbered companies that had bought up some of the homes. The numbers on the mural matched one of the companies.

SUNDAY WAS THE Day of the Dead when I was a kid, so much of the world closed. I still saw Sundays that way, despite the fact that everything was open now. There was a deadness in the air. The afternoon stretched out before me. I walked along Queen Street, stopped for a coffee at a hipster cafe and sat in the shade sipping my espresso and scrolling through emails and news stories.

Someone was prepared to burn a woman to death to get control of her property. The third guy to visit Bannich had been the arsonist. He walked around like he owned the place, she said, but he was casing it, assessing what he needed to torch it, which wouldn't have been much.

Whoever was doing this likely had cops on board—Toussaint and Pierce, maybe Max and Lloyd, as well as someone higher up. There would be someone in the city too. When they hired Fortier, they were hiring a seasoned thug, but they were also hiring a professional racist. I wondered if they had hired Maestro to create those murals. Maybe Angelique was Maestro. If she was, then why hire a Black woman? Unless they didn't know she was Black. People thought Maestro was male and maybe they also assumed she was white. She could have been hired through a cut-out and paid in bitcoin, as she said, an arrangement that would suit both parties. But now Maestro was turning on them, her murals becoming subversive. She would only do that if they didn't know her identity.

Which left three murders. I had no proof for any of my theories, nothing that would hold up in court. And at the centre of all this conjecture were Dashika and Angela, who might be part of it or be completely unrelated. I didn't even have a theory for them. All we had was Delroy, a ghost.

I should have been bouncing all of this off my partner, but Davis was too busy quietly running for mayor and she'd only tell me that I'd lost sight of what was important and was chasing the wind while the city was burning. And she might be right. She was putting a measurable distance between us, already the politician.

I sent an email to Mary Binetti from the graffiti squad to see if she had an address for Angelique, finished my coffee, and walked down Queen Street. There were a lot of people out on the street. No one here had cottages to escape to. Trinity Bellwoods Park was filled with couples pushing strollers, groups of people in circles on the grass, guys playing guitars, still leaning heavily on Neil Young.

I walked for more than an hour, then stopped at a restaurant with an outdoor patio. I ordered a beer, a Cuban burger made with pork, and coleslaw. I could taste smoked paprika and a spice I couldn't identify. It was pleasant on the patio. A parade of tattooed, pierced, wild-haired citizens walked by, snatches of a dozen musical genres. I finished my late lunch, had a Cuban coffee, tipped the heavily inked, vaguely hostile server, and left.

I checked my phone. Mary Binetti had sent me Angelique's address. Her place was a forty-minute walk. She might not be home, but I needed a walk after the burger and beer. She was farther west, north of Queen, a street that was a jumble of gracious Victorians, some smaller post-war homes, a mix of renovation and decline with old-growth trees forming a canopy over it all.

She was in one of the three-story Victorians. I walked up the steps onto the porch, which had two chairs and a small metal table on it. She was in number 2. I rang the buzzer and waited. I gave it a full minute and was about to ring again when she appeared at the door.

"Angelique," I said.

She looked over my shoulder to see if I was alone. "Shouldn't you be in church, Detective?"

"Maybe we both should be. I came to talk about art."

"On the Sabbath, a day of rest."

"Crime never rests."

"I thought you wanted to talk about art."

"I want to talk about the place where the two meet."

She considered this. "Caravaggio killed a man," she said. "He was also arrested for throwing stones at a policeman." She was wearing a white T-shirt, green linen shorts, sandals. "Should I be throwing stones at you, Detective?" I motioned to the chairs on the porch.

"Do you mind if I sit down?"

Her expression was noncommittal and I sat.

"Those pieces in St. James Town," I said. "The one with the crucified Jesus—real estate theme."

She laughed. "Shouldn't all real estate agents be crucified?"

"I have a theory."

"And you're dying to tell me."

"Someone bought up adjacent land around St. James Town using numbered companies. They hired a thug to assault and rob people in the area to help drive prices down and to make a case for urban renewal. Tear down the old buildings..."

"Move the brown people to the edges, safely out of sight," Angelique said. "They can take the bus back to clean the toilets, do the laundry, raise the children, suck the white man's dick."

"Something like that."

A woman walked by, pushing a stroller and looking at her phone.

"I think those same people hired a graffiti artist to put up those murals," I said.

Angelique smiled. "The broken window theory. You put up the tags, the art, let it stay up, you don't fix that broken window, then it's an invitation to other crime, it all escalates—assault, rape, murder. Isn't that how it works?"

"I think the person they hired is playing both sides of the street—taking their money but putting up subversive art."

"Isn't that the job of art? Being subversive. You can't blame the artist for that."

"I don't, but whoever hired Maestro might."

"I hear he keeps a pretty low profile, that he makes Banksy look like a social butterfly."

"I think it would be wise if he kept an even lower profile. Whoever is buying up those properties torched a place on Jarvis last night with the owner in it. She refused to sell and they burned her and her place to the ground."

Angelique still hadn't sat down.

"One of the keys to being a successful court jester is to make jokes that the king doesn't always understand," she said.

"I think even the slowest inbred royal can grasp that the numbers on one of the crosses matches a numbered company that is buying up the properties. If you bump into Maestro, you might tell him that now would be a good time to lie low, maybe stay with a friend for a while."

Angelique smiled. "Not all of us are lambs to the slaughter, Detective."

"I'd like to keep it that way."

I stood up. It was hot and I was tired from all the walking. I could have curled up on her porch and slept.

"When Caravaggio killed that man," she said, "he slashed him in the groin, severing his femoral artery, and he bled out. They were arguing over a prostitute."

"You should stay out of arguments for a while, Angelique."

"That's what art is, Detective. An argument with the world."

IT TOOK AN hour to walk back to my condo. It was too late for a nap now. And it was too hot to cook. I made an elaborate salad—baby spinach, shredded purple kale, arugula, avocado, diced apple, cherry tomatoes, raw broccoli, mint leaves, pomegranate seeds, and parsley. The recipe called for roasted sweet potato but I didn't want the oven on. The dressing had miso paste, ginger, rice vinegar, lime, agave syrup, hot peppers, soy sauce, toasted sesame oil, and sunflower oil. It took me half an hour to put everything together. I poured a large glass of the Sancerre and turned on the television.

Davis was on the screen. She said we were close to finding the killer, close to solving Dashika and Angela's murders. She said the force was preparing for Caribana, the annual celebration of Caribbean culture, which was coming up. She assured the viewers that it would be safe and peaceful and would celebrate a vibrant culture that had given the city so much. Thank you, Madam Mayor.

TWENTY-ONE

THERE WAS A TEXT from the accountant, Clement Ton: *Call me. Have something.* I called and he picked up right away.

"So it's a rat's nest," he said. "These companies—three dummy corps and four numbered companies—they all go back to the same place."

"China?"

"Lichtenstein. And it's an interesting journey."

I waited for the journey.

"There's a company called Phoenician Sky, incorporated in the Netherlands Antilles, that changed its name twice and is owned by two different companies—Botsford LLC, and Boyles Inc—that were incorporated in Panama, both controlled by a bank in Zurich. There are six mortgages held by a private foundation in Lichtenstein, which are linked to these companies. They add up to just north of $11 billion."

"So who holds those mortgages?"

"The private foundation has a moat around it. It could be anything—drug money, arms dealers, state-owned Chinese businesses, legitimate Swiss investors, a hedge fund."

"So this is all for tax purposes, or to disguise what's going on?"

"Could be a bit of both, but it's quite a bit of trouble and expense to disguise where this money is coming from."

"If you had to guess?"

"Accountants don't guess. That's why we have numbers."

"You'll send me everything you have?"

"You'll get it today, along with my invoice. There's something else."

"What's that."

"The property transfer records at the city. The sales of certain properties weren't registered. I noticed some anomalies and did some digging."

"Where are the properties?"

"Your area, Sherbourne, Jarvis. It looks like parts of the area have been sold, but the transfers are only registered for earlier ones."

"Someone is trying to keep this a secret."

"Someone who has some pull at city hall."

"All that offshore activity—where does it end up?"

"I don't know where it ends up, but it seems to run through Delaney Hutch."

JIMMY LLOYD CALLED a division meeting. He was standing at the front of the room. He felt this was his birthright, was soaking in the moment. Max was lurking behind him like an attack dog.

"We have an image problem," Lloyd said. "I know this because I read it in the papers. Let me be clear." He paused for effect. "I don't give a shit about image. It isn't a problem for me. What *is* a problem for me is *crime*. What I care about is solving them. What I care about is dead girls and grieving mothers. We solve this crime, and our image problem goes away. And let me tell you something. Outside of a handful of journalists and some bleeding hearts, no one really cares how we solve this murder. They just want us to catch the bad guy. If someone's feelings get hurt in the process of bringing a killer to justice, then we can deal with that afterward. We'll get them some therapy, an emotional support dog, a frozen daiquiri, whatever."

It was easy to read the crowd. Lloyd was roughly equal parts good news/bad news in the division. Half the cops thought he would take us back to getting results any way you had to and fuck the consequences and fuck the community, and that half felt this was the wrong way to police the city. The other half felt they had found their spiritual home.

Lloyd went on about Delroy Staples, built him up into public enemy number one, armed, dangerous. We needed him that week. We needed him before Caribana. We had four days. All hands on deck. For the next four days, every citizen within division boundaries could run red lights, speed through school zones, shoplift, threaten their husbands with knives, punch their annoying neighbours in the face and not have to worry about getting arrested. He wanted a full-court press: bring Staples in dead or alive.

Davis was at the back of the room, scrolling through her phone.

"Where have you been?" I asked.

She looked up. "Chasing bad people, going on TV and telling the world we are chasing bad people." She went back to her phone.

"You don't want to know what I've been up to?"

She kept texting. "I'm afraid of the answer. I'm afraid of your borderline conspiracy theories, I'm afraid you don't have a single piece of hard evidence that gets us any closer to closing this case."

I was afraid of the same things.

"Look," she said, looking up, "I'm out there every day, taking questions, *exposed*..."

"What if Staples isn't our guy."

"Who *is* our guy? You have another name."

"I'm just saying keep an open mind."

"I'm trying to do that. You don't always make it easy."

"The longer Staples is out there, the more pressure builds up, the greater the need for him to be guilty."

"I get that, but right now, he's the only game in town."

"I think the game is larger, much larger..."

"The game is murder, Abel."

"Maybc. What if murder is just a by-product. Maybe the game is real estate. Look, we're after the same thing, just coming at it from different angles."

Davis nodded, put her phone away. "Abel, I can back you on this, but you need something concrete, something *real*."

Very little of this seemed real. It seemed like one of those nightmares that doesn't have a plot, random images piling up, malevolent, mocking.

I looked over to see Mad Max staring at me. I walked to my desk, called Devin Nunes at Delaney Hutch and said I'd like to talk to him. He didn't want to talk to me. He knew I couldn't compel him. I called Tanya Willing and asked her to meet me for a drink at six.

WILLING WAS SITTING at the same table at Ursuline. She was wearing black linen pants, a long white shirt. It was too hot for much jewellery. She stood up, her hand extended.

"Detective."

"Tanya. How are you?"

She shrugged. "Waiting for the city to explode."

"You're not alone."

"Where are you with Dash and Angela?"

"I can't talk about the case, but I have something else for you."

"*Is* there anything else at the moment? I thought it was a full-court press to find the killer."

Davis must have given her Lloyd's speech. She might have been texting Tanya while we were chatting.

The server came by and Tanya ordered a white wine and I ordered a beer.

I told Tanya about Bannich and her house burning down and gave her the information on the business card that Bannich had given me. I told her about the graves, one of them holding the bones of an infant.

"You think the murders are connected to this somehow?" she asked.

"I don't know. Worth looking at. Even if it isn't connected, there's a story there."

"What's your take on Lloyd as division head?" she asked.

Tanya would already have Davis's assessment—that Lloyd was a well-connected thug, that he was a step backward, that he was exactly what the division didn't need, especially at this time.

"Lloyd is a thug with limited political skills, but he has half the division behind him."

"If he brings in Delroy Staples?"

"Staples is the holy grail. Lloyd will try and use it, maybe try for police chief, but he's too old-school, and not aware enough to realize it. Father and uncle both cops, Lloyd was raised in captivity and doesn't really have a grasp of the outside world."

We ordered two different appetizers—charred spicy broccoli and ceviche—and had a second drink. Tanya had long, graceful limbs, a pianist's hands, and a longshoreman's laugh: rich, full-throated. When she was listening, one hand massaged her throat gently, a tic almost. She was mildly flirtatious, but I guessed it was professional, the version she used on interview subjects, anyone she wanted to cultivate. It was subtle and welcome. We talked about city hall and police culture and real estate, then she said she had to go. She had a dog, she said, had to get back before it ate a pillow. We stood up, shook hands, and I sat down and watched her leave.

I had gotten into the habit of imagining my life with different women. This wasn't the same as falling in love, or maybe it was the fifty-two-year-old version. I had imagined my life with Helen (much better dressed, using her employee discount, living in my condo, trying out all the restaurants in the area with her), with the Italian woman in the olive oil shop (in that Tuscan farmhouse; the recent version had us making love on the wooden table in the kitchen in the middle of putting together *pappardelle al funghi*), with the French woman with the glorious accent where I bought croissants (a Provençal farmhouse, later amended to a house on the Brittany coast, where the weather was moody and cooler). These were disturbingly detailed, and now Tanya Willing was on the list, an untenable, unwise addition. I remembered Jefferson, the cop suicide, and what may have been his imagined romance with the East Asian woman, and wondered if this was a cop thing, that we drift so far from a normal life we're only capable of imagining a real one.

I took a look at the information that Clement Ton had sent. There was something in those company names that rang a bell.

TWENTY-TWO

ON FRIDAY EVENING, THE Caribana festivities started: fifty thousand people congregated in the plaza outside city hall. Bands on a stage, local entertainers whipping up the audience. There were food trucks and grills selling jerk chicken, rice and peas, chuletas, plaintain, tchaka, callaloo, chimichurri burgers. A marijuana haze over all of it. Police lingered on the fringes, waiting for someone to go off, but Friday night came and went without much in the way of incident—a few fights, a few drunks, the usual. On Saturday, there were private parties in clubs sponsored by rap artists, block parties, food trucks, outdoor concerts. Hundreds of thousands filled the streets. They were, for the most part, peaceful events. The crowds grew. Sunday was the parade.

Half the uniforms in the city were either on the parade route or standing nearby. The mounted guys on their horses, cops on bikes, foot patrol, cruisers parked on side streets. The mayor publicly appealed to the federal government to send in the army to stand by along the parade route, a request the feds sensibly turned down. This was always a delicate balance—if you had too many cops, it would look like a police state and there would be pushback. If there weren't enough and there was a problem, we'd get slammed.

I was watching the parade on television. Colourful, swaying, loud, a half million people feeling it. The sun was shining. I started the barbecue on the balcony and took a pork tenderloin out of the fridge to bring it to room temperature. I put soy sauce, chopped green onions, diced habanero peppers, garlic, dried thyme, and allspice into the food processor. I zested two limes and squeezed the juice in, then pulsed it so it was mixed but still had some personality. I brushed some onto the pork and put it on the barbecue. I opened the fridge, took out purple cabbage, a jalapeno, celery, carrots, fresh ginger, and another lime. I chopped the ingredients and made a vinaigrette with sesame oil, peanut butter, garlic, and ginger and mixed it all together and put it back into the fridge.

Other than faith, food is the most portable cultural artifact. It's what immigrants bring with them to the new country. It provides comfort, something familiar in an unfamiliar landscape. Food is the definition of self—we are what we eat. Our most temporary art, every masterpiece consumed.

The challenges of cooking for one are essentially twofold. One, you have to make a small amount, otherwise you're eating it all week, and two, there is no audience, either in the kitchen or at the table, no one to appreciate what you've done, no one to share with or cook for, no communion. An empty church. The six hundred cooking shows on cable TV arose from the fact that cooking is inherently communal. The open kitchen and the studio cameras let the chefs perform—ambitious, angry, sensual, chopping with flair, moving like ballerinas, tossing ingredients into skillets with a flourish, barking commands to flustered sous chefs. There are people who taste the result, who sit around the table and take in a forkful and stare upward and say it's heaven. Afterward, the chefs sit in their dark, empty restaurants or on the deserted set and sip a Calvados and light a cigarette and convince themselves they are the centre of the world, they create the fuel that keeps us marching toward extinction.

On the television, the camera was now in the parade, a handheld steadicam that moved with the dancers, doing a slow pirouette, like being inside a kaleidoscope—deep reds, hot pink, peacock blues and greens. There was a thumping bassline, gleaming bodies moving, sashaying. Colourful feathers, costumes someone had spent weeks working on. Bodies that had been honed, asses moving in rapid rhythms. It was both spectacle and catharsis.

I turned the pork over, brushed more jerk sauce onto it and closed the lid. I stood on the balcony and stared southwest, to where the parade was. I could see a glimpse of the lines of people, hear the music, faint, disjointed by distance. The sun was still high. Below me, the streets were almost empty. I turned the pork over again, prodded it with a knife. It was close. More glaze, another poke with the knife, then I took it off the grill, wrapped it in foil and let it sit on the cutting board for ten minutes. I opened a beer, poured it into a glass. I cut off six circles of the pork, put some of the remaining jerk sauce over it, spooned a large helping of the coleslaw and sat down on the balcony. The parade was a dark line in the distance. It was like watching the Kennedy caravan slowly snake through Dallas, waiting for history to happen.

IN THE END, nothing happened other than the usual—a few fights, public drunkenness, minor property damage. The parade was an unqualified success. There were two days of post-celebration celebration, the mayor reading from a prepared statement with a sense of discovery, proud of the city's ability to organize something on that scale, a chance to prove to the world who we were, the tens of millions of tourist dollars, the multicultural flowering and goodwill. If he were to organize a parade it would be a million middle-aged white men in hockey jerseys singing classic rock and weeping for a lost world.

I DROVE TO Rosedale to visit Titus Bishop again. He had represented St. James Town, had intimate knowledge about how it worked and how it didn't work. He was also someone who was very well connected, both to those higher up and those lower down. A lot flowed through Titus back in his days as a political bagman. Maybe a few things still flowed through him. The August sun was punishing. The streets of Rosedale were deserted except for a few professional dog walkers. Everyone was at their cottages, drinking gin on their docks. I knocked on his door. There were people working in his yard, a man with shears snapping at blades of grass. Titus opened the door. He was wearing shorts and a polo shirt. On his small plump body, it gave him the look of a decayed schoolboy. He offered a weak smile.

"Detective."

"Hello Titus. I wonder if we could chat a bit."

His look became brittle, a subtle shift in his eyes.

"What is it you would like to chat about, Detective?"

"St. James Town. You represented it for eight years. I could use the benefit of your expertise."

He nodded, turned away, and I followed him. We went to his study again, looked out the window to a man pruning a cedar hedge, squaring the edges, an enviable geometry.

"As you know, Detective, I haven't represented St. James Town or anywhere else for quite some time. It has changed. As everything must."

"You were part of the group that resisted its expansion south, as I recall."

"Fighting the good fight." He smiled, a politician's smile; there was nothing behind it.

"What is the good fight now?"

Another smile. "I don't know where the good fights are these days, Detective. That's one of the reasons I retired."

"And what now? Tear it all down?"

"St. James Town is a relic. Would it be good to fight to keep those crumbling towers, that exhausted idea, an idea of density that is now out of favour?"

"I think that kind of density is only out of favour for poor people. You can go up fifty stories as long as the penthouse sells for $10 million."

"Gentrification is inevitable. The best land will go for the highest price. It can take generations for that to play out, but it always does. It is a geological force."

"The glaciers slowly retreat and two million years later you have a Walmart."

"Something like that."

In the backyard, the man finished sculpting the hedge, a perfect wall of green. He was on to the flowering Japanese maple.

Sitting in his study, it was hard not to conjure the Family Compact. William Jarvis was a member of the ruling class whose grasp of democracy provided a model for the future of this city, a loose cabal bound by marriage, money, lakefront property, incompetence, and private schools. Jarvis was one of the few Toronto residents to own slaves.

We chatted a bit longer, then Titus said he was expecting a call. He stood up. I stood up, and he followed me to the door. He was able to connect people who needed to be connected but he didn't want any trace of that connection to see daylight. A valuable skill in both politics and crime. The sun was blinding. I heard the door close softly behind me.

TWENTY-THREE

TANYA WILLING'S PIECE ON St. James Town was in Saturday's paper. It outlined the complex ownership of St. James Town and the surrounding area. The sclerotic Ludlow Luckworth's Fairlane Properties had owned most of St. James Town, and Luckworth had been sued by his ex-wife, his son, and his daughter, and was in turn suing them. The kids were suing one another, and one of them was suing the mother. The son—Adrian—had recently gained control of the properties, successfully arguing that his ninety-four-year-old father had mismanaged the business, was suffering from dementia, and was unfit, in his description, to "manage a hot dog stand." He had used the ample list of management failings as proof. Adrian had wrested control from his father only a few weeks ago. Four days later, Fairlane Properties was acquired by Botsford LLC. I called Tanya and asked her about Luckworth. She probably knew more than appeared in the article, information that wouldn't run because of the threat of legal action.

"Adrian's a piece of work. They all are. The sister, Tessy, attacked her brother outside the courthouse a year ago. The old man probably does have dementia but wanted to hang on to the property just so his family wouldn't get it. He's a miserable old prick who thinks land is the only thing in this world worth owning. He was prepared to put up with all the headaches that eighteen thousand tenants bring. The kind of guy who didn't spend money on anything, lived in a modest house in Etobicoke, drove an old Toyota, dressed like a homeless guy. He survived cancer, had a heart attack last year. Too mean to die."

"What's your take on the son?"

"Looks like an accountant but tougher than he looks. Odd guy. Three ex-wives. Hard to say what turns his crank. I think he and the sister just wanted their father to sell the properties so they could get some money out of it."

We chatted a bit more and Tanya gave me Adrian Luckworth's address.

"He probably won't talk to you."

I drove out to Mississauga. Luckworth's street contained large suburban homes, most of them built in the 1960s. People leaving the city core looking for sunshine and space. Vinyl siding, big driveways, pristine lawns, two-car garages with basketball nets bolted above the doors. His house was a monster home, probably built in the last decade. He must have torn down two existing homes. It was a pastiche of Italianate, French chateau, and half-timbered Tudor, an architectural dog's breakfast that may have been built just to spite his father. There was a three-car garage. A pink Cadillac was in the driveway, the one with the giant fins that had twin taillights on them, the last of the 1950s' excesses before the sleek 60s arrived.

I parked in the driveway, rang the bell, heard a cute ten-note chime, a song I couldn't place. Through the yellow glass I could see a figure walking toward the door. He opened it slowly, examined me.

"That song," I said.

Luckworth stared blankly at me. He was mid-sixties, medium height, a skinny guy with a paunch and a weak chin, a horseshoe of black hair fringing his head. Pale, jowly, bright blue eyes.

"Your doorbell chime. That song…"

"'Afternoon Delight,'" he said.

I nodded and showed him my badge. "Mr Luckworth? Adrian Luckworth?"

"What's this about?"

"Real estate," I said. "I'm Detective Abel."

He stood there for a moment, then invited me in. The living room was cavernous, with two large leather couches facing one another across a massive black glass coffee table. It didn't look like it saw much use. He led me through a kitchen that looked like no one had ever cooked a meal in it and through to his back deck, shaded by a retractable awning. There was a large kidney-shaped pool, nicely tended grass, a seven-foot fence. His place looked like a show home, like no one actually lived in it. We sat down in the outdoor chairs, some kind of engineered wood that resembled teak.

"You sold Fairlane Properties," I said.

"If that's a question, the answer is it's a private company and any financial information is also private."

"You routinely made the list of worst landlords," I said.

"My father routinely made the list. He was the largest property owner in the city. He had the most complaints. Do the math."

"Those properties also had the most crime—the only part of the city that showed an increase in violent crime. And how many fires? Four in two months?"

"What are you suggesting, Detective?"

"You were ground zero for something."

"Chaos maybe."

"And your father was at the centre of St. James Town."

"St. James Town doesn't have a centre, Detective. My father is a miserly, unhappy man who tried to make those around him as unhappy as he is. Maybe his greatest success. I'd been trying to get him to sell those properties for a decade. Do you have any idea the damage that eighteen thousand renters cause? People raising live chickens in their living rooms, people who have twelve family members in a one-bedroom unit. The plumbing issues—tampons, drugs, and pets all flushed down toilets. Noise complaints, bedbug complaints. The buildings are sixty years old and were built to last fifty if they were well maintained, which they weren't. People are basically shit. You may have encountered that in your line of work."

"You got a good price."

"I wanted to get rid of it, they wanted to buy it. That's the definition of good. Real estate isn't houses or apartments, it's land. Houses are like cars, they start depreciating the minute after they're built. It's the land that appreciates." Luckworth smiled. "Anyway, it's someone else's headache now." He abruptly announced he had another engagement and stood up. I seemed to have that effect on people. I followed him to the front door.

The sun was high. Across the street a kid was shooting hoops, deking imaginary NBA stars, then the reverberating sound of the ball hitting the rim. There was no one else on the street. I got in my car and drove slowly through the quiet neighbourhood. Botsford and the other companies had what they needed now. They could start the eviction process, then tear down the towers. They would still need to get control of the few government buildings, and that would require some help from inside city hall. But they had help at city hall.

I drove to the station, then sat at my desk and scrolled through emails. The barometric pressure in the station had changed since Lloyd took over, that sudden drop before a storm. If Titus was involved, he would have gotten back to Lloyd or whoever his contact in city hall was and told them about my visits. Tanya Willing's piece about St. James Town had outlined the real estate deal. I had rattled Max's cage, had nudged Pierce, Toussaint, and Lloyd, and was without any political allies inside or outside the force. I was without even the psychological comfort of a partner; Davis would back me if I had something concrete, but I didn't have anything concrete. She couldn't align herself with a pile of unproven theories at a time when the pressure to find the girls' killer was mounting. There was no one more expendable. If I had gone to June Godfrey, my occasional therapist, and laid out this scenario, she would have suggested that subconsciously what I wanted was to blow things up and she would likely have been right.

Even when the station was located in the heart of Regent Park, when it was a cramped, dingy, two-story outpost instead of an architecturally relevant high-profile reno of a heritage building, it had had the quality of sanctuary. Just outside its doors were drug deals, assaults, robberies, racial conflict, homicide, domestic hell. A block away were sex workers who did tricks for a twenty piece of crack, wraiths who stood hollow-eyed on the street in dirty jeans and referred to crack as food. Inside the doors, you were in another world, part of the brotherhood; you were safe. But the station was no longer safe for me.

I went through my emails, made a few notes, ran P. Bannich's name through the system, checked to see if there was anything else on Luckworth or Phoenician Sky, then stood up and looked around. Max was staring at me, that unreadable reptile face. I left, got in my car, drove home. If they came at me, it would be on the job. It might come from a hired thug, whoever had taken Ambrose Fortier's place, someone they found through Bradley Weeks maybe.

I parked my car in the underground lot, went up to my unit, changed clothes, and walked to the liquor store. I had the names of six wines that were adjudged good value by someone who was likely bribed by the winemakers—sent a half-dozen cases or flown to France for a junket. I read through the list of descriptives: *barnyard notes*, *bold*, *funky*, *bright*, *smoke*, *subtle tannins*, *cured tea*, *licorice*, *herbal tones*, *a ferrous tang*, *leather funk*, *earthy*, *slightly feral with a dark mineral side*. A list that could be describing anything from wine to escaped convicts. The store had two of the wines, both under $20, and I bought two of each, then lingered over the exquisite Margauxs, finally choosing a $63 bottle.

Back in my unit I poured a large glass of one of the cheap Bordeauxs and tried unsuccessfully to taste leather or licorice or iron or cowshit or any of the other alleged secrets it held, then scaled and gutted a red mullet, cut red and yellow peppers into strips, and heated olive oil in my heavy expensive pan. I added onions and coriander seeds and let them brown for a few minutes before adding the peppers, garlic, bay leaves, curry powder, and cherry tomatoes. I added brown sugar, vinegar, salt, and pepper and cooked for five minutes. I covered the fish in a beaten egg and rolled it in flour and fried it in a separate pan, then added it to the vegetables and let it simmer for twelve minutes. I was supposed to put it in the oven but decided to stay strictly stove-top. I poured more wine, then arranged the mullet and vegetables in a shallow bowl and sat down in front of the television.

The news was grim. A glacier the size of Manhattan had calved off Greenland and was wandering the seas. Anomalous weather conditions were wreaking havoc in the American Midwest. Aquifers were drying up. A motorist had beaten a cyclist to death with a 9-iron, a woman in Kansas had murdered her bowling team with an assault rifle. I wondered if Davis would appear on my screen in her not-so-subtle run at the mayor's office. She might be trying to avoid the cameras right now; it had been eight weeks and we hadn't caught the killer and her association with the case might be viewed as a link to failure. Maybe she had a PR firm advising her on matters like this. After twenty minutes of looming disaster, Bobby Dale came on, standing in front of city hall, a handful of microphones in his face. "The elites have run this city for a hundred years," he said. He was sweating heavily, his face in the sun. "But what they don't understand is that it's the *people* who run this city—the guys that pick up the garbage, who clear the snow, the cops who keep us safe, the hockey dads and the mothers that look after the kids—that's who really runs this city. And let me tell you something, we ain't going away." He said we had to start doing things differently and the people deserved better and with one more term he could drown the Egyptians in the Red Sea and deliver us all to Canaan.

TWENTY-FOUR

THIS IS HOW IT happened. It was just after 9 p.m., a dank August evening, cloud cover, still hot but starting to cool. I got a call. Unknown number. I picked up. It was Toussaint, said he and Pierce were down at Cherry Beach. They had Delroy Staples, had a situation. He hung up before I had a chance to reply.

Maybe they had Staples. Either way, it might be an invitation to get ambushed. I was in my car, downtown. Cherry Beach was fifteen minutes away. I turned off my phone to prevent tracking; I didn't know what I'd find down there, didn't know if I wanted to be there. I drove east. Traffic was light. I could go straight down Cherry Street. That would be the fastest and most direct route, hopefully the one they assumed I'd take. Instead, I went east to Leslie, turned south, then west on Unwin, circling around. To my right was the industrial residue of an abandoned generating plant, a hulking brick building with a smokestack and cavernous spaces prized by the film business, a place to stage shoot-outs where all the bad guys miss at close range. To the left was heavy forest. On the other side of it was Lake Ontario. I drove slowly along Unwin, then stopped by a gravel road and backed down it into the trees about twenty metres. I turned off the engine, put on the gloves I kept in the glove compartment, and got out, closing the door quietly.

The clouds obscured the moon. The air was thick. I walked through the forest, heading to the lake as quickly and silently as possible, the way I used to walk through the ravine as a kid. I came out at the eastern edge of Cherry Beach. The wind was up, the waves folding heavily onto the beach, making enough noise to disguise my approach. The sky was dark but paled over the lake. I moved among the trees that were twenty metres from the water. For years cops used to bring people down here, suspects, sex workers, drug dealers. Nothing good happened here. It hadn't been in use for some time as far as I knew. But there are Cherry Beaches everywhere. I still had the image of that kid in Wisconsin in my head, all these years later. I wasn't sure of the precise site, but it wouldn't be far from the parking lot; cops didn't want to walk far with a perp.

I saw an outline, a half silhouette, the other half obscured by a tree. He wasn't tall. I was thirty metres away. It would be Pierce. Toussaint was too big to hide. Past Pierce there were two figures, another thirty metres farther down. Toussaint and Max.

I walked slowly toward Pierce. He was looking at Max and Toussaint. The soil was sandy, masking my footsteps. I had my gun out. A metre away, I raised my gun high and brought it down on Pierce's head with real force. It made a sick cracking sound. He collapsed onto the sand. I looked toward Max and Toussaint, but they didn't move. There was a lot of blood. I reached into Pierce's pocket and took out his service revolver, emptied the bullets and scattered them, then put the gun back into his holster. He had another gun in his jacket pocket. It wasn't regulation. It would be unregistered, something he took off the street. His breathing was shallow, laboured. I put two fingers on his neck and felt his pulse, then packed sandy soil around his head wound to staunch the bleeding. I took off his tie and wrapped it around his head to hold the dirt in place. I put my gun back in its holster and took Pierce's street gun and checked that it was loaded and the safety was off and moved toward Max and Toussaint. My heart was thumping hard and I worked to control my breathing. I was able to work behind the trees, moving softly. They were twenty metres away.

There was a third figure, slumped on the sand. I couldn't tell if it was Delroy Staples or not. Toussaint was smoking a cigarette, blowing the smoke upward. Max had a slight shimmy, like a fighter in his corner before the bell goes, staying loose. I got to the edge of the trees and took another step.

"Step away, hands on your head," I said. I had Pierce's gun aimed at Max. I figured he would be the most likely to make a move.

Max laughed, a chilling sound. I still couldn't tell who was on the ground, couldn't take my eyes off Toussaint and Max. Whoever it was, they were in an odd fetal position.

"Abel," Toussaint said. He looked behind me. He was slowly doing the math. I had come from the east, Pierce was waiting there in case anything went wrong. Pierce wouldn't be riding to the rescue.

"That's Staples," I said.

"There's your murderer," Toussaint said. "Case closed. We're all heroes."

I took one very fast glance at Staples. His hands were behind his back, probably tied. He was either unconscious or dead.

Max was subtly shifting his weight back and forth, his eyes on mine.

"We're all brothers, Abel, you can put your gun away," Toussaint said.

"You killed Infinity," I said to Max.

He didn't blink.

"You raped that kid, almost beat her to death."

Nothing from Max. Toussaint's posture changed slightly. He dropped his cigarette in the sand. If that was Staples lying there, and he was still alive, he would need a hospital right now.

"Hands behind your head, on your knees." Max still doing his subtle sway. I looked at Toussaint, who was looking at Max.

"Think about this, Abel," Toussaint said. "Think about this scene. Right now, right here, think about what this means. We all want to be in the same story, the one that has a happy ending. Murderer captured by brave cops, dies resisting arrest. City can sleep at night. Thank you, men in blue."

"He doesn't look like he's resisting," I said.

"Had a gun," Toussaint said.

I took a step closer to the body. I wanted to check for a pulse. Max was maybe three metres away. Toussaint was three metres to my left, a perfect equilateral triangle. Toussaint was too slow to charge and wasn't crazy enough. He'd try for his gun. Max would charge.

"I should call this in," Toussaint said thickly. "Ambulance. My phone." The words came out wrong, stiff. He reached into his jacket. I fired a shot that hit him in the chest. He slumped down at the same time Max charged. I got a shot off. Max was on me. I fired another shot. Max had both hands on my neck. His face was a rictus of pain and hate, red and twisted. A hellish sound came out. I dropped the gun, grappled with his hands. His face was inches away, an insane mask, teeth bared like an animal, froth at his mouth. His face didn't change expression but his grip loosened and I peeled his hands away. I rolled him off me, onto his back, with difficulty. Both shots had hit, the second one in the leg.

I stood up, went over to Toussaint, who was on his back. I opened his jacket. A gun was there. His phone wasn't. He wasn't breathing. I checked for a pulse. Toussaint was gone. I checked his pants pocket, found the burner phone he'd used to call me, checked to make sure it was turned off, disabled it, then threw it as far into the lake as I could. I approached the figure on the ground. It looked to be Delroy Staples, but it was hard to tell. He'd been severely beaten. I checked his pulse. Nothing. His hands were tied with a zip tie behind his back. Max was still breathing, shallow, laboured breaths. Blood bubbled on his lips. I stared at his face. All that madness dwindling to a close. When he stopped breathing, his eyes didn't register the change. His hands had been around my neck. I didn't think the skin was broken, but there could be DNA on his hands. I scrubbed his fingers with sand, rubbing hard. I hoped there wasn't anything under his fingernails. The sand wouldn't yield much in the way of footprints. If I left anything there, Belisle would find it.

I retreated along the sand, checked on Pierce—still breathing—then moved back into the trees. I moved quickly through the forest and ran to where I'd left my car. I opened the trunk, took out the gym bag that was there. I'd joined one of those discount gyms that are open 24/7 a year ago but hadn't been in months. I kept the bag in my car though, in case I suddenly got ambitious. I took off everything and put on the sweats, hoodie and running shoes. I crammed my suit, shirt, underwear, socks, shoes and Pierce's gun into the gym bag and put it in the car.

I took a slow, circuitous route east, to an all-night gas station run by Russians. They didn't have any security cameras. I went in, bought a lighter and lighter fluid. Then I drove north, to my childhood ravine.

I parked on a residential street, grabbed the gym bag, then popped the trunk, took out the folding army shovel I kept for digging out of snowbanks, and walked into the woods. the same path we'd used when I was a kid.

I walked down into the ravine, then turned off the path, through the trees. I walked for fifteen minutes then stopped, looked around. The forest was still. I stood and listened, made sure there weren't kids down here, drinking beer. It was 10:30, too late for dog walkers. There was a small creek three metres away and the soil was soft. I dug a hole with the army shovel. The earth had a decayed, vegetal smell. I took the gun out of the gym bag, placed the bag in the hole, sprayed lighter fluid on it, lit it, stood up, looked around.

I let it burn until the bag and clothes were half consumed, charred, then filled the hole with earth, tamped it down, and moved leaves and twigs over it. The woods were quiet. What would anyone make of a man burning and burying clothes in the middle of the night? I walked through the trees, climbing over deadfall strewn like children's toys, walking as quietly as possible. I stepped over a fallen poplar and stopped short. On the ground was the carcass of a deer. I walked up to it. A doe, dead for a week or more. Animals or birds or both had been at it, but not before a human had been. There were pieces hacked out, maybe with a hunting knife. Someone was in the forest.

I turned to the right, walked another fifty metres, then dug a second hole for the gun. I had gloves on but wiped it anyway, emptied the chamber and threw the bullets as far as I could. I placed the gun in the hole, covered it up, tamped it down and rearranged the leaves. I wiped the shovel down thoroughly and threw it into the creek.

As a kid, after we'd seen those men at their camp, my two friends had gotten new bikes but they didn't want to return to the ravine. I used to come on my own sometimes. There was a place I could hide my bike, under a large fallen tree, its branches forming a canopy that swallowed it. Then I'd continue through the woods on foot, walking with my jackknife in my hand, sometimes with the blade open, which heightened the adventure. I noted the different kinds of trees, the sounds of birds. I used to watch nature shows on TV, the ceaseless cycle of life, death, and decay, the scavengers, insects, and birds, a hidden world that never stopped. But all we saw was the stillness. And beyond that unseen natural world, there was an imagined world containing dark forces, older than the city, a magical, dangerous place.

One morning I'd gone back to where we'd seen those men. I might have been thirteen. It was after my father died, autumn, crisp weather, some of the leaves a pale yellow, a few fiery red maples. It has always been my favourite season, one that I associate with renewal, oddly. Some leaves had fallen and the forest floor had a soft covering. I came at the camp from the south, sneaking up slowly, looking for a sign of them. They might have a sentry. When I was ten metres away, I could see that most of the camp was gone. There was one remaining tarp, stained blue nylon strung across a fallen tree. There was a large firepit, blackened stones around it. I walked up to the tarp, my knife out, and crouched down. There was no one in there. Beside the fire there were two condoms and two empty mickeys of rum. Cigarette butts were strewn around. A few cans with their labels burned off. The men had moved on. This was like one of those ancient civilizations that are found in the jungle, all its people gone, a few monuments left that reveal how they prayed.

I drove to my gym, parked on a side street, walked in with my hood up, tapped my card, grabbed a towel and walked past the sleepy kid at the desk. There were a handful of people working out. I went to the locker room, undressed and went into the empty sauna. I sat down and waited for the heat to build. Gunshot residue can be detected on clothes for weeks but it's usually undetectable on the skin within eight hours. I waited until I couldn't stand any more then had a cold shower followed by a very long, very hot shower.

I got dressed and left and walked for three hours, winding through quiet neighbourhoods, thinking about what had happened, replaying the wrenching violence. Lives ended, my own changed forever. I went down a mental checklist of anything that could put me there.

It was close to 5 a.m. now, the sky starting to pale in the east. I drove back to the condo, parked on the street, took my sunglasses out of the glove compartment. I walked into the lobby, hood up, head down, just another suspect.

TWENTY-FIVE

THE ONLY OTHER SHOOTING I'd been involved in happened sixteen years ago. I had a partner named Samuels. We got a call that a bank robbery was in progress, a block away. Two men, both armed with shotguns. We put on the siren and lights, skidded to a stop in front of the bank. Two men came out wearing Disney masks, Goofy and Minnie Mouse. It was mid-afternoon. There were people on the street. I lost track of Samuels. I ran behind a parked car and yelled for them to drop their guns. Minnie stopped, looked around. You could see he was panicking, didn't know what to do. But Goofy brought his shotgun up to chest level. I fired two shots, both centre mass. He went down on the sidewalk. Minnie dropped his gun and Samuels moved on him, cuffed him. I moved up on Goofy. He was bleeding heavily from his chest. I nudged the shotgun away with my foot, holstered my weapon, knelt down, took off the mask. There were people tentatively walking toward us now. The uniforms were just arriving, hadn't set up a perimeter yet. He was still alive but couldn't talk. His eyes were filled with whatever they fill with when you're dying and you didn't plan on it. There was fear and something else, something unknowable. Then a spark of recognition. It was Jimmy Walsh, one of the kids I'd gone into the ravine with when I was a kid. We'd lost touch after my father's death and my mother and I moved to the apartment. I hadn't seen him in more than twenty years. I held his gaze for several seconds. I told him to breathe, to keep breathing, stupid advice. His eyes dimmed, and he bled out on the sidewalk.

I wondered if the other guy was Davey Fogel, my other childhood friend. He was in the back of a squad car. I took a look through the glass, but it wasn't him. I waited until the ambulance came and took Jimmy, watched them load him up, stared at the blood on the sidewalk. I remembered trading hockey cards with him in his basement, a saggy plaid sofa and an oval rug and boxes of things they didn't need and an old TV with a grey jumpy picture. I remembered sitting at his dining room table having dinner after my father died. His mother had invited me, felt it was the right thing to do. Hardly anyone spoke at the dinner table. You could hear the cutlery scraping on the plates as we sawed through pork chops. His father, mother, sister, and Jimmy, all of them silent, staring down at their food. Family life.

I went to Jimmy's funeral, a tense, conflicted event. I lingered at the back, away from family. A man delivered a eulogy, a friend of Jimmy's, said he was a good man, had found himself in a corner. He had a wife, a ten-year-old son. They were sitting with his mother in the front pew. I recognized her from that dinner, greyer, smaller looking. His death never left me, a complicated mourning for his lost life, our lost youth, and now another fatherless boy.

I wondered what happened to Davey Fogel. My childhood friends had slipped away after my father's death. I remembered that day in the ravine. Those men were our first glimpse of what we thought was evil. They probably weren't. They were likely just homeless men who'd found some kind of community in the woods, maybe guys from rural backgrounds who were more comfortable there than in the homeless shelters downtown. But they banded together with their anger and needs and who knew what manner of darkness happened in the ravine. But we were innocent.

TWENTY-SIX

IT WAS 8 A.M. Someone would have found them by now, early morning dog walkers, joggers. Two dead cops, one dead murder suspect, another cop critically injured, maybe dead as well. No witnesses, no murder weapon. Belisle might be there, combing through that conundrum. The investigators standing around asking the same question: *What the fuck happened here?*

I wondered the same thing. Maybe the idea was to have me take the rap for killing Delroy. They shoot me with the street gun, put it in Delroy's hand after they beat him to death: bad cop takes suspect down to Cherry Beach, beats him up, gets shot. But Belisle would have driven a forensic truck through that narrative. There must have been another plan. Maybe they hadn't meant to kill Staples, just rough him up, scare him, get him to give them another name if there was one. But Max got out of hand and Toussaint didn't have what it took to stop him. So bring me in as the patsy, the guy who beat Staples to death, and they end up shooting me because I was out of control. Maybe Lloyd set it up, but he'd want distance from this goat fuck.

I had two espressos, thought about eating something but didn't have an appetite. I drove to the station at 9. I had the news on. Warning of a heatwave, wildfires in California, a bad year for farmers. The perky morning host meticulously spelled out the unpronounceable word that had finally stumped a twelve-year-old spelling bee savant.

The news was just breaking in the station when I arrived. It came in blurts and frantic rumour. The desk cop told me five dead, which changed to three dead, killer on the loose. The room seemed to shimmer, a surreal quality to everyone's movements. I nodded hello to two bike cops, walked to my desk, surveyed the landscape, the chatter and disbelief, the palpable vacuum where Mad Max's psychosis had once been.

By 9:30 a.m. it had settled into disturbing fact: two dead cops, one dead murder suspect whose hands were tied and who may have been beaten to death, and one cop in intensive care with a severe brain injury.

Lloyd finally came out of his office. He would have been on the phone, talking to the police chief, to the mayor, maybe using a burner to make a few more calls. He had a shitshow on his hands and right now he was trying to create a narrative in which three cops weren't implicated in the death of a suspect whose hands had been tied behind his back, all discovered in a part of town that had been famous for police beatings of suspects whose hands had been tied behind their backs. What he needed was for Staples to be guilty. He would play up the cop killer angle, maybe try and claim it was friends of Staples's, maybe a Jamaican gang that killed Max and Toussaint. Ballistics would show that both cops had been killed with the same weapon, an unregistered .38 calibre pistol that likely came up from Detroit. But he'd need more than that. First create a narrative, then fashion good and evil to fit the story.

Lloyd asked for everyone's attention. His face was strained. "You've all heard," he said. "You all know that we lost two of our own today, that John Toussaint and Max Maxwell were brutally murdered, and that Jack Pierce is in intensive care right now and we're praying he pulls through. And you know Delroy Staples is dead. We don't know what happened down there. Maybe Jack can tell us when he comes out of intensive care. Maybe he won't be able to tell us. What we *do* know is that there is a cop killer out there. We find him, we find some answers. We'll have forensics by tomorrow morning. In the meantime, this is everyone's priority. I need everyone on this."

Lloyd scanned the room. His eyes met mine. "Good luck out there," he said to everyone and walked toward me. "Abel, my office," he said and turned and walked away.

I followed him into his office and closed the door behind me. Lloyd didn't sit down. He was walking in tight circles. He looked at me, stepped toward me.

"There's a killer out there, Abel," he said. His face was a foot away. His eyes were dark. He was still untangling all of it in his head.

I didn't say anything.

He took a breath. "You're big on theories, Abel. What's your theory. What went down?" It was more accusation than question.

"You tell me, Lloyd. Tell me why three cops take the most high-profile suspect in the city down to Cherry Beach and beat him to death."

"Dead *cops*, Abel. The First *fucking* Commandment."

They didn't get the dead cop they wanted.

Lloyd turned, walked a few steps, stared at the wall.

"Max was your pit bull," I said. "If you let him off the chain, this is on you. Your first act as superintendent. Congratulations."

"Go fuck yourself, Abel."

Either Max was obeying orders or he'd lost control. There was no way to tell which.

"We are bound together by blood," Lloyd said. "But not you, Abel. You're standing outside it all, aren't you? You're standing on your own little island, judging the rest of us. Two cops are *dead*."

Max was a psychopath. Getting shot was natural causes for him. There is a South American tribe that believes there is no such thing as natural causes. I vaguely remembered this from an anthropology course I took in second year. I'd taken the class because a girl I liked was taking it. I spent most of my time staring at her, but I still remembered that tribe who believed that virtually everyone died at the hands of their enemies. An old man lying in his bed, his heart failing, he wasn't dying of natural causes; he was bewitched by an enemy. It fell to his family to divine which enemy was responsible and seek revenge. So every death is a murder and every murder needs avenging with another murder, a society bound together by blood and revenge.

We were a foot apart, staring at one another. I wondered if Lloyd was part of it and he wondered if I'd been down there. A poker game where we couldn't see our own cards. Lloyd turned away and looked out the window. His career depended on a narrative that made some kind of sense and made him look like some kind of leader.

"You might be able to save Pierce," I said, "maybe Toussaint, but you're going to have to give Max up. You're a politician now."

"Get the fuck out of my sight, Abel."

I left his office, left the station, walked down to the Distillery District, away from the maelstrom. I called Davis.

"You heard."

"Christ, and we thought it was a shitshow before. You're at the station."

"Just left. Lloyd is panicking. He needs to come up with a narrative."

"You think he was in this?"

"I don't know. If he was, he would have created some distance. Either way, he needs a story. My guess is he revives the two-killer-theory. Staples didn't act alone, his partner is the one who kills Toussaint and Max."

"You still think it was two people? Belisle said same knife."

"Maybe two guys with the same kind of knife, but I don't think so. I think one guy, someone they knew, someone who got the knife in before either had time to react. Lloyd hasn't gotten in touch with you? He'll want you on the front lines, taking flak, keeping the villagers from torching the city."

"He called, I didn't pick up. Christ."

We hung up. Tanya Willing had left a phone message and sent three emails. I wrote back saying all we had at this point was two dead cops, one critically injured, a young male believed to be Delroy Staples dead, still awaiting confirmation. I had an espresso at a cafe and went back to the station. We got the confirmation on Staples early afternoon, his grandmother coming in to identify the battered body of her grandson. I saw her waiting outside the coroner's office, mouthing something to herself, a prayer, most likely. I thought about Delroy's mother. Was she still in town? I wondered about her grief for her abandoned child. There would be guilt; could she have saved him? A question she'd ask herself and a burden she'd carry. I walked over to the grandmother and offered condolences. Her face was streaked with tears.

I drove down to Cherry Beach. Belisle and his team were still there. They'd cordoned off a large part of the area. Belisle was staring out at the lake. I approached him. My heartbeat quickened. I'd been careful, but so had a thousand criminals who were now in jail. I'd scoured Max's fingers with sand. What else? There was always something else. Had any of my saliva landed on Max? Belisle was an artist.

"Belisle, I know you don't like talking until you have hard evidence but anything you can give me at this point would be extremely helpful," I said.

He kept staring out at the lake. His stare was unnerving.

Lloyd was searching for a narrative. I had already created my own: I could have stayed at the scene, phoned it in, gone with the bent cop angle, gone with what actually happened. But Lloyd would feed me to the wolves, look for criminal charges, the murder of two cops, attempted murder of a third. Any defence I could mount would crumble next to that pile of bodies. Belisle was struggling to find something that made sense.

"All three deaths at more or less the same time?" I asked.

Belisle shrugged. "Too soon to tell."

"Do we know if there is more than one shooter? Anything—shoe size, tire tracks?" I was trying to keep my voice neutral, to not sound like I was acting.

Belisle pointed to the sand. There were hundreds of divots that could be footprints, could be anyone's, could be new or old.

"Only in complete silence will you hear the desert," he said.

I waited for his explanation.

"It's a Bedouin saying," he said. "We don't have complete silence here. The sand won't reveal anything. Maybe something in the forest. Checking tire tracks. I wouldn't get my hopes up. We'll know the calibre of the gun. I can tell you the bullets were likely dumdum. Both Max and Toussaint were likely killed with the same weapon."

"What about Pierce?"

"Blunt force trauma. His gun was found at the scene, two bullets."

"So what is he doing thirty metres from the scene? Taking a leak? Sentry duty?"

"I don't know what he was doing. But here's something for you, Abel. His head wound. Someone packed it with wet sand. They used his tie to hold it."

"To stop the bleeding?"

"Most likely."

"Someone whacks him on the head, then dresses the wound? They don't want him to die."

Belisle shrugged. "I don't know what their thoughts were. Those appear to be their actions—they didn't have time to dress it properly."

Belisle stared at me, then stared at the lake.

Which left only Delroy Staples. "You have a cause of death for Staples? Was he killed here or was he already dead when they brought him here?"

Belisle kept up his staring contest with the lake. "It looks like blunt force trauma, but it might be suffocation. I won't know until tomorrow."

Maybe they beat him, he aspirates his own blood or vomit, he essentially drowns, not what they counted on. They needed a new story and that's when they called me.

They wouldn't find the burner, but they didn't need to. With two dead cops they would check phone records. They'd do a deep dive. I was hoping Toussaint's burner was clean, and couldn't be traced to him. But the record would show that an unregistered phone from this area—give or take 30 metres—was used to make a call at just after 9 and that call was to me. I put Toussaint's call at under five seconds. So someone calls, no number ID, I pick up, they don't say anything, five seconds of silence, a nuisance call, Maybe I turn off my phone so I don't get any more of them. But I couldn't get ahead of this, couldn't tell Belisle. How would I know the call was coming from here, that this was pertinent to the investigation? I'd have to wait until they came to me. But at some point, they would.

I lingered at the scene for a few more minutes, recreated the evening in my head, trying to piece together what had happened before I arrived. I got in my car and drove home and laid down on the couch. I felt a heaviness, a fatigue that went beyond the physical.

There wasn't much talk of morality in law school; it complicates things. I had just killed two men, critically injured a third.

Max or Toussaint or Pierce or some combination had beaten Delroy Staples to death. Max may have killed Infinity and had likely raped and beaten that girl. But this was merely my instinct. Coming into a court of law, what I had was my own amateur assessment of Max's mental health, a theory about him killing Infinity, and a one-word description of his eyes from a woman he had allegedly assaulted and who wouldn't be testifying. There was a balance of probabilities that he had killed Staples, but I had no real proof even of that. What if Toussaint was right, what if Staples was the killer, and what if he had a gun, maybe the gun that Pierce had on him? And if they beat him to death they may have been using the same logic I was using now: that Delroy Staples was a murderer, a bad man, and killing a bad man is different than killing a good man. I could fall down the same philosophical rabbit hole: How bad do we have to be to deserve death? Who decides what is good and bad? I was relieved that Max was dead. I didn't know much about Toussaint and Pierce's personal lives. I knew Toussaint was divorced, didn't know if either of them had kids. Maybe they never missed their son's hockey games, phoned their ailing mothers once a week. There is a weight you carry after taking a life. Jimmy Walsh's face never left me. Max's rabid face wouldn't either.

I slept for almost two hours, woke up, mixed a martini, and turned on the TV. Max and Toussaint's faces were all over the news. In the morning I'd call Jenny at Guiding Light and ask her to get the girl to confirm that it was Max who'd assaulted her.

There was a cop killer on the loose. That was this evening's news. Tomorrow's news would be: What happened to Delroy Staples down there?

TWENTY-SEVEN

THE CHIEF AND THE mayor decided to have the full-bore cop funeral for Max and Toussaint. Two hundred uniforms, a colour guard, police escort winding through the streets. There was black bunting at the station, flags at half mast, a piper. We gathered in the lush grounds of the Mount Pleasant cemetery in our comforting numbers. Max had no family, Toussaint had two ex-wives. There were no grieving widows. I'd gotten a text saying the girl positively IDed Max as her assailant. I was too far back to hear Max's eulogy. *We come together today to mourn not just a fallen officer, but a rapist, a murderer, a slaughterer of lambs, who walked with the devil and whose black heart embraced violence and hate. He touched many lives, left a dark indelible stain on this world. He left us too soon. Only Satan knows what he might have accomplished had he had his full three score and ten. He was sent upon this earth to devour goodness and we send his blackened soul back from whence it sprang, back to the fiery bowels of hell where his penance will be everlasting, his pain unrelenting, his cries unheeded. Dust unto dust, forever and ever amen, do not rest in fucking peace.*

I drifted away before the end of the ceremony, away from invocation, prayer, and benediction, and awkward conversations about good men gone. Dappled sunlight came through the trees. I passed grand Celtic crosses and glorious statuary. I passed the memorial for Mackenzie King, the country's longest-serving prime minister, a man who talked to his dead mother and made inaction an art form. I had parked six blocks away. Out on the sidewalk it was hot in the direct sun. I drove to the station. It was mercifully quiet, abandoned to a skeleton staff.

Belisle's autopsy results on Staples had come in and I scanned the sheet: blunt force trauma, ruptured spleen, pulmonary embolism—a list of internal injuries. Max must have started kicking and didn't stop. They hadn't intended to kill him. But they were stuck with that body on the beach and that's when they called me.

IT DIDN'T TAKE long for them to get phone records. I was sitting in an interview room with Lloyd and two detectives I didn't know and who didn't introduce themselves. Both were beefy guys, slab-faced. They looked like brothers.

"Night of, you get a call, 9:04." Detective One.

"If that's what you've got..."

"Who did you talk to?" Detective Two.

"I don't recall talking to anyone. What does the record say? Who called."

"Five seconds," Lloyd said. "Some fucking body said something."

"Five seconds," I repeated. "Yeah, I picked up, no caller ID, asked who's there, no one answers, I hang up."

"And you have no idea..."

"My idea is someone I arrested five years ago, carries a grudge, somehow got my cell number, possibly leaked by one of my close friends on the force. What the fuck is this?"

"The call came from Cherry Beach, Abel." Lloyd was staring hard.

"An hour later we have three dead bodies." Detective One.

"Two of them cops." Detective Two.

"I'm guessing the phone's a burner," I said.

"The fucking fact *remains,* Abel, that someone at the scene called you." Lloyd was ready to blow.

"So you're thinking it's either Toussaint, Pierce, or Max, or a fourth party."

"Why does the killer call you, Abel?"

"I don't know who called me, Lloyd..."

"If any of those guys needed help, you would be the last fucking guy *on this earth* they would call. Which leaves the killer."

"And you think I masterminded a triple homicide, two cops and the city's most wanted murder suspect. For fuck's sake Lloyd, what is the possible motive here."

"You had beefs with all three cops." Detective One.

"They had beefs with me. Lloyd, no one knows what happened down there but the most logical explanation, the one that is moving around this division like the flu, is that Max went off the leash and killed Staples. The only question is who killed Max and Toussaint."

The interrogation lasted more than an hour, turning in circles and landing at the same place: an unidentified caller called me before a triple homicide from somewhere in the vicinity. Lloyd felt I knew more than I was telling, but he also knew it didn't make sense that I was involved. And it didn't. He clearly didn't have any forensics that tied me to the scene. And he would have checked the geolocation of my phone, which put me downtown during the murders. He might have pulled the security footage from my building, which would only show an unidentified male in a hoodie getting into the elevator after an early morning run. I'd gotten rid of the running shoes, sweatpants and hoodie. The only cameras were in the lobby and parking area. Lloyd also had a political dilemma. He had papered over the cracks in his dead cops, barely. If I was guilty, then that paper would be torn off and he could have four very dirty cops that would produce a media frenzy and a call for serious police reform, likely starting with him losing his job. If there was a killer still out there, it gave him leverage to ask for more, more money, more resources, a little leeway in his methods. In the end, what he had was 4.7 seconds of silence and another mystery. Lloyd would wait until this case was either solved or gone cold then get the chief to quietly offer me a retirement package.

I'D GONE THROUGH the transcribed interviews with Peter Manning, a.k.a. Lord Yo. There were three, one conducted by me, two by Davis. The transformation from Lord Yo to Pete Manning for the benefit of the courts was impressive—not just the clothes and hair, but the voice, mannerisms, attitude. He'd been well coached. I called the prison, asked for any record of visitors for Peter Manning, told them to text me the list.

I called Davis, and we met at a cafe on Queen East, sitting outside under an awning. I decided not to tell her about the interrogation.

"I know you've got one foot out the door," I said, "that you're taking a run at the mayor's office. Wonderful, brilliant, you have my vote, but you're officially expendable now that Delroy's dead."

"If you mean the crude boilerplate politics that made me the poster girl for this racial shitshow are no longer needed by a paternalistic, lily-white, paramilitary, cynical cabal of motherfuckers, then I already put that together, Abel."

I took a sip of my espresso, which was authentically sour.

"This war of narratives," I said, "if Lloyd and the mayor win that battle, you could lose the tough-on-crime white suburbs and the wary immigrants in the exurbs and you'll get Jane and Finch and all the liberals in the core and it won't be enough."

"I'm a cop and my parents were immigrants."

"I'm just saying it's going to be tricky positioning yourself in that debate. It tends to be black and white, no grey areas. Bobby Dale and Lloyd will label you progressive, which is code for soft on crime, and they'll start with the dog whistle. You need a different story for this to work for you."

They would take clips of her speaking publicly, splice them in a way that made her sound more sociology major than cop.

"And you've got another story for me. Well, let's hear it, Mr Masterpiece Theatre."

"I think Staples was innocent."

"Yeah, you mentioned that, but for Staples to be innocent, someone else has to be guilty. Crime and politics are zero sum."

"You did a third interview with Lord Yo, two days after I talked to him."

"And..."

"And you asked him if the name Delaney Hutch meant anything to him, and he answered, and I quote, 'Wasn't he wide receiver for the Bills?' And at that point, the esteemed Legal Aid lawyer Lilly Tam ended the interview."

"*And*..."

"I asked him the same question and he said he thought she might be a porn star, but that's when Tam ended our interview as well."

I could see the impatience in Davis's face.

"What if Lilly Tam is on retainer with Delaney Hutch and they're paying her under the table, what if there's a link between Lord Yo and Delaney Hutch."

"'What if, what if.' What the fuck, Abel."

"But if I've guessed right, and everything is connected, and Manning is our killer, then this is your ticket. You busted Manning. If he killed those girls, you're the hero."

"I don't need to be a hero, I just need to be the voice of reason."

"Like the voice of reason that got Bobby Dale elected? Politics is emotion, not reason."

"But police work *is* reason, and I need more than your guesses."

A mentally ill man was shrieking something a block away, walking toward us.

"They put the two of us together," I said, "with the hope that one of us would fuck up and if he or she..."

"He."

"... if he did, then he would drag her down with him. Two birds, one stone. Which is why you've created a healthy distance between us."

"Abel, you create distance naturally. That's your superpower. You've managed to create distance between you and every single person in the department. Everyone on earth for all I know. Right now, your idea of police work is to go around, rattle every cage, hope someone cracks and supports your theories. But you don't actually have anything concrete."

"We prove Lord Yo killed those girls, you win the mayor's job. We're still partners, Davis. I'm trying to help you here."

Her face softened. "I understand that, Abel. And I appreciate it, I do. If you can find proof, it would be good for all of us. Let me know what you find out."

We lingered for a few more minutes in the shade. Davis checked her phone, said she had a meeting. Maybe Davis was right about my superpower. The mentally ill guy was three metres away, dressed in a track suit, no shoes.

Davis stood up. The guy pointed at her and yelled "Caliban the Taliban, Caliban the Taliban," then drifted down the street.

I checked my phone. There was a text from correctional services. Other than his lawyer, Pete Manning had only had one visitor: his father. I called correctional services, had them pull Eddy Manning's records from when he was in, behaviour, cellmates. I got up and got another coffee even though I didn't need it. I sat down and watched the pedestrian parade: a cyclist in a hazmat suit, four toddlers holding on to a blue rope following a teenager, six breeds of dog, clouds of weed.

The city streets were like the forest in the ravine. There was a stillness and order to the untrained eye, but beneath that stillness was a furious cycle of growth and death and decay. People walked by containing guilt and fear and dreams of revenge. They carried debt and perversion and health scares and the sins of their fathers and the doubts of their children. Worlds sashayed by, unglimpsed.

If we could see into the soul of everyone in the subway car with us, we wouldn't be able to bear it.

I got a text back from correctional services: Eddy Manning's cellmate had been Bradley Weeks.

Manning's house was only six blocks away. I drove into the alley behind his house. The alley was deserted. His garage was leaning westward, there was a pile of rotting wood in the backyard, a blackened firepit with a half-dozen empty bottles. I knocked on the back door. The inside door was open. Through the screen door I could see Manning's charming partner start down the three steps from the kitchen to the door, see her see me and then turn and walk quickly back up the stairs. The screen door was unlocked. I opened it and walked in.

They were both in the living room. The television was on, the volume loud. Manning was sprawled on the couch wearing only shorts. I'd put him at 6′3″, maybe 230, an acre of spoiled white flesh, four-day beard, damaged red nose. He looked like a Lucian Freud painting. A beer in one meaty hand.

"You can't just…" his partner started. "We have rights." Her voice went higher when she was indignant, an unpleasant sound.

I picked up the remote and turned off the TV. "You and Bradley Weeks did time together."

Manning stared up at the ceiling.

"Then Weeks gets in touch, says he has a job, might be something for your boy Pete. Pays well."

"The only time cops start telling you a story is when they don't have shit," Manning said. He took a sip of his beer.

"You visited your son in prison, told him to keep his mouth shut, you'd get him the best lawyer."

"Father visiting his son in prison isn't a crime. Getting a lawyer. What the fuck."

"No, but if you were the link between Weeks and your son, and your son killed those two girls in St. James Town, then that's accessory, that's fourteen years. And with your record, you'll likely pull all fourteen of them, Eddy."

Manning took another sip of his beer.

"You got no proof," his partner said.

"Yeah, or I'd be downtown, in a cell, and you'd have a warrant and wouldn't have to violate the rights of a tax-paying citizen. Either arrest me or get the fuck out of my house."

Another cage rattled. I left through the back door, walked to my car, called in an APB on Bradley Weeks, description, address, and licence number on file. He'd be on the move as soon as Eddy Manning called him, which would be right now. Weeks may have been a bigger part of this picture than I'd originally thought. He was taking orders from someone, someone high up. They would keep the cut-outs to a minimum. Weeks was an ex-con, he wouldn't trust those above him to protect him. He'd be protecting himself. He'd have evidence of that connection somewhere.

TWENTY-EIGHT

THE FUNERAL FOR Delroy Staples drew more people than Max and Toussaint's. The official estimate was eight hundred people in the church and another two thousand filling the street. A screen was set up outside, projecting the service. Charles Tait gave one of the eulogies. *An innocent child beaten to death by those who were supposed to serve and protect. Who do they serve? Who do they protect? Not you. Not me. Not Delroy Staples.* It was the rousing, soul-stirring speech of an evangelist, a circuit preacher bringing angels and devils into the tent and making them dance.

I was outside, hovering at the periphery. There was a woman standing near me, beautiful, delicate, sobbing uncontrollably. She was being comforted by a man, both expensively dressed. I wondered if this was Delroy's mother. If this was where his beauty came from. She had come to the city on her own, as so many do, and the city is a crucible, the poets and actors and writers who arrive from the hinterland eventually going into advertising and teaching. We become something else, sometimes someone else. She abandoned her husband and son and found a new life. Relieved to be rid of her husband, her old life, devastated to leave her son. A steep price.

And as people arrived in the city, it adapted, a neighbourhood gentrified, another abandoned, the different tribes moving through the city, settling in one place, migrating to another. The Italians moving from the East End across the river to College Street, the Greeks taking their place. The East Asians gathering along Gerrard, then heading north to Brampton. The cycle like nature, a process of decay and revival, everyone seeking the sunlight.

THAT NIGHT, THE city burned. There were forty-six fires. It was a hot night, Day 5 of a heatwave, and the eight and a half hours of darkness were a fever dream of ruin. I was on Yonge at 8 p.m. and I could see it start to form, clusters of young men, moving, shifting, the clusters growing larger, merging—that restlessness. The atmosphere was charged, waiting for a cue, comforted by the mob mantra: *They can't arrest all of us.* There was something else, what Elias Canetti called the invisible crowd, the spirits of the dead gathering unseen, but their presence felt. There were maybe a thousand people on the square, waiting for that first brick. Something launched through a window, the glass falling to the sidewalk, the starter's gun. A dozen police cruisers pulled up. Traffic was stopped. Some of the stopped cars became targets. Sirens filled the air.

I started to walk home, heading west. People passed me, some jogging toward the action, otherwise peaceable young men who would catch the fever. I passed a group of what looked like students. They tipped a metal newspaper box over. They would smash a window, reach through broken glass to grab a pair of Nikes, would jostle and yell and move through the streets like liquid with the crowd.

A group walked toward me, two guys, two girls, maybe eighteen. One of the girls had a look of religious ecstasy, feeling the electricity. Her boyfriend threw his shoulder into me as they walked by. I turned and saw him push a younger kid into the brick wall. I went back. The boy had crumpled into a pile on the sidewalk. I asked him if he was okay. Mostly just frightened. I helped him up and he walked west quickly.

There was a light hovering over the square, something on fire. I walked back toward the action. The uniforms had their sticks out, swinging. I saw one connect with a kid, his knees giving out, hitting the pavement. Kids threw rocks at the cops. There would be tear gas soon. The crowd kept growing.

Crowds are amoral, without conscience. They march and loot and maim and scream then disperse, turned once more into individuals, burdened by consequence and regret. Everyone is equal in a crowd, all the hierarchies gone.

As cops, we approach people singly or in pairs. But massed together, herded toward a civic threat, we become a crowd too, with all its attendant traits. And when two crowds meet, you have war. This one would be caught on a thousand cell phones, an eight-hour montage of random violence, all our civic demons let out in the darkness. I turned and headed west again. Maybe Lloyd was right; I wasn't part of the brotherhood. I was on my own little island.

It took forty-five minutes to walk home. I mixed a martini and stared out. I could see the pale light, hear the sirens. The city was in permanent twilight. I slept in dream-laden fits, ugly images dredged up from my subconscious.

AT 5:30 A.M. I got up and made a coffee, then went for a walk. By 6:15 the light was red in the east. I walked north and turned onto Queen Street. There was garbage and glass and half-dressed mannequins with missing limbs on the sidewalk, a trail of clothes. I walked up Spadina to Bloor, the smell of acrid smoke in the air. There was a line of spray paint that stretched along a half-dozen stores.

On Bloor, I picked up a paper at a convenience store, went to a cafe and ordered a double espresso and a healthy muffin that tasted like a handful of dirt. There were eight pages of photos in the paper, a civic wilding. Seven people were dead. Stores had been looted, people assaulted cops, who in turn had cracked heads, pepper spray and tear gas had filled the night air.

I walked east for half an hour, past St. James Town, two buildings still smouldering, yellow police tape strung for a hundred metres, three fire trucks still on the scene. Hundreds of people were out, milling around, assessing the damage, trying to make some sense. A news truck was parked. There would be a producer looking for the best backdrop, a blackened building, the journalist set up in front, giving a solemn tally of the damage. *What we know at this point . . .*

Tanya Willing left two email messages and two phone messages. I called her and we met at an outdoor cafe and I gave her a slightly edited version of Mad Max, Toussaint, and Pierce, enough for her to write something that would balance the sainthood the department was trying to confer on them. Willing was wearing a wrinkled linen dress and sandals and looked damp and exhausted. A tendril of hair stuck to her face and she brushed it away.

"How dirty were Max and Toussaint?"

"Max was a psychopath, basically the department's id." I told her about complaints from sex workers who said he'd demanded sex, had threatened them, occasionally assaulted them. I didn't tell her about the girl.

"Which would be rape," Tanya said. "Toussaint and Pierce?"

"There were formal complaints against both of them. You'd have to check the numbers, but some of them were buried, is my guess, and most of the citizens in our division wouldn't launch a formal complaint. They're immigrants who distrust the police, who aren't sure how things work here, who don't want to be in the system. Or low lifes who know nothing is going to happen, so what's the point, you just get the cops angrier. So if they have, I don't know, three formal complaints, it could mean ten more people have something to complain about."

"What about Lloyd? He's running the show. Where does he stand with these guys?"

"These are his homies, but he's political now. Maybe creating a little space between him and them. At least publicly."

"What the hell happened down there?"

I shrugged. "Could be that Max went off the chain. I'd put him as most likely to have killed Staples. Who killed Max and Toussaint, anyone's guess. We don't have anything at the moment."

We talked for half an hour. I didn't mind the heat. If you weren't moving, it brought a certain comfort. I left Tanya to her notes and drove to Titus Bishop's house.

After I'd put out the APB on Bradley Weeks, he'd been picked up by two uniforms, booked as an accomplice to murder, and was now in a cell downtown. A warrant issued to search his apartment and car and an off-site storage locker yielded a computer that had emails and a phone that had calls to Titus, Mullins, Fortier, and Pete Manning. Weeks had kept them as insurance or to lean on Titus if he had to.

Rosedale had been exempt from the revolution. The pitched battles had taken place on the main streets. I knocked on Titus's door.

He answered. This time he didn't try to disguise his distaste.

"I'm busy, Detective," he said.

Titus didn't look healthy. He may never have looked healthy, but now his face had collapsed, forming new lines and ridges, as if the weight of his jowls had dragged it down. His eyes were ringed with red, his face preternaturally pale. He seemed to have aged a decade in little more than a week.

"I don't care if you're busy, Titus. I need to talk about Pete Manning. You can choose where we talk and how many lawyers are present, but we will talk."

He examined me and inside his head a half-dozen calculations were simultaneously running. How much did I know? Was there any evidence? What were his options? What would the fallout be and how close would it fall?

A sound came out of his mouth and he turned and walked down the hallway. I took it as an invitation and followed. We went back to the now familiar study. There were no gardeners in the backyard today, no one fussing over the geometry of the cedar hedges. The house was silent. We sat down.

"You're not well, Titus," I said.

One hand fluttered in dismissal. "I'm fine."

"You hired Peter Manning."

"I'm not in the mood for your fishing expedition, Detective."

"The money came from you, it went through Bradley Weeks, and it landed in Manning's drug-addicted, racially confused lap, and it was all in cash and you're an experienced bagman, so there isn't a money trail."

Titus waited.

"The money was to wreak havoc in St. James Town, maybe murder was the plan all along or maybe this was Manning going rogue, but either way, Titus, you're implicated."

"I've never met a Peter Manning."

"I'd be surprised if you had. He's a piece of work. Like Ambrose Fortier was a piece of work, like Randy Mullins was a piece of work. You may want to re-examine your hiring practices."

Titus looked out onto his yard. It had the sterility of a George Stubbs painting. I half-expected a horse and someone in English riding gear to appear.

"When you were in politics, Titus, you were the man who knew where all the bodies were buried. You scurried between the rats, clutching your briefcase filled with good news. But you didn't rise up in the ranks. You had your own problems of course, and enough people knew about them, so you were vulnerable. You were the guy who took orders, a faithful soldier."

"Your assessment of my political career, of which I am immensely proud, is of no interest to me, Detective."

"It's of no interest to me either, Titus. I bring it up only as evidence that you weren't the one calling the shots here. You were in the middle. You gave money to Weeks and he gave it to Fortier and Manning and Mullins, the man who stabbed Fortier to death in prison."

"Perhaps you could speak to the evidence you've managed to gather to support these fictions, Detective."

"There is a witness who will attest that you were behind the money, Titus." Weeks would likely roll on him for a reduced sentence.

Titus gave me a long look. I could almost see a crack in his composure.

"I *defended* my constituents. I worked for them."

"And now you're working to move them out of the neighbourhood."

Titus stared out the window. "I'd like you to leave, Detective."

"The companies that are buying up the land around St. James Town," I said. "I was struck by something."

I paused, trying to read Titus's face, a poker face honed over nearly forty years in politics.

"Botsford and Boyles. Two of the companies. Those names mean anything to you?"

I thought there was a flicker of something. So subtle it was almost invisible to the untrained eye, the visual equivalent of a dog whistle.

"I'm afraid they don't ring any bells, Detective."

"Botsford was William Jarvis's middle name. Boyles was his wife Mary's middle name." I paused briefly. "The sheriff of the Home District, the founder of Rosedale, the..."

"I'm familiar with Jarvis. The middle names, I'm sure you'll agree, are a bit of a stretch, and any further discussion will, in fact, involve my lawyers. You can leave now, Detective Abel."

Titus stared out his window. Sitting in his shorts and sweater, a grotesque schoolboy waiting to be punished. I stood up and left.

CHOOSING THE TIME of our own death can mean greater control over the obituary. Time is often what divides the hero from the villain. Sir John A. Macdonald was the founder of the nation, imperfect, drunk, a brilliant, complex man who was able to craft a country out of a giant wilderness and a dozen disparate interests. He used fear and cunning and starved Crowfoot's people, then gave Crowfoot a lifetime pass aboard the railway he had etched into the new country. Crowfoot outlived all twelve of his own children, who mostly died of starvation or tuberculosis, casualties of Confederation. With his children gone, Crowfoot had no more use for life. "From nowhere we came," he said on his deathbed, "into nowhere we go." But like Macdonald, he went into history, with its judgments and fictions.

Three days later, Titus Bishop was found hanged in his garage. One of the gardeners found him and called the police. The newspapers were kind: *Titus Bishop gave himself to civic life, a dedicated man who touched many lives in this city and left a grieving wife.*

The obituary mentioned something else, the last piece of the puzzle.

TWENTY-NINE

THE THICK BLUE LINE

TANYA WILLING | The damage was estimated at "more than a hundred million dollars." And what do we talk about when we talk about damage? The estimates come from insurance companies, who may want to keep the losses low, and they are based on material damage—buildings damaged and/or burned, cars turned over and/or burned, merchandise taken from stores, damage to civic and private property.

But there was other damage, other losses, losses that aren't as easily quantified. It wasn't the police department's finest hour. All those jumpy cell phone videos of raised batons coming down on the heads of fifteen-year-olds, cops dragging people across the concrete. Not a good look.

The other side (this is assuming there is an actual other side and not just a random mob) doesn't fare any better. Those angry faces, throwing rocks, smashing cars, torching buildings. Why throw a brick through the window of Holt Renfrew? Perhaps the summer sale was a disappointment. Everything was a target.

And it was a target because the real target is complicated and elusive.

It started decades ago, with the education system, lack of affordable housing, and the subtle (and not-so-subtle) racism that greeted many new arrivals. But you can't throw a brick through that. You can't torch history.

Instead, we are moved to revolt by what happened at Cherry Beach.

Except we don't know what happened down there.

We know that Delroy Staples was found with his hands tied behind his back with a zip tie, beaten to death.

We know that two detectives, "Mad" Max Maxwell and John Toussaint, were both shot dead, and that a third detective, Jack Pierce, was found near the scene and is still in intensive care. Perhaps Detective Pierce will recover fully and will volunteer the events of that evening and his version will be detailed and accurate. And perhaps the Maple Leafs will win the next six Stanley Cups in a row.

We don't know what happened at Cherry Beach. We may never know.

But here's what we do know. Mad Max Maxwell came by his name honestly. He was a violent man who routinely demanded sexual favours from sex workers, who assaulted them, who assaulted suspects, and at least two of those suspects have recounted the physical assault and humiliation they suffered at his hands.

His eulogy gave us a different man, but then that's the point of eulogies, isn't it.

John Toussaint and Jack Pierce weren't angels either. They managed to collect several formal complaints. And the thing about formal complaints is: they are usually the tip of the iceberg. How many people would have liked to complain but were too frightened or didn't know how, or were immigrants who didn't want to rock the boat, or were basically disenfranchised and didn't think anything would happen anyway, so what was the point.

And what of Delroy Staples? What do we know about him?

We know he came here from Jamaica at the age of eleven, that he lived with his father, then his grandmother, that he dated Dashika Moore. It gets a bit thin after that.

Almost as thin as the case against him. He is the de facto murderer of two girls because a) he dated one of them, and b) he's dead. Evidence-wise, that's pretty much what we're looking at here, folks.

But what if he isn't the murderer? What if he went into hiding because he feared that he would be railroaded into a guilty verdict.

What if he was right?

This is the city's Gordian knot. Alexander the Great untied that knot and went on to conquer Asia. It's unlikely that there are any Alexanders out there, and given the number of condos sold to absentee Chinese buyers, Asia may be conquering us. At the heart of this whole mess—two dead girls, one dead suspect, two dead cops—there lies an answer. It won't be an answer that everyone likes. Right now it is in the interests of the department for Delroy to be guilty and for Maxwell and Toussaint to be sterling, dedicated detectives.

It is in the interests of the Black community for Delroy to be innocent and the cops to be dirty.

We are, at heart, tribal people. This is a city of tribes—blue (the police), Black, white, red, yellow. Anthropologists will tell you that we tend to retreat to our tribe in times of danger or scarcity or war. And now it appears we are at war, though it isn't always easy to pick a side.

When we talk about damage and loss, we don't say the city lost a piece of itself. But we all lost something, we are all damaged.

THIRTY

TANYA'S PIECE HAD TWO sidebars, one detailing Delroy's transgressions, which included the knife incident at his school, the other a detailed list of complaints against Max, Toussaint, and Pierce, which she may have gotten from Davis.

The next day there was the threat of legal action from the police department, alleging libel re: the dead officers, *a travesty*, et cetera, though this was strictly for show and the newspaper knew that and publicly defended Willing and her reporting. Any actual legal action would dredge up a dozen misdeeds on the part of Max, possibly Toussaint and Pierce as well. The threat of legal action was strictly for the press conference.

There were complaints to the paper's ombudsperson from the Jamaican Canadian Society, a dozen letters to the editor, including one from Charles Tait, arguing that a privileged white woman wasn't in a position to preside over the life and death of a Black man. The city lining up on various sides.

I CALLED DAVIS, told her I'd talked to Manning's father, that we had Weeks and I was going to interview him, that he was looking to make a deal. She came to the station. We stood behind the glass. Weeks was sitting with Lilly Tam in the interview room. He was a heavy guy, but now seemed heavier.

"He wants to make a deal?" Davis asked.

"Not sure it isn't Tam who wants to make the deal, keep Delaney Hutch out of the headlines."

We went into the room. Weeks was an ex-con, he knew what we had, knew his best hope was some kind of deal. And Lilly Tam wanted to avoid a trial because it could reveal some unfortunate connections for her real client.

"Ms Tam," I said.

"We are prepared to make a deal," she said.

I spoke directly to Weeks. "Pete Manning was hired to kill a white girl. You delivered the money."

This was the plan—hire Manning in his Lord Yo phase to kill a white girl in St. James Town, create fear, racialize it. Angela Blair was the target; Dashika Moore was collateral damage. Manning knew Dashika from when she dated Delroy and used her to get at Blair, then Yo was identified as a Black assailant. But they didn't need Yo; they had the happy accident of an actual Black suspect in Delroy Staples. "Titus Bishop gave the money to you, Brad, and you delivered it to Manning."

"Don't answer that," Tam said.

"Let me guess," I said. "You'll give up Manning, but you didn't know what the money was for or who it came from."

"There is nothing in Mr Weeks's records that indicates he was aware of who was financing this. And Mr Bishop, tragically, is dead."

"There are emails to Titus Bishop." Albeit carefully worded.

"They are, as you know, insubstantial, Detective," Tam said. "And prosecuting a dead man, one who was a pillar of the community, is a non-starter. Peter Manning wasn't paid to kill anyone."

This was possible. He may have done it on his own. At any rate, it would be difficult to prove otherwise in court.

"You want a deal, Ms Tam. I strongly suggest your client start telling me a story, one that keeps Delaney Hutch out of court. And I wouldn't bet too heavily on Titus being a pillar of anything."

Weeks sat there, shoulders slumped, hands folded on the table: Exhibit A. He knew he'd be back inside, knew how to do time.

"Titus. Tight *Ass*," Weeks said. "That Rosedale dumpling fuck. Guys like that, they stand on the sidelines throwing money onto the field. They never get their uniform dirty."

"He gave you money."

"Yeah, never enough, but he gave me money."

"And that money was for..."

"This would be a good time to nail down the terms of my client's deal," Tam said.

"His deal depends on the quality of the information," Davis said.

Tam didn't need much of a deal; she didn't care how long Weeks stayed behind bars. Maybe the longer the better. She was going through the motions.

"Titus gave you cash?"

"Always cash."

"You hired Pete Manning."

Weeks nodded.

"He was hired to kill a white girl."

Weeks shrugged. "It wasn't that specific. Far as I knew, his job was, you know, shake things up."

"He certainly did that."

The central mystery was solved—the man who killed two innocent girls would go to trial, accused of murder. Tam had probably already convinced Weeks to take a deal. If his sentences were concurrent, he could be out in six years, and there was probably some kind of payoff from Delaney Hutch for taking the deal. Weeks and Tam left.

"Interesting piece of theatre," Davis said.

"We get Weeks, reduced sentence, we have the case against Manning."

"That's all we get. After, what, nine weeks of hell, two dead girls, three if we include Infinity, Delroy's murder, half the city burned. Delaney Hutch, they skate. God knows who else. You figure Lloyd, got to be others. Fuck me."

It wasn't the resounding victory we'd hoped for. Manning had likely acted alone, although he might try and pin it all on Delroy. But all we had were the bottom feeders. There wasn't enough to go after the puppet masters.

"Hollow victory," I said.

"They don't get any hollower."

"When you're mayor..."

"Don't start, Abel."

I DROVE HOME, parked, and walked to the market and bought a half-dozen prawns, chicken thighs, some half-cured chorizo sausage, mussels, bomba rice, and red and yellow peppers. I stopped at the olive oil store and bought an eight-ounce bottle of arbequina olive oil that advertised artichoke and green apple notes. The black-haired woman was there. She was dressed the same as the last time, in a black dress and heels. She was standing, talking to a woman, the only other customer. Her feet were slightly splayed, her posture rigid, like a defiant dancer. I took my bottle to the cash and she rang me up without any hint of recognition. A brief, practised smile as she handed me the bottle. There was something elemental about her, the darkness of her eyes, her hair. Another love gone.

Back home, I sautéed the chicken, then the chorizo briefly, then the prawns, removing everything from the pan and adding the onions for ten minutes. Then the peppers, garlic, snow peas, paprika, kosher salt, saffron. I added a cup of stock, stirred in the rice, and put the chicken thighs back in. I had opened a bottle of Rioja and was sipping as I cooked. Paella wasn't really a hot-weather dish, but I hadn't eaten much in the last few days and felt like something robust. When the rice was tender I put the prawns and chorizo back for five minutes. I went to the balcony and cut some basil from the plant I had growing there. I tore the basil, did a quick spritz with lemon over the plate. I had been to Spain once, after my mother died. Europe is where young men go to reinvent themselves and fall in love. I fell in love with a hundred women, all of whom walked by me without a glance, and to some degree I reinvented myself. I wasn't bound by any family. Neither parent had any siblings. I had already quit law school, become someone else.

I sat on the couch with my dinner. On the news, there was a young woman who said she was with Delroy Staples the night the girls were murdered. She was nineteen, a plain girl bewitched by Delroy's beauty and notoriety. She was tearful and looked like she'd rehearsed her speech, stopping to compose herself, a subtle shake of her head as if she was summoning the courage. A part of her was acting, borrowing tics from her favourite movies, but it didn't mean she wasn't telling the truth. It just meant she was part of the social media stage that had engulfed the globe, everyone a performer, showing us how to repair an iPhone, how to play "Hey Jude" on a ukelele, sobbing as they tell us about their personal struggles and about finally finding what is important in life.

She said Delroy told her no one would believe them, they had to stay hidden. But now that he was gone, she felt she had to come forward. The interviewer leaned in, empathized, said she knew how hard this was for her. The girl said they were in love. The interview lasted ten minutes, five less than Warhol predicted.

THIRTY-ONE

MANNING'S TRIAL TOOK PLACE in early October. I went, curious to see what he'd say on the stand. The newspapers were filled with images of Pete Manning, both the recent version and the Lord Yo version, as well as pictures of Angela and Dashika. There was a good photo of Davis, identified as the arresting officer.

Manning had pleaded not guilty. The two versions I had seen of him had both been manufactured: the gangster rapper and the Brady Bunch ingénue. I wondered what I'd see in court. It was, it turned out, a third version. His hair was a bit longer, somewhere between his dreads and the Superman haircut. He had a scraggly beard. The glasses were gone. The Crown prosecutor was Mary Wiggins, sharp, well prepared. She asked him what he had been doing the night of the murders. Manning said he was "flying with homies."

"If you mean you were out with friends, Mr Manning, we have testimony from those friends. They all deny being with you. Three of the four denied being friends with you."

Manning looked upward, as if seeking inspiration, and his reply was slow. "Stabbed in the back, suffering children, people on the street talking crazy shit," he said, finally.

Wiggins took this in stride. "And where were you when all this was happening, Mr Manning?"

"Knocking on the door of absolute death."

Wiggins kept up her deliberate questions, unfazed by Manning's increasingly unhinged responses. I wondered if he was angling for an insanity defence.

"You said in a statement you sometimes hear voices, Mr Manning?"

Manning nodded.

"Witness nods, affirmative. Who do you think is talking to you? The devil?"

This would have been a good time for Lilly Tam to protest, but she stayed quiet.

"*Tired* of the hustling failure, bleeding on the cross, bro," Manning said.

Manning wandered through his testimony as though it were an experimental film, quick cuts that referenced childhood, drugs, girlfriends, racism. The judge let him roam. It was a grim, rarely coherent view into his fractured psyche.

I looked at the two mothers sitting with one another, examining the man who had taken their lives away, trying to make sense of what was becoming increasingly senseless. Manning invoked movies and song lyrics, a personality composed of random cultural touchstones, video games and dark websites. He described himself as heroic and tragic and misunderstood. He said he would wade across the River Jordan, that he was an avenging angel. I stayed for an hour, then left, relieved to be out in the sunlight. Maybe Manning was mentally ill, or maybe he was simply a modern mess, an ugly pastiche of twitchy impulse and everything he'd seen on the internet.

THE DEAL FOR a new development where St. James Town stood was announced. The full-page newspaper ad said it would be one of the largest urban development projects in the nation's history—seventy acres of luxury condos, with retail and office space as well as parkland. It would re-define the mid-town area.

I drove over to Dorothy Bishop's home, knocked on the door. She answered. She was wearing high-waisted tan pants, a white blouse. Her silver hair was pulled back, showcasing her patrician face, lines etched heavily over that rigid bone structure.

"Detective."

"I wonder if I could have a word with you, Ms Bishop."

She gave this a second's thought.

"Do come in."

I followed her in, closed the door. We sat in their very formal living room, something out of Regency England: pink striped wallpaper, oval family portraits on the walls, an oversized, unused fireplace.

"I'm sorry for your loss," I said.

She nodded. "Yes." The word drawn out a bit.

The silence felt complicated. It was hard to calculate how much she had really lost. It may have been a marriage of convenience, and Titus had become inconvenient. He may not have gone to prison, but his life would have been ruined. You can bear the ruin if you have the right partner. You saw it with politicians all the time. Those unsmiling wives who stood beside their husbands as they publicly apologized for letting down their families, letting down the nation and letting down God, and said how they had learned an important lesson about strippers and cell phones. Who knew what bargains were struck. But Dorothy Bishop wasn't one of those wives.

"You have your development," I said.

Titus's obit said he was married in 2005 to Dorothy Hutch. I ran her name and got her parents, Bentley and Theresa Hutch. Bentley "Bent" Hutch was the founding member of Delaney Hutch.

"It's hardly my development, Detective."

"But you're involved. You're connected to Botsford, to Boyles. Delaney Hutch helped bring the deal together. Your maiden name."

"My involvement with Delaney Hutch is titular, at best, Detective."

"Like the queen."

She smiled, a faint smile. "Without all those troublesome children."

"It looks impressive. The rendering that was in the paper. A city unto itself. Simcoe Village. Did you choose the name?"

"Perhaps my greatest contribution to this enterprise."

Lord Simcoe was Upper Canada's first lieutenant governor, a staunch monarchist who sang "God Save the King" each night before he went to sleep. He wanted to recreate Britain here in the colonies with all its attendant manners, foibles, and class divisions. Dorothy's role was more than titular. She'd used Titus as the bagman. She had a significant stake.

"Was it worth starting a war, I wonder."

"I would hardly call it a war, Detective. Throughout history, wars have always been about land. We attach noble causes to them afterward, of course, but war is about real estate. It always has been."

Angelique had been right. The plan was to move all the brown people away from the centre, push them out to edges, to the Soviet-inspired high-rises that dotted the suburbs, and each morning they would crowd the subways to come to the centre to clean bathrooms and push strollers and trim the hedges into unnatural shapes.

"I'm afraid I have another appointment, Detective," Dorothy said, standing up.

I stood up and walked to the door. "When the Family Compact built their homes on Jarvis and Sherbourne 160 years ago," I said, "they didn't foresee the way the city would grow, how the underclass would swallow up their grand houses. And now you're reclaiming them. War isn't the only thing that is about real estate. History is about real estate, too. Who is shunted off the land, where they go, what's left behind."

This time there was a genuine smile. "History is something my people are very good at, Detective."

She closed the door and I stood on the porch and looked down the street. She was right; her people were good at history. But they were on the wrong side of it now. History might show this to be a final stand, before the collapse of the WASP empire. The condos would go up, but the upper class, at least as determined by money, had shifted. I would bet that Dorothy Hutch had given the orders to create mayhem in St. James Town to force Luckworth to sell and bring the price down, and to cement the idea that the city was safer with all the immigrants safely corralled on the outskirts. If I was right, then she bore responsibility for the deaths of Dashika Moore and Angela Blair, for the deaths of P. Bannich and Ambrose Fortier, for the twenty or so people who had died in fires, the seven who had died in the riot. She had used her husband's contacts to carry it out with impunity. She would never be charged with a crime, would never be held responsible. Here was the banality of evil. I wondered if she would have been horrified if she'd actually witnessed the stabbings, if she'd seen those people burn, seen a fifteen-year-old felled by a police baton, bleeding onto Yonge Street. I wondered if it would have made a difference. I had the deaths of Max and Toussaint on my hands, the maiming of Pierce. I bore some responsibility for Titus's death. Lord John Graves Simcoe had once said he would die by torture in order to restore his king to his just inheritance, by which he meant several million square kilometres of the New World. They hadn't inherited it, of course, but the imperial mind is endlessly elastic.

EPILOGUE

DAVIS RAN FOR MAYOR and won by the narrowest margin of victory in the city's history. I congratulated her and she thanked me for Manning. Bobby Dale declared the election stolen by the elites, the class of which Davis was now apparently a member. Lloyd stepped down as superintendent of 51. I heard he'd gone into private security, consulting. Jack Pierce never fully recovered and retired on a disability pension. He wasn't able, or was unwilling, to shed any light on that night. Peter Manning was found guilty and sentenced to two concurrent terms of twenty-five years. Bradley Weeks got seven years. The case of two dead cops wasn't solved. Angelique had a gallery showing in the West End and I went and looked at her stark charcoal drawings and bought one for $1,700.

I dated Tanya Willing for a bit. She had left the newspaper and was writing an angry book. She was bitter and fun and I was grateful for her company, but I could see that I wasn't Mr Right. She turned fifty and I made an elaborate dinner for her. She was intensely carnivorous, almost paleolithic, and I made a beef Wellington, roasting beef bones for the broth, then reducing the broth by two-thirds to make a Madeira sauce. I worked on the fussy laminated dough, something that is easier to buy than create, but I wanted to do everything from scratch. Then the duxelles—a mixture of chopped mushrooms mixed with shallots, herbs, and a worrisome amount of butter. I made crepes, patted the beef dry, seared it on all sides in yet more butter, mixed the duxelles with wild boar pâté, spread it on the crepes and wrapped the crepes around the beef, then wrapped it all in the pastry. I brushed an egg wash over it, scored it with a knife, and put it in the oven. This whole operation took almost three hours. If I overcooked it, it would be a heartbreak I would never recover from, but it came out rare, the way Tanya preferred. I served it with charred brussels sprouts and a beet salad (red, yellow, and candy striped) with walnuts and goat cheese. For dessert I made macaroons, which were almost as labour intensive as the Wellington and took longer because I screwed up two batches before getting the whole sugar-almond meal-egg white mixture to a perfect, humidity-free, airy consistency and getting it into the oven before it fucking deflated. The result was six cookies I could have bought down the street for fifteen bucks and they were wildly underappreciated, given the effort that went into them.

Had she been turning sixty rather than fifty, Tanya might have settled for me. But she wasn't ready to settle yet. The parting was amicable.

The murders at Cherry Beach passed into the city's history. Tanya was right; it was the city's Gordian knot. I was the only one who could untie it.

What is justice? Revenge is an act of passion, Samuel Johnson noted, vengeance an act of justice, a subtle distinction. I had killed two men, maimed a third, and I roamed free. Dorothy Hutch was one of those people who would die in her sleep in her own bed at the age of one hundred, untouched by need or doubt, unburdened by guilt. Delroy Staples and Dashika Moore and Angela Blair had died for nothing. Eighteen thousand people were displaced as the towers came down, scattered to the edges of town. There is no just society. Justice is a fantasy, the place where the falling angel meets the rising ape.

I left the department with a pension that was comfortable. I booked a trip to Italy to take a three-week cooking class in Tuscany. Marcella Hazan, an Italian chef whose books I'd enjoyed, says that cooking has to express taste, not technique, because technique doesn't communicate anything; it's like mastering the grammar of a language in which you have nothing to say. She was a great believer in basics. I wanted to return to something basic, to embrace another history—blood-addled memories of empire and decline and genius, a land that prized revenge, had turned it, as it turned everything, into art. I wanted the taste of history and olive oil on my lips, to stare into dark eyes and find love.

DON GILLMOR is the author of *To the River*, which won the Governor General's Award for nonfiction. He is the author of five novels, *Cherry Beach*, *Breaking and Entering*, *Long Change*, *Mount Pleasant*, and *Kanata*; a two-volume history of Canada, *Canada: A People's History*; and nine books for children, two of which were nominated for the Governor General's Award. He was a senior editor at *The Walrus*, and his journalism has appeared in *Rolling Stone*, *GQ*, *Saturday Night*, *Toronto Life*, the *Globe and Mail*, and the *Toronto Star*. He has won twelve National Magazine Awards and numerous other honours. He lives in Toronto.

Printed by Imprimerie Gauvin
Gatineau, Québec